The Nameless Castle

Translated From The Hungarian
Under The Author's Supervision

by

S. E. Boggs

Double 9
BOOKS

The Nameless Castle

by S. E. Boggs

Copyright © 2024

All Rights reserved.

ISBN: 978-93-63051-84-3

Published by

DOUBLE 9 BOOKS

2/13-B, Ansari Road
Daryaganj, New Delhi – 110002
info@double9books.com
www.double9books.com
Tel. 011-40042856

This book is under public domain

ABOUT THE AUTHOR

S. E. Boggs, an enigmatic figure of literary intrigue, unveils his chilling masterpiece, "The Nameless Castle," with an eerie blend of Gothic allure and psychological suspense. Set against the backdrop of a desolate landscape shrouded in mystery, Boggs's narrative unfolds with atmospheric prose and tantalizing ambiguity, drawing readers into a labyrinth of secrets and shadows. In "The Nameless Castle," Boggs deftly explores the darkest recesses of the human psyche, delving into themes of isolation, obsession, and the uncanny. Through vivid characterization and atmospheric world-building, he creates a chilling tableau where reality blurs with the supernatural, and every shadow holds a whispered secret. As a master of the Gothic genre, S. E. Boggs's "The Nameless Castle" stands as a testament to his talent as a storyteller and his ability to evoke a sense of dread and fascination in equal measure. With its labyrinthine plot and haunting imagery, this novel is sure to ensnare readers in its web of mystery, leaving them spellbound until the final, chilling revelation.

--

CONTENTS

INTRODUCTION..9

DR. MAURUS JOKAI 11

PART I
CYTHERA'S BRIGADE
CHAPTER I 15

CHAPTER II 23

CHAPTER III 27

CHAPTER IV 39

PART II
THE HOME OF ANECDOTE
CHAPTER I 45

CHAPTER II 53

CHAPTER III 62

PART III
THE MISTRESS OF THE CATS
CHAPTER I 68

CHAPTER II 72

CHAPTER III 79

CHAPTER IV 86

PART IV
SATAN LACZI
CHAPTER I 95

CHAPTER II 101

CHAPTER III 106

CHAPTER IV 120

PART V
ANGE BARTHELMY

CHAPTER I 125

CHAPTER II 130

CHAPTER III 145

PART VI
DEATH AND NEW LIFE IN THE
NAMELESS CASTLE

CHAPTER I 151

CHAPTER II 159

CHAPTER III 163

CHAPTER IV 169

CHAPTER V 175

CHAPTER VI 178

PART VII
THE HUNGARIAN MILITIA

CHAPTER I 186

CHAPTER II 190

CHAPTER III 195

PART VIII
KATHARINA OR THEMIRE?

CHAPTER I 203

CHAPTER II 209

CHAPTER III 212

PART IX
SATAN AND DEMON

CHAPTER I 217

CHAPTER II 225

CHAPTER III 229

CHAPTER IV 235

PART X
CONCLUSION
CHAPTER I 238

CHAPTER II 242

CHAPTER III 247

INTRODUCTION

TO THE ENGLISH TRANSLATION OF MY WORKS

This is not the first occasion upon which it has been my good fortune to win appreciation and approval for my works from the reading public of the United States. Up to the present, however, it has often been under difficulties; for many of my works which have been published in the English tongue were not translated from the original Hungarian text, while others, through want of a final perusal, were introduced to the public marred by numerous faults.

In the present edition we have striven to give the English reading public a correct translation, for which an authorized text has been utilized by the Doubleday & McClure Co., who have sole right for publishing future English translations of my books.

Between the United States and Hungary we discover many common traits: the same state-creative energy in the predominant people, which finds expression in constitutional forms, relying upon the love of freedom, which unites so many different races in one uniform whole; the same independent institutions; the same ideas in religion, in ethics; the same respect for women, the same esteem of labor, the same mental culture; a striving after progress, yet side by side with this a high respect for traditions; the same poetry of agriculture, the same prose of industry; rapid progress of both, and in consequence thereof an impetuous growth of towns.

Yet, while we find so many common traits between America and Hungary in the great field of theory, those typical figures which here in Hungary represent such theories must make a novel and extraordinary *entrée* in the New World, that they may deserve to win the interest of the foreign reader.

Hungary still represents a piece and parcel of the Old World; she is not so much Europe as a modern Asia. My novels centre round those peculiar figures of Hungarian common life; and in every work of mine a bit of history of true common life will be found described. I have had a particular delight, however, in occupying myself with foreign countries, especially with the East. There have been years when I was compelled to choose subjects for novel-writing in foreign parts.

In English and in Hungarian literature we find a common trait in that humor which is discovered also in the tragic; a characteristic of the nation itself.

It is with perfect confidence and in good hope that I present my present work (translated so faithfully) before the much-esteemed English reading public. May God bless that home of freedom, by whose example we have learnt how to unite the greatness of the state with the welfare of the people.

DR. MAURUS JOKAI.

BUDAPEST, May 11th, 1898.

DR. MAURUS JOKAI

A Sketch

To a man who has earned such titles as "The Shakespeare of Hungary" and "The Glory of Hungarian Literature"; who published in fifty years three hundred and fifty novels, dramas, and miscellaneous works, not to mention innumerable articles for the press that owes its freedom chiefly to him, it seems incredible that there was ever a time of indecision as to what career he was best fitted to follow. The idle life of the nobility into which Maurus Jókay was born in 1825 had no attractions for a strongly intellectual boy, fired with zeal and energy that carried him easily to the head of each class in school and college; nor did he feel any attraction for the prosaic practice of law, his father's profession, to which Austria's despotism drove many a nobleman in those wretched days for Hungary. It was Pétofi, the poet, who was his dearest friend during the student-life at Pápa; idealism ever attracted him, and, by natural gravitation toward the finest minds, he chose the friendship of young men who quickly rose into eminence during the days of revolution and invasion that tried men's souls.

For a time Jókay, as he then wrote his name, was undecided whether to choose literature or art as an outlet for the idealism, imagination, and devotion that overflowed in two directions from this boy of seventeen. With some of the inherited artistic talent, which in his relative Munkacsy amounted to genius, he felt most inclined toward painting and sculpture, and finally consecrated himself to them. In his library at Budapest there now stands a small, well-executed bust of his wife in ivory; and on the walls hang several landscapes and still-life paintings, which he showed with a smile to an American visitor, who stood silent before them last winter, hoping for some inspiration of speech that would reconcile politeness with veracity and her own ideals of good art. If a "deep love for art and an ardent desire to excel" will "more than compensate for the want of method," to quote Sir Joshua Reynolds, then Jókay would have been a great painter indeed. While he never was that, his chisel and brushes have remained a recreation and delight to him always.

Apparently he was diverted from art to literature by a trifle; but in the light of later developments it is simple enough to see which was really the greater force working within. The Academy of Arts and Sciences, founded by Szécheni, offered a prize for the best drama, and Jókay won it. He was then seventeen, for careers began early in olden times. When twenty-one his first novel, "Work Days," met with great applause; other romances quickly followed, and, as they dealt with the social and political tendencies that fanned the revolution into flame two years later, their success was instantaneous. His true representations of Hungarian life and character, his passionate love of liberty, his lofty idealism for his crushed and lethargic country, aroused a great wave of patriotism like a call to arms, and consecrated him to work with his pen for the freedom of the common people. Henceforth paint-brushes were cast aside.

Pétofi and Jókay, teeming with great ideas, quickly attracted other writers and young men of the university about them, and, each helping the other, brought about a bloodless revolution that secured, among other inestimable boons, the freedom of a censored, degraded press. And yet the only act of violence these young revolutionists committed was in entering a printing establishment and setting up with their own hands the type for Pétofi's poem, that afterward became the war-song of the national movement. At that very establishment was soon to be printed a proclamation granting twelve of their dearest wishes to the people. From this time Jókay changed the spelling of his name to Jókai, y being a badge of nobility hateful to disciples of the doctrine of liberty, fraternity, equality.

About this time Jókai married the Rachel of the Hungarian stage, Rosa Laborfalvy. The portrait of her that hangs in her husband's famous library shows a beautiful woman of intense sensitiveness, into whose face some of the sadness of her rôles seems to have crept. It was to her powers of impersonation and disguise that Jókai owed his life many years later, when, imprisoned and suffering in a dungeon, he was enabled to escape in her clothes to join Kossuth in the desperate fight against the allied armies of Austria and Russia. Since her death he has lived in retirement.

The bloodless revolution of 1848, which suddenly transformed Hungary into a modern state, possessing civil and religious liberty for which the young idealists led by Kossuth had labored with such passionate zeal, was not effected without antagonizing the old aristocracy, all of whose cherished institutions were suddenly swept away; or the semi-barbaric people of the peasant class, who could little appreciate the beneficent reforms. Into the awful civil war that followed, when the horrors of an Austrian-Russian invasion were added to the already desperate situation, Jókai plunged with magnificent heroism. Side by side with Kossuth, he fought with sword and pen. Those who heard him deliver an address at the Peace Congress at Brussels two years ago felt through his impassioned eloquence that the man had himself drained the bitterest dregs of war.

While Kossuth lived in exile in England and the United States, and many other compatriots escaped to Turkey and beyond, Jókai, in concealment at home, writing under an assumed name and with a price on his head, continued his work for social reform, until a universal pardon was granted by Austria and the saddened idealists once more dared show their faces in devastated Hungary.

Ripe with experience and full of splendid intellectual power, Jókai now turned his whole attention to literature. The pages of his novels glow with the warmth of the man's intensity of feeling: his pen had been touched by a living coal. He knew his country as no other man has known it; and transferred its types, its manners, its life in high degree and low, to the pages of his romances and dramas with a brilliancy and mastery of style that captivated the people, whose idol he still remains. Scenes from Turkish life—in which, next to Hungarian, he is particularly interested; historical novels, romances of pure imagination, short tales, dramatic works, essays on literature and social questions, came pouring from his surcharged brain and heart. The very virtues of his work, its intensity, and the boundless scope of its imagination, sometimes produce a lack of unity and an improbability to which the hypercritical in the West draw attention with a sense of superior wisdom; but the Hungarians themselves, who know whereof he writes, can see no faults whatever in his work. It is essentially idealistic; the true and the beautiful shine through it with radiant lustre, in sharp distinction from the scenes of famine and carnage that abound. His Turkish stories have been described as "full of blood and roses."

Of his more mature productions, the best known are: "A Magyar Nabob"; "The Fools of Love"; "The New Landlord"; "Black Diamonds"; "A Romance of the Coming Century"; "Handsome Michael"; "God is One," in which the Unitarians play an important part; "The Nameless Castle," that gives an account of the Hungarian army employed against Napoleon in 1809; "Captive Ráby," a romance of the times of Joseph II.; and "As We Grow Old," the latter being the author's own favorite and, strangely enough, the people's also. Dr. Jókai greatly deplores that what the critics call his best work should not have been given to the English-speaking people.

In 1896 Hungary celebrated the completion of his fifty years of literary labor by issuing a beautiful jubilee edition of his works, for which the people of all grades of society subscribed $100,000. Every county in the country sent him memorials in the form of albums wrought in gold and precious stones, two hundred of these souvenirs filling one side of the author's large library and reception-room. Low bookcases running around the walls are filled only with his own publications, the various editions of his three hundred and fifty books making a large library in themselves. The cabinets hold sketches and paintings sent by the artists of Hungary as a jubilee gift; there are cases containing carvings, embroidery, lace, and natural-history specimens sent him by the peasants, and orders in gold and silver, studded with jewels, with autograph letters from the kings and queens of Europe. In the midst of all this inspiring display of loving appreciation, Dr. Jókai has his desk; a pile of neatly written, even manuscript ever before him, for in his seventy-fourth year he still feels the old-time passion for work calling him to it early in the morning and holding him in its spell all the day long. A small room adjoining his library contains the books of reference he consults, a narrow bed like a soldier's, and a few window plants. It might be the room of a monk, so bare is it of what the world calls comforts. One devoted man-servant attends to Dr. Jókai's simple wants with abundant leisure to spare.

While in Budapest Dr. Jókai is seldom seen away from home, except in Parliament, where he has a seat in the Upper House, or at the theatre where his plays are regularly performed, or at the table of a few dear relatives and old-time friends. His life is exceedingly simple and well ordered.

Just a little way back on the hills that rise beyond Buda, across the Danube and overlooking wide stretches of beautiful, fertile country, stands Dr. Jókai's summer-home. His garden is a paradise. Quantities of roses climb over the unpretentious house, the paths are lined with them; gay beds of poppies and other familiar favorites in our Western gardens, but many new to American eyes, crowd the fruit that grows in delightful abundance everywhere, for Dr. Jókai tends his garden with his own hands, and his horticultural wisdom is only second to his knowledge of the Turkish wars. His apples, pears, and roses win prizes at all the shows, and his little book, "Hints on Gardening," propagates a large crop of like-minded enthusiasts year after year. Now, as ever, any knowledge he has he shares with the people. After a long life of bitter stress and labor, abundant peace has come in the latter days.

Hungary boasts four great men: Liszt, Munkacsy, Kossuth, and Jókai, who was the intimate friend of the other three.

NELTJE BLANCHAN.

NEW YORK, JUNE, 1898.

PART I
CYTHERA'S BRIGADE

CHAPTER I

A snow-storm was raging with such vigor that any one who chanced to be passing along the silent thoroughfare might well have believed himself in St. Petersburg instead of in Paris, in the Rue des Ours, a side street leading into the Avenue St. Martin. The street, never a very busy one, was now almost deserted, as was also the avenue, as it was yet too early for vehicles of various sorts to be returning from the theatre.

The street-lamps on the corners had not yet been lighted. In front of one of those old-fashioned houses which belong to a former Paris a heavy iron lantern swung, creaking in the wind, and, battling with the darkness, shed flickering rays of light on the child who, with a faded red cotton shawl wrapped about her, was cowering in the deep doorway of the house. From time to time there would emerge from the whirling snowflakes the dark form of a man clad as a laborer. He would walk leisurely toward the doorway in which the shivering child was concealed, but would turn when he came to the circle of light cast on the snowy pavement by the swinging lantern, and retrace his steps, thus appearing and disappearing at regular intervals. Surely a singular time and place for a promenade! The clocks struck ten—the hour which found every honest dweller within the Quartier St. Martin at home. On this evening, however, two belated citizens came from somewhere, their hurrying footsteps noiseless in the deep snow, their approach announced only by the lantern carried by one of them—an article without which no respectable citizen at the beginning of the century would have ventured on the street after nightfall. One of the pedestrians was tall and broad-shouldered, with a handsome countenance, which bore the impress of an inflexible determination; a dimple indented his smoothly shaven chin. His companion, and his senior by several years, was a slender, undersized man.

When the two men came abreast of the doorway illumined by the swinging lamp, it was evident that they had arrived at their destination. They halted and prepared to enter the house.

At this moment the child crouching in the snow began to sob.

"See here!" exclaimed the taller of the two gentlemen. "Here is a little girl."

"Why, so there is!" in turn exclaimed the elder, stooping and letting the light of his lantern fall on the child's face. "What are you doing here, little one?" he asked in a kindly tone.

"I want my mama! I want my mama!" wailed the child, with a fresh burst of sobs.

"Who is your mama?" queried the younger man.

"My mama is the countess."

"And where does she live?"

"In the palace."

"Naturally! In which avenue is the palace?"

"I—don't—know."

"A true child of Paris!" in an undertone exclaimed the elder gentleman. "She knows that her mother is a countess, and that she lives in a palace; but she has never been told the name of the street in which is her home."

"How come you to be here, little countess?" inquired the younger man.

"Diana can tell you," was the reply.

"And who may Diana be?"

"Why, who else but mama's Diana?"

"Allow me to question her," here interposed the elder man. Then, to the child: "Diana is the person who helps you put on your clothes, is she not?"

"It is just the other way: she took off my clothes—just see; I have nothing on but this petticoat and this hideous shawl."

As she spoke she flung back the faded shawl and revealed how scantily she was clad.

"You poor child!" compassionately ejaculated the young man; and when he saw that her thin morocco slippers were buried in the snow, he lifted her hastily in his arms. "You are half frozen."

"But why did Diana leave you half clothed in this manner?" pursued the elder man. "Why did she undress you? Can't you tell us that much?"

"Mama slapped her this morning."

"Ah! then Diana is a servant?"

"Why, of course; what else could she be?"

"Well, she might be a goddess or a hound, you know," smilingly returned the old gentleman.

"When mama went to the opera, this evening," explained the little one, "she ordered Diana to take me to the children's ball at the marquis's. Instead, she brought me to this street, made me get out of the carriage, took off my silk ball-gown and all my pretty ornaments, and left me here in this doorway—I am sure I don't know why, for there is n't any music here."

"It is well she left this old shawl with you, else your mama would not have a little countess to tell the tale to-morrow," observed the elder man. Then, turning to his companion, he added in a lower tone: "What are we to do with her?"

"We can't leave her here; that would be inhuman," was the reply, in the same cautious tone.

"But we can't take her in; it would be a great risk."

"What is there to fear from an innocent prattler who cannot even remember her mother's name?"

"We might take her to the conciergerie," suggested the elder gentleman.

"*I* think we had better not disturb the police when they are asleep," in a significant tone responded his companion.

"That is true; but we can't take the child to our apartments. You know that we—"

"I have an idea!" suddenly interposed the young man. "This innocent child has been placed in our way by Providence; by aiding her we may accomplish more easily the task we have undertaken."

"I understand," assented the elder; "we can accomplish two good deeds at one and the same time. Allow me to go up-stairs first; while you are locking the door I will arrange matters up there so that you may bring this poor little half-frozen creature directly with you." Then, to the child: "Don't be afraid, little countess; nothing shall harm you. To-morrow morning perhaps you will remember your mama's name, or else she will send some one in search of you."

He opened the door, and ran hastily up the worn staircase.

When the young man, with the little girl in his arms, reached the door at the head of the stairs, his companion met him, and, with a meaning glance, announced that everything was ready for the reception of their small guest. They entered a dingy anteroom, which led, through heavily curved antique sliding-doors, into a vaulted saloon hung with faded tapestry.

Here the child exhibited the first signs of alarm. "Are you going to kill me?" she cried out in terror.

The old gentleman laughed merrily, and said:

"Why, surely you don't take us to be *croquemitaines* who devour little children; do you?"

"Have you got a little girl of your own?" queried the little one, suddenly.

"No, my dear," replied the old gentleman, visibly affected by the question. "I have no wife; therefore I cannot have a little girl."

"But my mama has no husband, and she 's got me," prattled the child.

"That is different, my dear. But if I have not got a little girl, I know very well what to do for one."

As he spoke he drew off the child's wet slippers and stockings, rubbed her feet with a flannel cloth, then laid her on the bed which stood in the alcove.

"Why, how warm this bed is!" cried the child; "just as if some one had been sleeping here."

The old man's face betrayed some confusion as he responded:

"Might I not have warmed it with a warming-pan?"

"But where did you get hot coals?"

"Well, well, what an inquisitive little creature it is!" muttered the old man. Then, aloud: "My dear, don't you say your prayers before going to sleep?"

"No, indeed! Mama says we shall have plenty of time for that when we grow old."

"An enlightened woman, truly! Well, I dare say, my little maid, your convictions will not prevent you from drinking a cup of egg-punch, and partaking of a bit of pasty or a small biscuit?"

At mention of these dainties the child's countenance brightened; and while she was eating the repast with evident relish, the younger man rummaged from somewhere a large, beautifully dressed doll. All thought of fear now vanished from the small guest's mind. She clasped the toy in her arms, and, having finished her light meal, began to sing a lullaby, to which she very soon fell asleep herself.

"She is sleeping soundly," whispered the elder man, softly drawing together the faded damask bed-curtains, and walking on tiptoe back to the fireplace, where his companion had fanned the fire into a fresh blaze.

"It is high time," was the low and rather impatient response. "We can't stop here much longer. Do you know what has happened to the duke?"

"Yes, I know. He has been sentenced to death. To-morrow he will be executed. What have you discovered?"

"A fox on the trail of a lion!" harshly replied the young man. "He who aroused so many hopes is, after all, nothing more than an impostor—Leon Maria Hervagault, the son of a tailor at St. Leu. The true dauphin, the son of Louis XVI., really died a natural death, after he had served a three years' apprenticeship as shoemaker under Master Simho; and in order that a later generation might not be able to secure his ashes, he was buried in quick-lime in the Chapel of St. Margarethe."

"They were not so scrupulous concerning monsieur," [1] observed the old man, restlessly pacing the floor. "I received a letter from my agent to-day; he writes that monsieur was secretly shot at Dillingen."

[1] Count de Provence, afterward Louis XVIII.

"What! He, too? Then—"

"Hush!" cautiously interposed the elder man. "That child might not be asleep."

"And if she were awake, what could she understand?"

"True; but we must be cautious." He ceased his restless promenade, and came close to the young man's side. "Everything is at an end here," he added in a lower tone. "We must remove our treasure to a more secure hiding-place—this very night, indeed, if it be possible."

"It is possible," assented his companion. "The plan of flight was arranged two days ago. The most difficult part was to get away from this house. It is watched day and night. Chance, however, has come to our aid."

"I understand," nodded the old gentleman, glancing significantly toward the bed.

"The most serious question now is, where shall we find a secure hiding-place? Even England is not safe. The bullets of Dillingen can reach to that country! Indeed, wherever there are police no secret is safe."

"I 'll tell you something," after a moment's deliberation observed the elder man. "I know of a country in Europe where order prevails, and where there are no police spies; and, what is more, the place of which I speak is beyond the range of a gunshot!"

"I confess I am curious to learn where such a place may be found," with an incredulous smile returned the young man.

"Fetch the map, and I will point it out to you. Afterward we will arrange your route toward it." The two men spread a large map of Europe on the table, and, bending over it, were soon deeply absorbed in examining it, the while exchanging whispered remarks.

At last they seemed to have agreed on something. The map was folded up and thrust into the younger man's pocket.

"I shall start at once," he said, with an air of decision.

"That is well," with evident satisfaction assented his companion. "And take with you also the steel casket. In it are all the necessary documents, some articles of clothing on which the mother with her own hands embroidered the well-known symbol, and a million of francs in English bank-notes. These, however, you will not use unless compelled to do so by extreme necessity. You will receive annually a sufficient sum from a certain banking-house which will supply all your wants. Have our two trusty friends been apprised?"

"Yes; they await me hourly."

"So soon as you are beyond the French boundary you may communicate with me in the way we have agreed upon. Until I hear from you I shall be in a terror of anxiety. I am sorry I cannot accompany you, but I am already suspected. You are, as yet, free from suspicion—are not yet registered in the black book!"

"You may trust my skill to evade pursuit," said the young man, producing from a secret cupboard a casket richly ornamented with gold.

"I do not doubt your skill, or your ability to accomplish the undertaking; but the task is not a suitable one for so young a man. Have you considered the fate which awaits you?"

"I have considered everything."

"You will be buried; and, what is worse, you will be the keeper of your own prison."

"I shall be a severe jailer, I promise you," with a grim smile responded the young man.

"Jester! You forget your twenty-six years! And who can tell how long you may be buried alive?"

"Have no fear for me. I do not dread the task. Those in power now will one day be overthrown."

"But when the child, who is only twelve years old now, becomes in three or four years a blooming maiden—what then? Already she is fond of you; then she will love you. You cannot hinder it; and yet, you will not even dare to dream of returning her love. Have you thought of this also?"

"I shall look upon myself as the inhabitant of a different planet," answered the young man.

"Your hand, my friend! You have undertaken a noble task—one that is greater than that of the captive knight who cut off his own foot, that his sovereign, who was chained to him, might escape—"

"Pray say no more about me," interposed his companion. "Is the child asleep?"

"This one is; the one in the other room is awake."

"Then let us go to her and tell her what we have decided." He lifted the two-branched candlestick from the table; his companion carefully closed the iron doors of the fireplace; then the two went into the adjoining chamber, leaving the room they had quitted in darkness.

The elder gentleman had made a mistake: "this" child was *not* asleep. She had listened attentively, half sitting up in bed, to as much of the conversation as she could hear.

A ray of light penetrated through the keyhole. The little girl sprang nimbly from the bed, ran to the door, and peered through the tiny aperture. Suddenly footsteps came toward the door. When it opened, however, the little eavesdropper was back underneath the covers of the bed. The old gentleman entered the room. He had no candle. He left the door open, walked noiselessly to the bed, and drew aside the curtains to see if "this" child was still asleep. The long-drawn, regular breathing convinced him. Then he took something from the chair beside the bed, and went back into the other room. The object he had taken from the chair was the faded red shawl in which the stray child had been wrapped. He did not close the door of the adjoining chamber, for the candles had been extinguished and both rooms were now dark.

To the listening child in the bed, however, it seemed as if voices were whispering near her—as if she heard a stifled sob. Then cautious footsteps crossed the floor, and after an interval of silence the street door opened and closed.

Very soon afterward a light was struck in the adjoining room, and the elder man came through the doorway—alone.

He flung back the doors of the fireplace, and stirred the embers; then he proceeded to perform a singular task. First he tossed a number of letters and papers into the flames, then several dainty articles of girls' clothing. He watched them until they had burned to ashes; then he flung himself into an arm-chair; his head sank forward on his breast, in which position he sat motionless for several hours.

CHAPTER II

When the younger of the two men stepped into the street he carried in his arms a little girl wrapped in a faded red shawl, to whom he was speaking encouragingly, in tones loud enough for any passer-by to hear:

"I know the little countess will be able to find her mama's palace; for there is a fountain in front of it in which there is a stone man with a three-pronged fork, and a stone lady with a fish-tail! Oh, yes; we shall be sure to find it; and very soon we shall be with mama."

Here the child in his arms began to sob bitterly.

"For heaven's sake, do not weep; do not let your voice be heard," whispered the young man in her ear.

At this moment a man wearing a coarse blouse, with his cap drawn over his eyes and a short pipe between his lips, came staggering toward them. The young man, in order to make room for him, pressed close to the wall, whereupon the new-comer, who seemed intoxicated, began in drunken tones:

"Hello, citizen! What do you mean? Do you want me to walk in the gutter?—because you have got on fine boots, and I have only wooden sabots! I am a citizen like yourself, and as good as you. We are alike, are n't we?"

The young man now knew with whom he had to deal—a police spy whose duty it was to watch him. He therefore replied quietly:

"No, we are not alike, citizen; for I have in my arms an unfortunate child who has strayed from its mother. Every Frenchman respects a child and misfortune. Is not that so, citizen?"

"Yes, that is so, citizen. Let 's have a little conversation about it"; and the pretended drunkard seized hold of the young man's mantle to detain him.

"It is very cold," returned the young man. "Instead of talking here, suppose you help me get this child to its home. Go to the nearest corner and fetch a coach. I will wait here for you."

The blouse-wearer hesitated a moment, then walked toward the street-corner, managing, however, to keep an eye on the young man and his charge. At the corner he whistled in a peculiar manner, whereupon the rumbling of wheels was heard. In a few moments the leather-covered vehicle drew up beside the curb where the young man was waiting.

"I am very much obliged to you for your kindness, citizen," he said to the blouse-wearer, who had returned with the coach. "Here," pressing a twenty-sou piece into the man's palm, "is something for your trouble. I wish you would come with me to help hunt for this little girl's home. If you have time, and will come with me, you shall be paid for your trouble."

"Can't do it, citizen; my wife is expecting me at home. Just you trust this coachman; he will help you find the place. He 's a clever youth—are n't you, Peroquin? You have made many a night journey about Paris, have n't you? See that you earn your twenty francs to-night, too!"

That the coachman was also in the service of the secret police the young man knew very well; but he did not betray his knowledge by word or mien.

The blouse-wearer now shook hands cordially with the young man, and said:

"Adieu, citizen. I beg your pardon if I offended you. I 'll leave you now. I am going to my wife, or to the tavern; who can tell the future?"

He waited until the young man had entered the coach with his charge; then, instead of betaking himself to his wife or to the tavern, he crossed the street, and took up his station in the recess of a doorway opposite the house with the swinging lantern. . . .

"Where to?" asked the coachman of the young man.

"Well, citizen," was the smiling response, "if I knew that, all would be well. But that is just what I don't know; and the little countess, here, who has strayed from her home, can't remember the street, nor the number of the house, in which she lives. She can only remember that her mama's palace is on a square in which there is a fountain. We must therefore visit all the fountains in turn until we find the right one."

The coachman made no further inquiries, but climbed to the box, and drove off in quest of the fountains of Paris.

Two fountains were visited, but neither of them proved to be the right one. The young man now bade the coachman drive through a certain street to a third fountain. It was a narrow, winding street—the Rue des Blancs Manteaux.

When the coach was opposite a low, one-storied house, the young man drew the strap, and told the driver he wished to stop for a few moments. As the vehicle drew up in front of the house, the door opened, and a tall, stalwart man in top-boots came forth, accompanied by a sturdy dame who held a candle, which she protected from the wind with the palm of her hand.

"Is that you, Raoul?" called the young man from the coach window.

There was no response from the giant, who, instead, sprang nimbly to the box, and, flinging one arm around the astonished coachman, thrust a gag into his mouth. Before the captive could make a move to defend himself, his fare was out of the coach, and had pinioned his arms behind his back. The giant and the young man now lifted the coachman from the box and carried him into the house, the woman followed with the trembling child, whom she had carefully lifted from the coach.

In the house, the two men bound their captive securely, first removing his coat. Then they seated him on the couch, and placed a mirror in front of him.

"You need not be alarmed, citizen," said the man in the top-boots. "No harm shall come to you. We are only going to copy your face—because of its beauty, you know!"

The young man also seated himself in front of the mirror, and proceeded, with various brushes and colors, to paint his cheeks and nose a copper hue, exactly like that of the coachman's reflection in the glass. Then he exchanged his own peruke and hat for the shabby ones of the coachman. Lastly, he flung around his shoulders the mantle with its seven collars, and the resemblance was complete.

"And now," observed the giant, addressing the captive, "you can rest without the least fear. At the latest, to-morrow about this time your coach, your horses, your mantle, and whatever else belongs to you will be returned. For the use of the things we have borrowed from you we shall leave in the pocket of your coat twenty francs for every hour, and an extra twenty francs as a *pourboire*; don't forget to look for it! To-morrow at eleven o'clock a girl will fetch milk; she will release you, and you can tell her what a singular dream you had! If you can't go to sleep, just repeat the multiplication table. I always do when I can't sleep, and I never have to go beyond seven times seven. Good night, citizen!"

The door of the adjoining room opened, and the woman appeared, leading by the hand a pretty little boy.

"We are ready," she announced.

The two men thrust pistols into their pockets. Then the woman and the little boy entered the coach, the two men took seats on the box, and the coach rolled away.

CHAPTER III

At ten o'clock the next morning the old gentleman paid a visit to his little guest. This time the child was really asleep, and opened her eyes only when the curtains were drawn back and the light from the window fell on her face.

"How kind of you to waken me, monsieur!" she said, smiling; she was in a good humor, as children are who have slept well. "I have slept splendidly. This bed is as good as my own at home. And how delightful not to hear my governess scolding! You never scold, do you, monsieur? I deserve to be scolded, though, for I was very naughty last night, and you were so kind to me—gave me such nice egg-punch; see, there is a glass of it left over; it will do for my breakfast. I love cold punch, so you need not trouble to bring me any chocolate." With these words, the little maid sprang nimbly from the bed, ran with the naïveté of an eight-year-old child to the table, where she settled herself in the corner of the sofa, drew her bare feet up under her, and proceeded to breakfast on the left-over punch and biscuits.

"There! that was a good breakfast," she said, after she had finished her meal. "Oh, I almost forgot. Has mama sent for me?"

"Certainly not, my dear! We are going, by and by, to look for her. The countess very likely has not yet learned of your disappearance; and if she does know that you did not return home last night, she believes you safe with the marquis. She will think you were not allowed to return home in the storm, and will not expect to see you before noon."

"You are very clever, monsieur. I should never have thought of that! I imagined that mama would be vexed, and when mama is cross she is *so* disagreeable. At other times, though, she is perfectly lovely! You will see how very beautiful she is, monsieur, for you are coming home with me to tell her how you found me—you are so very kind! How I wish you were my papa!"

The old gentleman was touched by the little one's artless prattle.

"Well, my dear little maid," he said tenderly, "we can't think of showing ourselves on the street in such a costume. Besides, it would frighten your mama to see you so. I am going out to one of the shops to buy you a frock. Tell me, what sort was it Diana took from you?"

"A lovely pink silk, trimmed with lace, with short sleeves," promptly replied the little maid.

"I shall not forget—a pink silk, trimmed with lace. You need not be afraid to stay alone here. No one will come while I am away."

"Oh, I am not the least bit afraid. I like to be alone sometimes."

"There is the doll to keep you company," suggested the old gentleman, more and more pleased with his affable little visitor.

"Is n't she lovely!" enthusiastically exclaimed the child. "She slept with me last night, and every time I woke up I kissed her."

"You shall have her for your own, if you like her so much, my dear."

"Oh, thank you! Did the doll belong to your dear little daughter who is dead?"

"Yes—yes," sorrowfully murmured the old gentleman.

"Then I will not play with her, but keep her locked in my little cupboard, and call her Philine. That was the name of my little sister who is dead. Come here, Philine, and sit by me."

"Perhaps you might like to look at a book while I am away—"

"A book!" interrupted the child, with a merry laugh, clapping her hands. "Why, I am just learning the alphabet, and can't bring myself to call a two-pronged fork 'y.'"

"You dear little innocent rogue!" tenderly ejaculated the old gentleman. "Are you fond of flowers?"

He brought from the adjoining room a porcelain flowerpot containing a narcissus in bloom.

"Oh, what a charming flower!" cried the child, admiringly. "How I wish I might pluck just one!"

"Help yourself, my dear," returned her host, pushing the plant toward her.

The child daintily broke off one of the snowy blossoms, and, with childlike coquetry, fastened it in the trimming of her chemise.

"What is this beautiful flower called, monsieur?"

"The narcissus."

At mention of the name the little maid suddenly clapped her hands and cried joyfully:

"Why, that is the name of our palace! Now don't you know where it is?"

"The 'Palace of Narcissus'? I have heard of it."

"Then you will have no trouble finding my home. Oh, you dear good little flower!" and she kissed the snowy blossom rapturously.

The old gentleman surveyed her smilingly for a few moments, then said:

"I will go now, and buy the frock."

"And while you are away I shall tell Philine the story of Gargantua," responded the child.

"Lock the door after me, my dear, and do not open it until I mention my name: Alfred Cambray—"

"Oh, I should forget the second one! Just say, 'Papa Alfred'; I can remember that."

When the child was certain that the old gentleman had left the house, she began hastily to search the room. She peered into every corner and crevice. Then she went into the adjoining chamber, and opened every drawer and cupboard. In returning to the first room she saw some scraps of paper scattered about the floor. She collected them carefully, placed them on the table, and dexterously fitted the pieces together until the entire note-sheet lay before her. It was covered with writing which had evidently been traced by a hurried hand, yet the child seemed to have no difficulty in reading it.

When she heard the old gentleman's footstep on the staircase, she brushed the scraps of paper from the table, and hastened to open the door before the signal was given; and when he exhibited his purchase she danced for joy.

"It is just like my ball-gown—exactly like it!" she exclaimed, kissing the hands of her benefactor. Then the old gentleman clothed the child as skilfully as if he were accustomed to such work. When the task was finished he looked about him, and saw the scraps of paper on the floor; he swept them together, and threw them into the fire.

Then, with the hand of his little companion clasped in his own, he descended to the street in quest of a cab to take them to the Palace of Narcissus.

The Palace of Narcissus had originally been the property of the celebrated danseuse, Mlle. Guimard, for whom it had been built by the

Duke de Soubise. Like so many other fine houses, it had been confiscated by the Revolution and sold at auction—or, rather, had been disposed of by lottery, a lady who had paid one hundred and twenty francs for her ticket winning it.

The winner of the palace sold it to M. Périgaud, a banker and shrewd speculator, who divided the large dwelling into suites of apartments, which became the favorite lodgings of the young men of fashion. These young men were called the "narcissi," and later, the "incroyables" and "petits crevés." The building, however, retained the name of the Palace of Narcissus.

When the fiacre stopped at the door of the palace which led to her mama's apartment, the little countess alighted with her escort, and said to the coachman:

"You need not wait; the marquis will return home in my mama's carriage."

M. Cambray was obliged to submit to be called the "marquis." The harmless fib was due to the rank of the little countess; she could not have driven through the streets of Paris in the same fiacre with a pékin!

"We will not go up the main staircase," said the child, taking her companion's arm and leading him into the palace. "I don't want to meet any of the servants. We will go directly to mama's boudoir, and take her by surprise."

The countess mother, however, was not in her boudoir; only a screaming cockatoo, and a capuchin monkey that grimaced a welcome. Through the folding-doors which opened into an adjoining room came the melancholy tones of a harmonium; and M. Cambray recognized a favorite air—Beethoven's symphony, "Les adieux, l'absence, et le retour." He paused a moment to listen to it.

"That is mama playing," whispered the child. "You go in first, and tell her you have brought me home. Be very careful; mama is very nervous." M. Cambray softly opened the door, and halted, amazed, on the threshold.

The room into which he had ventured unannounced was a magnificent salon, filled with a brilliant company. Evidently the countess was holding a matinée.

The assembled company were in full toilet. The women, who were chiefly young and handsome, were clad in the modest fashion of that day, which draped the shoulders and bust with embroidered kerchiefs, with priceless lace adorning their gowns and genuine pearls twined among their tresses.

The men also wore full dress: Hungarian trousers, short-waisted coat, with large, bright metal buttons, opening over an embroidered waistcoat.

Surrounded by her guests, the mistress of the house, an ideal of beauty, Cythera herself, was seated at the harpsichord, her neck and shoulders hidden by her wonderfully beautiful golden hair. When M. Cambray, in his plain brown coat buttoned to the chin, with black gloves and dull buckle-shoes, appeared in the doorway of the boudoir, which was not open to all the world, every eye was turned in surprise toward him.

The lady at the harpsichord rose, surveyed the intruder with a haughty stare, and was about to speak when a lackey in silver-embroidered livery came hastily toward her and said something in a low tone.

"What?" she ejaculated, with sudden terror. "My daughter lost?"

The guests crowded around her, and a scene of great excitement followed.

Here M. Cambray came forward and said:

"I have found your daughter, countess, and return her to you."

The lovely woman made one step toward the child, who had followed M. Cambray into the room, then sank to the floor unconscious. She was tenderly lifted and borne into the boudoir. Two physicians, who were of the company, followed.

When the door closed behind them, the entire company remaining in the salon gathered about M. Cambray. The ladies seized his hands; and while a blonde houri on his right sought to attract his attention, a brunette beauty claimed it on his left—both women ignoring the attempts of the men to shake hands with the hero of the hour.

One of the men, an elderly and distinguished-looking personage with a commanding mien, now pressed forward to introduce himself. "Monsieur, I am the Marquis Lyonel de Fervlans," he repeated in a patronizing tone.

"I am Alfred Cambray," was the simple response.

"Ah? Pray, have the kindness to tell us—the friends of the countess— what has happened?"

M. Cambray related how and where he had found the lost child, the company listening with eager attention. All were deeply affected. Some of the women wept. When M. Cambray concluded his recital, the marquis grasped both his hands, and, pressing them warmly, said in a trembling voice:

"Thanks, many thanks, you brave, good man! We will never forget your kindness."

One of the physicians now came from the boudoir, and announced that the countess was better, and desired to speak to the deliverer of her child.

The countess was reclining on an ottoman, half buried in luxurious cushions. Her little daughter was kneeling by her side, her head resting on her mother's knee. It was a charming tableau.

"I am not able to express my gratitude, monsieur," began the countess, in a faint voice, extending both hands toward M. Cambray. "I hope you will allow me to call you my friend. I shall never cease to thank you! Amélie, my love, kiss this hand; look at this face; impress it on your heart, and never, *never* forget it, for this brave gentleman rescued you from a most horrible fate."

M. Cambray listened to these profuse expressions of gratitude, but with heedless ear. His thoughts were with the fugitives. He longed to know if they had escaped pursuit. While the countess was speaking he could not help but think that a great ado was being made because a little countess had been abandoned half clad in the public street. *He* knew of another little maid who had been treated with far greater cruelty.

His reply was brief:

"Your little daughter is very charming."

The mother sat upright with sudden decision, and unfastened the ivory locket from the black ribbon around her neck. It contained a portrait of the little countess Amélie.

"If the memory of the little foundling you rescued is dear to you, monsieur, then accept this from me, and think sometimes of your protégée."

It was a noble gift indeed! The lovely countess had given him her most valued ornament.

M. Cambray expressed his thanks, pressed his lips to the countess's hand, and kissed the little Amélie, who smilingly lifted her face for the caress. Then he bowed courteously, and returned to the salon. He was met at the door by the Marquis de Fervlans, who exclaimed reproachfully:

"What, you are going to desert us already? Then, if you will go, you must allow me to offer you my carriage." He gave his arm to the old gentleman, and conducted him to the vestibule, where, among a number of liveried servants, stood a trim hussar in Swiss uniform.

The marquis ordered the hussar to fetch his carriage, and, when it drew up before the door, himself assisted M. Cambray to enter it. Then he shook hands cordially with the old gentleman, stepped back to the doorway, and watched the carriage roll swiftly across the square.

When the servant Jocrisse had closed the boudoir door behind M. Cambray, the suffering countess sprang lightly from her couch, and pressed her handkerchief to her lips to smother her laughter; the little Amélie, overwhelmed by merriment, buried her face in her mother's skirts; the maid giggled discreetly; while Jocrisse, clasping his rotund stomach with both hands, bent his head toward his knees, and betrayed his suppressed hilarity by his shaking shoulders. Even the more important of the two physicians pursed his lips into a smile, and proffered his snuff-box to his colleague, who, smothering with laughter, whispered:

"Are we not capital actors?"

Meanwhile M. Cambray drove rapidly in the Marquis de Fervlans's carriage through the streets of Paris. He was buried in thought. He glanced only now and then from the window. He was not altogether satisfied with himself that he was riding in a carriage which belonged to so important a person—a gentleman whose name he had never heard until that day.

Suddenly he was surprised to find the carriage entering a gateway. A carriage could not enter the gate at his lodgings! The Swiss hussar sprang from the box, opened the carriage door, and M. Cambray found himself confronted by a sergeant with a drawn sword.

"This is not my residence," said the old gentleman.

"Certainly not," replied the sergeant. "This is the Prison of St. Pélagie."

"What have I to do here? My name is Alfred Cambray."

"You are the very one we have been expecting."

And now it was M. Cambray's turn to laugh merrily.

When M. Cambray's pockets had been searched, and everything suspicious confiscated, he was conducted to a room in the second story, in which he was securely locked. He had plenty of time to look about his new lodgings.

Apparently the room had been occupied by many an important personage. The walls were covered with names. Above some of them impromptu verses had been scribbled; others had perpetuated their profiles; and still others had drawn caricatures of those who had been the means of lodging them here. The guillotine also figured among the illustrations.

The new lodger was not specially surprised to find himself a prisoner; what he could not understand was the connection between the two events. How came it about that the courteous and sympathetic Marquis de Fervlans's carriage had brought him here from the palace of the deeply grateful countess?

He was puzzling his brain over this question when his door suddenly opened, and a morose old jailer entered with some soup and bread for the prisoner.

"Thanks, I have dined," said M. Cambray.

The jailer placed the food on the table, with the words: "I want you to understand, citizen, that if you have any idea of starving yourself to death, we shall pour the soup down your throat."

Toward evening another visitor appeared. The door was opened with loud clanking of chains and bolts, and a tall man crossed the threshold. It was the Marquis de Fervlans.

His manner now was not so condescending and sympathetic. He approached the prisoner, and said in a commanding tone that was evidently intended to be intimidating:

"You have been betrayed, and may as well confess everything; it is the only thing that will save you."

A scornful smile crossed the prisoner's lips. "That is the usual form of address to a criminal who has been arrested for burglary."

The marquis laughed.

"I see, M. Cambray, that you are not the sort of person to be easily frightened. It is useless to adopt the usual prison methods with you. Very well; then we will try a different one. It may be that we shall part quite good friends! What do I say? Part? Say, rather, that we may continue together, hand in hand! But to the point. You have a friend who shared the same apartment with you. This gentleman deserted you last night, I believe?"

"The ingrate!" ironically ejaculated M. Cambray.

"Beg pardon, but there was also a little girl secreted in your apartment, whom no one ever saw—"

"Pardon me, monsieur," interrupted Cambray, "but it is not the custom for French gentlemen to spy out or chatter about secrets which relate to the fair sex."

"I am not talking about the sort of female you refer to, monsieur, but about a child—a girl of perhaps twelve years."

"How, pray, can one determine the age of a lady whom no one has seen?"

"Certain telltale circumstances give one a clue," retorted De Fervlans. "Why, for instance, do you keep a doll in your rooms?"

"A doll? I play with it myself sometimes! I am a queer old fellow with peculiar tastes."

"Very good; we will allow that you are telling the truth. What have you to say to the fact that you took to your apartment yesterday evening a stray child, and an hour later your friend came out of the house with another child, wrapped in the shawl which had enveloped the lost child when you found her—"

"Have they been overtaken?" hastily interrupted Cambray, forgetting himself.

"No, they have not—more 's the pity!" returned the marquis. "My detective was not clever enough to perceive the difference between the eight-year-old girl who was carried to your apartments at ten o'clock, and the twelve-year-old little maid whom your friend brought downstairs at eleven, pretending that he was going in search of the lost child's mother. Besides, everything conspired to aid your friend to escape. He was too cunning for us, and got such a start of his pursuers that there was no use trying to follow him. We do not even know in what direction he has gone."

Cambray repressed the sigh of relief which would have lightened his heart, and forced himself to say indifferently:

"Neither the young man nor the child concern me. It is his own family affair, in which I never meddled."

"That is a move I cannot allow, M. Cambray!" sharply responded the marquis. "There are proofs that you are perfectly familiar with his affairs."

Again Cambray smiled scornfully.

"You have evidently searched my lodgings."

"We have done our duty, monsieur. We even tore up the floors, broke your furniture and ornaments,—for which we apologize,—and found nothing suspicious. Notwithstanding this, however, we know very well that you received a letter yesterday warning you of approaching danger. We know very well that you and your friend traced out the route of his flight;

we have a witness who listened to your plans, and who fitted together the scraps of the torn letter of warning, and read it."

"And who may this witness be?" queried Cambray.

"The child you picked up in the street."

"What!" ejaculated Cambray, incredulously. "The little girl who sat shivering in the snow?"

"Yes; she is our most skilful detective, and has entrapped more than one conspirator," triumphantly interrupted De Fervlans.

"Then"—and M. Cambray brought his hands together in a vehement gesture—"what I have believed a myth is really true. The police authorities really employ a number of beautiful women, handsome young men, and clever children to spy out and entrap suspected persons? 'Cythera's Brigade' really exists?"

"You had the pleasure of meeting that celebrated brigade this morning," replied De Fervlans.

"And those grateful men and women, who gathered about me with tearful eyes and sympathetic words—"

"Were members of Cythera's Brigade," supplemented the marquis.

"And the mistress of the house—the beautiful woman who fainted at sight of her child?"

"Is the fair Cythera's substitute! She taught her little daughter the part she played so successfully."

With sudden fury M. Cambray tore from his breast the ivory locket containing the little Amélie's portrait, and was about to fling it on the floor and trample upon it. On second thought, he restrained himself, returned the locket to his breast, and muttered:

"The child is not to blame. Those who have made her such a monster are at fault. I will keep the miniature as a talisman for the future."

"And now, M. Cambray," pursued the marquis, "we want to learn what has become of your young friend. In fact, we *must* know what has become of him and his charge."

"I don't know where he is."

"You do know. According to the report from our witness, he has fled to a 'country where order prevails, and where there are no police.' Where is this country, M. Cambray?"

"In the moon, perhaps!" was the laconic response.

"Our witness heard these words from your own lips, and you pointed out the spot on the map to your friend."

"Your witness dreamed all this!"

"M. Cambray, let us talk sensibly. You are a banker—at least, that is what you are registered in the police records. It is to the interest of the state to discover your secret. If you will reveal the hiding-place of your friend you may demand your own reward. Do you wish to be intrusted with the management of the state's finances? Or—"

"I regret, monsieur le marquis," interrupted Cambray, "that I must refuse so handsome an opportunity to enrich myself. Although I am a banker, I am no swindler."

"Very good! Then you require no money. You are *not* a banker, M. Cambray; that is merely a fable. What is your ambition? Should you prefer to be a governor? Name any office; let it be what it may, you shall receive the appointment to-morrow."

"Thank you again, monsieur. I must repeat what I said before: I know nothing about the future residence of the fugitive gentleman."

"And if I tell you, M. Cambray, that your refusal may cost you your head?"

"I should reply," returned Cambray, smiling calmly, as he took up the piece of bread lying on the table, "that it is a matter of perfect indifference to me if this daily portion of bread is enjoyed by some one else to-morrow. That which I do not know I cannot tell you."

"Very well, then," in a harsh tone rejoined De Fervlans. "I will tell you that Cambray the banker may say what is not true; but the nobleman cannot lie. *Marquis d'Avoncourt*, do you know to what country your friend has flown?"

At this question the old gentleman rose from his chair, drew himself up proudly, and gazing defiantly into the eyes of his questioner, replied:

"I do."

Instantly De Fervlans's manner changed. He became the embodiment of courtesy. He bowed with extreme politeness, then, slipping his arm familiarly through that of the prisoner, whispered insinuatingly:

"And what can we do to win this information from you?"

The gray-haired man released himself from De Fervlans's arm, and answered with quiet irony:

"I will tell you what you can do: have my head cut off, and send it to M. Bichet, the celebrated professor of anatomy; perhaps he may be able to discover the information in my skull—if it is there! And now I beg you to leave me; I wish to be alone."

De Fervlans took up his hat, but turned at the door to say, in a meaning tone:

"Marquis d'Avoncourt, we shall forget that you are a prisoner so long as it shall please you to remain obstinate. As for the fugitives, Cythera's Brigade will capture them, sooner or later. *Au revoir!*"

That same night the old nobleman was removed to the prison at Ham.

CHAPTER IV

While the ensnared conspirators against the state were receiving sentence in one district of Paris, in another district the inhabitants were entertaining themselves.

Paris does not mourn very long. Paris is like the earth: one half of it is always illumined by the sun. On this fateful evening the incroyables and the merveilleuses were amusing themselves within the walls of the Palace of Narcissus.

The members of Cythera's Brigade took great pains to make outsiders believe that they never troubled themselves about that half of the world which was in shadow—that half called politics.

In the salon of the fascinating Countess Themire Dealba not a word was heard relating to affairs of state. The beautiful women who were banded together to learn the secrets which threatened the present order of government worked in an imperceptible manner. They did not belong to the ordinary class of spies—those who collect every ill-natured word, every trifling occurrence of the street. No, indeed! *They* did nothing but amuse themselves. They were merry society women, trusty friends and confidantes. They moved in the best circles; no one ever saw them exchange a word with a police commissioner. If any one in the company happened to speak of anything even remotely connected with politics, some one quickly changed the subject to a more innocent theme; and if a stranger chanced to mention so delicate a matter as, say, the dinner which had been given by the emperor's nephew at Very's, which cost seventy-five thousand francs, while forty thousand laborers were starving, then the witty Countess Themire herself turned the conversation to the "toilet rivalry" between the Mesdames Tallien and Récamier.

On this particular evening the Countess Dealba was discussing the beauties of the latest opera with a few of her most intimate friends, when the Marquis de Fervlans approached, and, bending over her, whispered: "I must see you alone; find an opportunity to leave the room, and join me in the conservatory."

At that time it was the fashion to clothe children in garments similar to those worn by their elders. A company of little ones, therefore, looked like an assemblage of Lilliputian merveilleuses and incroyables. The little men and women also accompanied their mamas to receptions and the theatre, where they joined in the conversation, danced vis-à-vis with their elders, made witty remarks, criticized the toilets and the play, gave an opinion as to whether Hardy's confections or those of Riches were the better, and if it were safe to depend on the friendship of the Czar Alexander.

In this company of little ones the Countess Amélie was, beyond a doubt, the most conspicuous.

One could not have imagined anything more interesting or entertaining than the manner of this miniature dame when left by her mama to do the honors of the house. The dignity with which the child performed her duties was enchanting. She understood perfectly how to entertain her mother's guests, how to spice her conversation with piquant anecdotes, how to mimic the manner of affected personages. She was, in a word, a prodigy!

Countess Themire, knowing she might safely trust her little daughter to perform the duties of hostess, followed De Fervlans to the conservatory.

"We have been outwitted," he began at once. "They vanished twelve hours before we learned that they had flown."

The countess shrugged her shoulders and tossed her head.

"Why do you think it necessary to tell me this?" she inquired, with a touch of asperity. "Have you not got enough police to arrest the fugitives, who must pass through the entire country in their flight?"

"Yes, we have quite enough spies, and they are very skilful; but the fugitives are a trifle more skilful. They have disguised themselves so effectually that it is impossible to trace them. They seized a public coach by force, changed the number on it, and sent it back from the boundary by an accomplice, who left it in the Rue Muffetard. Even should we succeed in tracing their flight, by the time we discovered them they would have crossed the boundary of Switzerland, or would be sailing over the ocean. No; we must begin all over again. There is but one expedient: *you* must travel in search of the fugitives, and bring them back."

"I go in search of them and bring them back?" repeated the countess, in a startled tone.

"The first part of your task will not be so difficult," continued De Fervlans. "The imprisoned marquis will not reveal the destination of the fugitives; but we have learned, through your clever little daughter, that they have gone to a country where there is order, but where there are no police. That, methinks, is not a very difficult riddle to solve. You need only journey from place to place until you find such a country. The fugitives will be certain to betray themselves by their secrecy, and I have not the least doubt but your search will be rewarded before the year is out. For one year you shall have the command of three hundred thousand francs. When you discover the fugitives you will know very well what to do. The man is young and an enthusiast—an easy conquest, I should fancy; and when you have ensnared him the maid's fate is decided. We want the man, the maid, and the steel casket; any one of the three, however, will be of great value to us. You will keep us advised as to your progress, and we, of course, will assist you all we can. You know that we have secret agents all over Europe. And now, you will do well to prepare for an immediate departure; there is not a moment to be lost."

"But good, heavens! how can I take Amélie on such a journey?"

"You are not to take her with you—of what are you thinking? That man has already seen the child, and would recognize her at once."

"You surely cannot mean that I am to desert my daughter?"

"Don't you think Amélie will be in safe hands if you leave her in *my* care?" asked De Fervlans, with a glance that would have made any one who had not heard his words believe he was making a declaration of love. "Besides, it will not be the first time you leave her to the care of another."

"That is true," sighed the countess; "I ought to be accustomed to parting with her. Have not I trusted her to the care of a police spy? and all for my own advantage! Oh, what a wretched profession I have chosen for myself and my child!"

"A profession that yields a handsome income, madame," supplemented the marquis, a trifle sharply. "You ought not to complain. Surely the régime is not to blame that you married a roué, who squandered your fortune, and then was killed in a duel about a rope-dancer, leaving you a clever little daughter and a half-million of debts! What else could you have done to have earned a living for yourself and child?"

"I might have sent the child to a foundling asylum, and sought employment for myself in the gobelin factory. It would have been better had I done so!"

"I doubt it, countess. The path of virtue is only for those women who— have large feet! You are too fairy-like, and would have found the way too rough. It is much better, believe me, to serve the state. What would you? Is there not a comforting word due to the conscience of the soldier who has killed a fellow-being in the interest of his country? Don't you suppose his heart aches when he looks upon the death-struggles of the man he has killed without having a personal grudge against him? We are all soldiers of the state. When we assault an enemy, we do not inquire if we hurt him; we kill him! and the safety of our fatherland hallows the deed."

"But that which we are doing is immoral," interposed the countess.

"And that which our enemy is doing is not immoral, I presume? Are not their beautiful women, their polished courtiers, acting as spies in our salons? We are only using their own weapons against them."

"That may be; but it was a repulsive thought that prompted the using of children as instruments in this deadly game."

"Were not they the first to set us an example? Was not it a repulsive thought which prompted them to hold over the heads of an entire people that hellish machine of torture in the shape of a smiling child? No, madame; we need not be ashamed of what we are doing. Our men are engaged in warfare against their men; our lovely women are engaged in warfare against their lovely women; and our little children are engaged in warfare against their little children. Your little Amélie is a historical figure, and deserves a monument."

The marquis, perceiving that his sophistry was not without its effect on the lovely woman, continued:

"And then, madame, if you are weary of the rôle you and your little daughter are playing with such success, the opportunity is now offered to you to quit your present mode of life. Your financial affairs are utterly ruined; you are only the nominal possessor of the estate you inherited from your ancestors. If you succeed in the task which you are about to undertake, the entire sum of money, the interest of which you receive annually, becomes your own. Five millions of francs deserve some sacrifice. With this sum you can become an independent woman, and your daughter will never be reproached with having been, in her childhood, a member of Cythera's Brigade."

Countess Themire deliberated a few moments; then she asked:

"May I not kiss my daughter farewell?"

"Leave your kiss with me, and I will deliver it faithfully!" smilingly responded the marquis.

"How can you jest at such a moment? Suppose my absence lasts a long time?"

"That is very probable."

"Am I not even to hear from my child—not even to let her know that I am living?"

"Certainly, countess; you may communicate with her through me. Moreover, it rests with yourself how soon you will return. Until that time it shall be my pleasure to take care of Amélie; you may rest in peace as to that!"

"Yes; she could not be in worse hands than in those of her mother!" bitterly rejoined the countess. "The first letter, then, must be one of farewell."

She rose, went into her boudoir, and wrote on a sheet of paper:

"MY DEAR CHILD: I am compelled to take a journey. I shall write to you when I am ready to return. Until then, I leave you to perform the duties of hostess, and intrust my money-chest to your care. I embrace you a thousand times.
"Your old friend and little mama,
"THEMIRE."

She folded and sealed the letter, and handed it to De Fervlans.

"I shall be sure to deliver it," he said. "And now, send Jocrisse for a fiacre; you must not use your own carriage for this. You can leave the palace unperceived by the garden gate. Speak German wherever you go, and remember that you do not understand a word of French. I think you would better begin your search in Switzerland. And now, adieu, madame, until we meet again—"

"If only I might take one last look at my little daughter!" pleadingly interrupted the countess.

"Themire! You are actually beginning to grow sentimental. That does not become a soldier!"

"Had I suspected this," returned Themire, "I would not have given Amélie's portrait to M. Cambray in that ridiculous farce. I wonder if I might not get it from him?"

"No; he will not part with it; he says he is going to keep it as a talisman. Only M. Sanson has the privilege of relieving prisoners of their trinkets, and Cambray is still far enough from Sanson's reach! I shall have another portrait painted of Amélie, and send it to you."

"But this picture was painted while yet she was an innocent child."

"Upon my word, madame, you are as sentimental as a professor's daughter! I begin to fear you will not accomplish your mission—that you will end by falling in love with the man you are to capture for us, and betray us to him."

Themire did not say another word, but hurried into her dressing-room.

De Fervlans wrote an order for one hundred and fifty thousand francs for the Countess Themire Dealba for the first six months, added his wishes for a pleasant and successful journey, then returned to the salon, where he gave the missive which had been intrusted to his care to Jocrisse.

Jocrisse placed it on a silver tray, and presented it to the tiny lady of the house.

"Pray allow me, ladies and gentlemen," said the Lilliputian *grande dame*, as she broke the seal, "to read this letter—although I am only just learning the alphabet!"

There were a number of persons in the company who understood and enjoyed the concluding words.

The little countess lifted her gold-rimmed lorgnette to her eyes, and read her mother's letter.

She shook her head, shrugged her shoulders, and opened wide her blue eyes.

"Ladies and gentlemen," she proceeded to explain, "mama has been called suddenly away. She sends her greetings to you" (this was not in the letter, but the little diplomatist thought it best to atone for her mama's neglect) "until she returns, which will be very soon" (this also was a thought of her own). "I am to fulfil the duties of lady of the house."

Then she turned toward De Fervlans, and whispered, holding the lorgnette in front of her lips:

"Mama leaves her money-chest in my care"—adding, with naïve sarcasm, "which means that she has left me to battle with her creditors."

PART II
THE HOME OF ANECDOTE

CHAPTER I

The entire population of Fertöszeg was assembled on the public highway to welcome the new proprietress of the estate. Elaborate preparations had been made for the reception. An arch of green boughs—at the top of which gleamed the word "Vivat" in yellow roses—spanned the road, on either side of which were ranged twelve little girls in white, with flower-baskets in their hands. They were under the superintendence of the village cantor, whose intention it was to conclude the ceremonies with a hymn of welcome by these innocent little creatures.

On a sort of platform, a bevy of rosy-cheeked maids were waiting to present to the new-comer a huge hamper heaped to the brim with ripe melons, grapes, and Ostyepka cheeses of marvelous shapes. Mortars crowned the summit of the neighboring hill. In the shadow of a spreading beech-tree were assembled the official personages: the vice-palatine, the county surveyor, the village pastor, the district physician, the justice of the peace, and the different attendants, county and state employees, belonging to these gentlemen. The vice-palatine's assistant ought also to have been in this company, but he was busy giving the last instructions to the village beauties whose part it was to present the hamper of fruit and cheeses.

These gentlemen had wives and daughters; but *they* had stationed themselves along the trench at the side of the road. *They* did not seek the shadow of a tree, because *they* wished people to know that *they* had parasols; for to own a parasol in those days was no small matter.

Preparations were making in the market-place for an ox-roast. The fat young ox had been spitted, and the pile of fagots underneath him was ready for the torch. Hard by, on a stout trestle, rested a barrel of wine. In front of the inn a gypsy band were tuning their instruments, while at the window of the church tower might have been seen two or three child faces; they were on the lookout for the new lady of the manor, in order that they might be ready to ring the bells the moment she came in sight. There was only that one tower in the village, and there was a cross on it; but it was not a Romish church, for all that. The inhabitants were adherents of Luther—Swabians, mixed with Magyars.

The municipal authorities, in their holiday attire of blue cloth, had grouped themselves about the town hall. The older men wore their long hair brushed back from the temples and held in place by a curved comb. The young men had thrust into the sides of their lambskin caps gay little nosegays of artificial flowers. *They* proposed to fire a grand salute from the pistols they had concealed in their pockets.

Meanwhile, the dignitaries underneath the umbrageous beech-tree were passing the time of waiting pleasantly enough. Maple wine mixed with mineral water was a very refreshing drink in the intense heat; besides, it served as a stimulant to the appetite—*appetitorium*, they called it.

Three wooden benches, joined together in a half-circle, formed a comfortable resting-place for the committee of reception, the chief of whom, the vice-palatine, was seated on the middle bench, drawing through the stem of his huge carved meerschaum the smoke of the sweet Veker tobacco. His figure was the living illustration of the ever true axiom: "*Extra Hungariam non est vita*,"—an axiom which his fat red face by no means confuted,— while his heavy, stiffly waxed mustache seemed to add menacingly: "Leave the Hungarian in peace."

He shared his seat with the clergyman, whose ecclesiastical office entitled him to that honor. The reverend gentleman, however, was an extremely humble person, whom erudition had bent and warped to such a degree that one shoulder was lower than the other, one eyelid was elevated above its fellow, and only one half of his mouth opened when he gave utterance to a remark. His part in the festive ceremony was the performance of the *beneventatio*; and although he had committed the speech to memory, he could not help but tremble at thought of having to repeat it before so grand a dame as the new mistress of the manor. He always trembled whenever he began his sermons; but once fairly started, then he became a veritable Demosthenes.

"I only hope, reverend sir," jestingly observed the vice-palatine, "that it will not happen to you as it did to the *csokonai*, not long ago. Some wags exchanged his sermon-book for one on cookery, and he did not notice it until he began to read in the pulpit: 'The vinegar was—' Then he saw that he was reading a recipe for pickled gherkins. He had the presence of mind, however, to continue, '—was offered to the Saviour, who said, "It is finished."' And on that text he extemporized a discourse that astounded the entire presbytery."

"I shall manage somehow to say my speech," returned the pastor, meekly, "if only I do not stumble over the name of the lady."

"It is a difficult name," assented the vice-palatine. "What is it? I have already forgotten it, reverend sir."

"Katharina von Landsknechtsschild."

The vice-palatine's pointed mustaches essayed to give utterance to the name.

"Lantz-k-nek-hisz-sild—that's asking a great deal from a body at one time!" he concluded, in disgust at his ill success.

"And yet, it is a good old Hungarian family name. The last Diet recognized her ancestors as belonging to the nobility."

This remark was made by a third gentleman. He was sitting on the left of the vice-palatine, and was clad in snuff-colored clothes. His face was covered with small-pox marks; he had tangled yellow hair and inflamed eyelids.

"Are you acquainted with the family, doctor?" asked the vice-palatine.

"Of course I am," replied the doctor. "Baron Landsknechtsschild inherited this estate from his mother, who was a Markoczy. The baron sold the estate to his niece Katharina. You, Herr Surveyor, must have seen the baron, when the land was surveyed around the Nameless Castle for the mad count?"

The surveyor, who was seated beside the doctor, was a clever man in his profession, but little given to conversation. When he did open his lips, he rarely got beyond: "I—say—what was it, now, I was going to say?"

As no one seemed willing to-day to wait until he could remember what he wanted to remark, the doctor, who was never at a loss for words, continued:

"The Baroness Katharina paid one hundred thousand florins for the estate, with all its prerogatives—"

"That's quite a handsome sum," observed the vice-palatine. "And, what is handsomer, it is said the new proprietress intends to take up a permanent residence here. Is not that the report, Herr Justice? You ought to know."

The justice had an odd habit, while speaking, of rubbing together the palms of his hands, as if he were rolling little dumplings between them.

"Yes—yes," he replied, beginning his dumpling-rolling; "that is quite true. The baroness sent some beautiful furniture from Vienna; also a piano, and a tuner to tune it. All the rooms at the manor have been hung with new tapestry, and the conservatory has been completely renovated."

"I wonder how the baroness came to take such a fancy to this quiet neighborhood? It is very strange, too, that none of the neighboring nobles have been invited here to meet her. It is as if she intended to let them know in advance that she didn't want their acquaintance. At any other celebration of this sort half the county would have been invited, and here are only ourselves—and we are here because we are obliged, *ex officio*, to be present."

This speech was delivered over the mouthpiece of the vice-palatine's meerschaum.

"I fancy I can enlighten you," responded the doctor.

"I thought it likely that the 'county clock' could tell us something about it," laughingly interpolated the vice-palatine.

"You may laugh as much as you like, but I always tell what is true," retorted the "county clock." "They say that the baroness was betrothed to a gentleman from Bavaria, that the wedding-day was set, when the bridegroom heard that the lady he was about to marry was—"

"Hush!" hastily whispered the justice; "the servants might hear you."

"Oh, it isn't anything scandalous. All that the bridegroom heard was that the baroness was a Lutheran; and as the *matrimonia mixta* are forbidden in Vienna and in Bavaria, the bridegroom withdrew from the engagement. In her grief over the affair, the *sposa repudiata* said farewell to the world, and determined to wear the *parta* [2] for the remainder of her days. That is why she chose this remote region as a residence."

[2] A head-covering worn only by Hungarian maidens.

Here the bell in the church tower began to ring. It was followed by a roar from the mortars on the hilltop.

The gypsy band began to play Biharis's "Vierzigmann Marsch"; a cloud of dust rose from the highway; and soon afterward there appeared an outrider with three ostrich-plumes in his hat. He was followed by a four-horse coach, with coachman and footman on the box.

The committee of reception came forth from the shade of the beech and ranged themselves underneath the arch. The clergyman for the last time took his little black book from his pocket, and satisfied himself that his speech was still in it. The coach stopped, and it was discovered that no one occupied it; only the discarded shawl and traveling-wraps told that women had been riding in the conveyance.

The general consternation which ensued was ended by the agent from Vienna, who drove up in a second vehicle. He explained that the baroness and her companion had alighted at the park gate, whence they would proceed on foot up the shorter foot-path to the manor. And thus ended all the magnificent preparations for the reception!

A servant now came running from the village, his plumed *czako* in one hand, and announced that the baroness awaited the dignitaries at the manor.

This was, to say the least, exasperating! A whole week spent in preparing—for nothing!

You may be sure every one had something to say about it, audibly and to themselves, and some one was even heard to mutter:

"This is the *second* mad person come to live in Fertöszeg."

And then they all betook themselves, a disappointed company, to their homes.

The baroness, who had preferred to walk the shorter path through the park to driving around the village in the dust for the sake of receiving a ceremonious welcome, was a lovely blonde, a true Viennese, good-humored, and frank as a child. She treated every one with cordial friendliness. One might easily have seen that everything rural was new to her. While walking through the park she took off her hat and decorated it with the wild flowers which grew along the path. In the farm-yard she caught two or three little chickens, calling them canaries—a mistake the mother hen sought in the most emphatic manner to correct. The surly old watch-dog's head was patted. She brushed with her dainty fingers the hair from the eyes of the gaping farmer children. She was here and there in a moment, driving to despair her companion, whose gouty limbs were unable to keep pace with the flying feet of her mistress.

At the manor the baroness was received by the steward, who had been sent on in advance with orders to prepare the "installation dinner." Then she proceeded at once to inspect every corner and crevice—the kitchen as well as the dining-room, astonishing the cooks with her knowledge of their art. She was summoned from the kitchen to receive the dignitaries.

"Let there be no ceremony, gentlemen," she exclaimed in her musical voice, hastening toward them. "I detest all formalities. I have had a surfeit of them in Vienna, and intend to breathe natural air here in the country, without 'fuss or feathers,' with no incense save that which rises from burning tobacco! This is why I avoided your parade out yonder on the highway. I want nothing but a cordial shake of your hands; and as regards the official formalities of this 'installation' business, you must settle that with my agent, who has authority to act for me. After that has been arranged, we will all act as if we were old acquaintances, and every one of you must consider himself at home here."

To this gracious speech the vice-palatine gave utterance to something which sounded like:

"Kisz-ti-hand!"

"Ah!" returned the baroness, "you speak German?"

"Well, yes," replied the descendant of the Scythians; "only, I am likely to blunder when speaking it, as did the valiant Barkocz. When our glorious Queen Maria Theresa recovered from the chicken-pox, she was bemoaning the disfiguring scars left on her face, when the brave soldier, in order to comfort her, said: 'But your Majesty still has very beautiful *leather*.'"

"Ha, ha, ha!" merrily laughed the baroness. "You are the gentleman who has an anecdote to suit every occasion. I have already heard about you. Pray introduce the other gentlemen."

The vice-palatine proceeded to obey this request. "This is the Rev. Herr Tobias Mercatoris, our parish clergyman. He has a beautiful speech prepared to receive your ladyship; but he can't repeat it here, as it begins, 'Here in the grateful shadow of these green trees.'"

"Oh, well, your reverence, instead of the speech, I will listen to your sermons on Sundays. I intend to become a very zealous member of your congregation."

"And this, your ladyship," continued the master of ceremonies, "is Dr. Philip Tromfszky, resident physician of Fertöszeg, who is celebrated not only for his surgical and medical skill, but is acknowledged here, as well as in Raab, Komorn, Eisenburg, and Odenburg, as the greatest gossip and news dispenser in the kingdom."

"A most excellent accomplishment!" laughingly exclaimed the baroness. "I am devoted to gossip; and I shall manage to have some ailment every few days in order to have the doctor come to see me!"

Then came the surveyor's turn.

"This, your ladyship, is Herr Martin Doboka, county surveyor and expert mathematician. He will measure for you land, water, or fog; and if your watch stops going, he will repair it for you!"

"And who may this be?" smilingly inquired the lady, indicating the vice-palatine's assistant, who had thrust his long neck inquisitively forward.

"Oh, he is n't anybody!" replied the vice-palatine. "He is never called by name. When you want him just say: 'Audiat!' He is one of those persons of whom Cziraky said: 'My lad, don't trouble yourself to inquire where you shall seat yourself at table; for wherever you sit will always be the lowest place!'"

This anecdote caused "Audiat" to draw back his head and seek to make himself invisible.

"And now, I must present myself: I am the vice-palatine of this county, and am called Bernat Görömbölyi von Dravakeresztur."

"My dear sir!" ejaculated the baroness, laughing heartily, "I could n't commit all that to memory in three years!"

"That is exactly the way your ladyship's name affects me!"

"Then I will tell you what we will do. Instead of torturing each other with our unpronounceable names, let us at once adopt the familiar 'thou,' and call each other by our Christian names."

"Yes; but when I enter into a 'brotherhood' of that sort, I always kiss the person with whom I form a compact."

"Well, that can also be done in this instance!" promptly responded the baroness, proffering, without affectation of maidenly coyness, the ceremonial kiss, and cordially shaking hands with the vice-palatine. Then she said:

"We are now Bernat *bácsi*, and Katinka; and as that is happily arranged, I will ask the gentlemen to go into the agent's office and conclude our official business. Meanwhile, I shall make my toilet for dinner, where we will all meet again."

"What a perfectly charming woman!" exclaimed the justice, when their hostess had vanished from the room.

"I wonder what would happen," observed the doctor, with a malicious grin, "if the vice-palatine's wife should hear of that kiss? Would n't there be a row, though!"

The heroic descendant of the Scythians at these words became seriously alarmed.

"The Herr Doctor, I trust, will be honorable enough not to gossip about it," he said meekly.

"Oh, you may rest without fear, so far as *I* am concerned; but I would n't say as much for the surveyor, here. If ever he should succeed in getting beyond 'I say,' I won't answer for the safety of your secret, Herr Vice-palatine! When your wife hears, moreover, that it is 'Bernat' and 'Katinka' up here, it will require something besides an anecdote to parry what will follow!"

CHAPTER II

When the baroness appeared at the dinner-table, she was attired simply, yet with a certain elegance. She wore a plain black silk gown, with no other ornamentation save the string of genuine pearls about her throat. The sombre hue of her gown signified mourning; the gems represented tears; but her manner was by no means in keeping with either; she was cheerful, even gay. But laughter very often serves to mask a sorrowful heart.

"Thy place is here by my side," said the baroness, mindful of the "thee-and-thou" compact with Herr Bernat.

The vice-palatine, remembering his spouse, sought to modify the familiarity.

"I forgot to tell you, baroness," he observed, as he seated himself in the chair beside her own, "that with us in this region 'thou' is used only by children and the gypsies. To those with whom we are on terms of intimacy we say 'he' or 'she,' to which we add, if we wish, the words *bácsi*, or *hugom*, which are equivalent to 'cousin.'"

"And do you never say 'thou' to your wife?"

"To her also I say 'she' or 'you.'"

"What a singular country! Well, then, Bernat bácsi, if it pleases 'him,' will 'he' sit here by me?"

Baroness Katinka understood perfectly how to conduct the conversation during the repast—an art which was not appreciated by her right-hand neighbor, Herr Mercatoris. The learned gentleman had bad teeth, in consequence of which eating was a sort of penitential performance that left him no time for discourse.

But the doctor and the vice-palatine showed themselves all the more willing to share the conversation with their hostess.

"The official business was satisfactorily arranged without me, was it not, Bernat bácsi?" after a brief pause, inquired the baroness.

"Not altogether. We are like the gypsy who said that he was going to marry a countess. He was willing, and all that was yet necessary was the consent of a countess. Our business requires the consent of a baroness—that is, of Katinka hugom."

"To what must I give my consent?"

"That the conditions relating to the Nameless Castle shall continue the same as heretofore."

"Nameless Castle?—Conditions?—What does that mean? I should like very much to know."

"Katinka hugom can see the Nameless Castle from the terrace out yonder. It is a hunting-seat that was built by a Markoczy on the shore of Lake Neusiedl, on the site of a primitive pile-dwelling. Three years ago, a gentleman from a foreign country came to Fertöszeg, and took such a fancy to the isolated house that he leased it from the baron, the former owner, on condition that no one but himself and servants should be permitted to enter the grounds belonging to the castle. The question now is, will Katinka hugom consent to the conditions, or will she revoke them?"

"And if I should choose to do the latter?" inquired the baroness.

"Then your ladyship would be obliged to give a handsome bonus to the lessee. Shall you revoke the conditions?"

"It depends entirely on the sort of person my tenant proves to be."

"He is a very peculiar man, to say the least—one who avoids all contact with his fellow-men."

"What is his name?"

"I don't think any one around here knows it. That is why his residence has been called the Nameless Castle."

"But how is it possible that the name of a man who has lived here three years is not known?"

"Well, that is easily explained. He never goes anywhere, never receives visitors, and his servants never call him anything but 'the count.'"

"Surely he receives letters by post?"

"Yes, frequently, and from all parts of the known world. Very often he receives letters which contain money, and for which he is obliged to give a receipt; but no one has yet been able to decipher the illegible characters on the letters addressed to him, or those of his own hand."

"I should think the authorities had a right to demand the information?"

"Which authorities?"

"Why—'he,' Bernat bácsi."

"I? Why, what business is it of mine?"

"The authorities ought to inquire who strangers are, and where they come from. And such an authority is 'he'—Bernat bácsi!"

"Hum; does 'she' take me to be a detective?"

"But you surely have a right to demand to see his passport?"

"Passport? I would rather allow myself to be thrown from the window of the county-house than demand a passport from any one who comes to Hungary, or set my foot in the house of a gentleman without his permission!"

"Then you don't care what people do here?"

"Why should we? The noble does as he pleases, and the peasant as he must."

"Suppose the man in the Nameless Castle were plotting some dreadful treason?"

"That would be the affair of the king's attorney, not mine. Moreover, nothing whatever can be said against the tenant of the Nameless Castle. He is a quiet and inoffensive gentleman."

"Is he alone? Has he no family?"

"That the Herr Justice is better able to tell your ladyship than am I."

"Ah! Then, *Herr Hofrichter*," inquired the lady of the manor, turning toward the justice, "what do *you* know about this mysterious personage? Has he a wife?"

"It seems as if he had a wife, your ladyship; but I really cannot say for certain if he has one."

"Well, I confess my curiosity is aroused! How is it possible not to know whether the man is married or not? Are the people invisible?"

"Invisible? By no means, your ladyship. The nameless count and a lady drive out every morning at ten o'clock. They drive as far as the neighboring village, where they turn and come back to the castle. But the lady wears such a heavy veil that one can't tell if she be old or young."

"If they drive out they certainly have a coachman; and one might easily learn from a servant what are the relations between his master and mistress."

"Yes, so one might. The coachman comes often to the village, and he can speak German, too. There is a fat cook, who never leaves the castle, because she can't walk. Then, there are two more servants, Schmidt and his wife; but they live in a cottage near the castle. Every morning at five o'clock they go to the castle gate, where they receive from some one, through the wicket, orders for the day. At nine o'clock they return to the gate, where a basket has been placed for the things they have bought. But they never speak of the lady, because they have never seen her face, either."

"What sort of a man is the groom?"

"The people about here call him the man with the iron mouth. It is believed the fat cook is his wife, because he never even looks at the girls in the village. He will not answer any questions; only once he condescended to say that his mistress was a penniless orphan, who had nothing, yet who got everything she wanted."

"Does no one visit them?"

"If any one goes to the castle, the count alone receives the visitor; the lady never appears; and no one has yet had courage enough to ask for her. But that they are Christians, one may know from their kitchen: there is always a lamb for dinner on Easter; and the usual *heiligen Stritzel* on All Saints'. But they never go to church, nor is the pastor ever received at the castle."

"What reason can they have for so much mystery, I wonder?" musingly observed the baroness.

"That I cannot say. I can furnish only the data; for the deductions I must refer your ladyship to the Herr Doctor."

"Ah, true!" ejaculated her ladyship, joining in the general laughter. "The doctor, to be sure! If you are the county clock, Herr Doctor, surely you ought to know something about our mysterious neighbors?"

"I have two versions, either of which your ladyship is at liberty to accept," promptly responded the doctor. "According to the first 'authentic' declaration, the nameless count is the chief of a band of robbers, who ply their nefarious trade in a foreign land. The lady is his mistress. She fell once into the hands of justice, in Germany, and was branded as a criminal on her forehead. That accounts for the heavy veil she always wears—"

"Oh, that is quite too horribly romantic, Herr Doctor!" interrupted the baroness. "We cannot accept that version. Let us hear the other one."

"The second is more likely to be the true one. Four years ago the newspapers were full of a remarkable abduction case. A stranger—no one knew who he was—abducted the wife of a French officer from Dieppe. Since then the betrayed husband has been searching all over the world for his runaway wife and her lover; and the pair at the castle are supposed to be they."

"That certainly is the more plausible solution of the mystery. But there is one flaw. If the lovers fled here to Fertöszeg to escape pursuit, the lady has chosen the very worst means to remain undiscovered. Who would recognize them here if they went about in the ordinary manner? The story of the veil will spread farther and farther, and will ultimately betray them to the pursuing husband."

By this time the reverend Herr Mercatoris had got the better of his bad teeth, and was now ready to join the conversation.

"Gentlemen and ladies," he began, "allow me to say a word about this matter, the details of which no one knows better than myself, as I have for months been in communication with the nameless gentleman at the castle."

"What sort of communication?"

"Through the medium of a correspondence, which has been conducted in quite a peculiar manner. The count—we will call him so, although we are not justified in so doing, for the gentleman did not announce himself as such—the count sends me every morning his copy of the Augsburg 'Allgemeine Zeitung.' Moreover, I frequently receive letters from him through Frau Schmidt; but I always have to return them as soon as I have read them. They are not written in a man's hand; the writing is unmistakably feminine. The seal is never stamped; only once I noticed on it a crest with three flowers—"

"What sort of flowers?" hastily interposed the baroness.

"I don't know the names of them, your ladyship."

"And what do you write about?" she asked again.

"The correspondence began by the count asking a trifling favor of me. He complained that the dogs in the village barked so loud; then, that the children robbed the birds' nests; then, that the night-watchman called the hour unnecessarily loud. These complaints, however, were not made in his own name, but by another person whom he did not name. He wrote merely: 'Complainant is afraid when the dogs bark.' 'Complainant loves birds.' 'Complainant is made nervous by the night-watchman.' Then he sent some money for the owners of the barking dogs, asking that the curs be shut indoors nights; and some for the children, so they would cease to rob the birds' nests; and some for the watchman, whom he requested to shout his loudest at the other end of the village. When I had attended to his requests, he began to send me his newspaper, which is a great favor, for I can ill afford to subscribe for one myself. Later, he loaned me some books; he has the classics of all nations—the works of Wieland, Kleist, Börne, Lessing, Locke, Schleiermacher. Then we began to write about the books, and became entangled in a most exciting argument. Frau Schmidt, who was the bearer of this exchange of opinions, very often passed to and fro between the castle and the parsonage a dozen times a day; and all the time we never said anything to each other, when we happened to meet in the road, but 'good day.' From the letters, however, I became convinced that the mysterious gentleman is neither a criminal, nor a fugitive from justice, nor yet an adventurous hero who abducts women! Nor is he an unfortunate misanthrope. He is, on the contrary, a philanthropist in the widest sense—one who takes an interest in everything that goes on about him, and is eager to help his suffering fellows. In a word, he is a philosopher who is happy when he is surrounded by peace and quiet."

The baroness, who had listened with interest to the reverend gentleman's words, now made inquiry:

"How does this nameless gentleman learn of his poor neighbors' needs, when neither he nor his servants associate with any one outside the castle?"

"In a very simple manner, your ladyship. He has a very powerful telescope in the tower of the castle, with which he can view every portion of the surrounding region. He thus learns when there is illness or death, whether a house needs repair; and wherever anything is needed, the means to help are sent to me. On Christmas he has all the children from the village up at the castle, where he has a splendid Christmas tree with lighted tapers, and a gift for every child,—clothes, books, and sweets,—which he distributes with his own hand. I can tell you an incident which is characteristic of the man. One day the county arrested a poor woman, the wife of a notorious thief. The Herr Vice-palatine will remember the case—Rakoncza Jutka, the wife of the robber Satan Laczi?"

"Yes, I remember. She is still in prison," assented the gentleman referred to.

"Yes. Well, she has a little son. When the mother was taken to prison, the little lad was turned away from every door, was beaten and abused by the other children, until at last he fled to the marshes, where he ate the young shoots of the reeds, and slept in the mire. The nameless count discovered with his telescope the little outcast, and wrote to me to have him taken to Frau Schmidt, where he would be well taken care of until his mother came back."

By this time the tears were running down the baroness's cheeks.

"Poor little lad!" she murmured brokenly. "Your story has affected me deeply, Herr Pastor."

Then she summoned her steward, and bade him fill a large hamper with sweets and pasties, and send it to Frau Schmidt for the poor little boy. "And tell Frau Schmidt," she added, "to send the child to the manor. We will see to it that he has some suitable clothes. I am delighted, reverend sir, to learn that my tenant is a true nobleman."

"His deeds certainly proclaim him as such, your ladyship."

"How do *you* explain the mystery of the veiled lady?"

"I cannot explain it, your ladyship; she is never mentioned in our correspondence."

"She may be a prisoner, detained at the castle by force."

"That cannot be; for she has a hundred opportunities to escape, or to ask for help."

Here the surveyor managed to express his belief that the reason the lady wore a veil was because of the repulsiveness of her face.

At this, a voice that had not yet been heard said, at the lower end of the table:

"But the lady is one the most beautiful creatures I ever saw—and quite young."

Every eye was turned toward the speaker.

"What? Audiat? How dares he say such a thing?" demanded the vice-palatine.

"Because I have seen her."

"You have seen her? When did you see her? Where did you see her— her whom no one yet has seen?"

"When I was returning from college last year, *per pedes apostolorum*, for my money had given out, and my knapsack was empty. I was picking hazelnuts from the bushes in the park of the Nameless Castle, when I heard a window open. I looked up, and saw in the open sash a face the like of which I have never seen, even in a picture."

"Ah!" ejaculated the baroness. "Tell us what is she like. Come nearer to me."

The clerk, however, was too bashful to leave his place, whereupon the baroness rose and took a seat by his side.

"She has long, curling black hair," he went on. "Her face is fair as a lily and red as a rose, her brow pure and high, with no sign of the branding-iron. Her mouth is small and delicate. Indeed, her entire appearance that day was like that of an angel looking down from heaven."

"Is she a maid or a married woman?" inquired one of the company.

A maid, in those days, was very easily distinguished from her married sister. The latter was never seen without a cap.

"A young girl not more than fifteen, I should say," was the reply. "A cap would not suit her face."

"Ha, ha, ha!" laughed Bernat bácsi. "And this enchanting fairy opened the window to show her lovely face to Audiat!"

"No; she did not open the window on my account," retorted the young man, "but for the beasts that were luckier than I—for four cats that were playing in the gutter of the roof; a white one, a black one, a yellow one, and a gray one; and all of them scampered toward her when they heard her call."

"The cats are her only companions—that much we know from the servants," affirmed the justice.

The laurels which his clerk had won made the vice-palatine jealous.

"Audiat," he said, in a reproving tone, "you ought to learn that a young person should speak only when spoken to; indeed,—as the learned Professor Hatvani says,—even then it is not necessary to answer all questions."

But the company around the dinner-table did not share these views. The clerk was assailed on all sides—very much as would have been an aëronaut who had just alighted from a montgolfier—to relate all that he had seen in those regions not yet penetrated by man. What sort of gown did the mysterious lady wear? Was he certain that she had no cap on? Was she really no older than fifteen years?

The vice-palatine at last put an end to his clerk's triumph.

"Tut, tut! what can you expect to learn from a mere lad like him?—when he saw her only for an instant! Just wait; I will find out all about this nameless gentleman and lady."

"Pray how do you propose to accomplish that?" queried the baroness, who had returned to her former seat.

"I shall go to the Nameless Castle."

"Suppose you are not permitted to enter?"

"What? I, the vice-palatine, not permitted to enter? Wait; I will explain my plan to you over the coffee."

When the time came to serve the black coffee, the amiable hostess suggested that it would be pleasant to enjoy it in the open air; whereupon the company repaired to the veranda where, on several small tables, the fragrant mocha was steaming in the cups. Here the baroness and the vice-palatine seated themselves where they could look directly at the Nameless Castle; and Herr Bernat Görömbölyi proceeded to explain how he intended to take the castle without force—which was forbidden a Hungarian official.

Then the two ladies withdrew to make their toilets for the evening; and the gentlemen betook themselves to the smoking-room, to indulge in a little game of chance, without which no "installation" ceremony would have been complete.

CHAPTER III

The following morning, after a very satisfactory breakfast, the gentlemen took leave of their amiable hostess, Bernat bácsi lingering behind the rest to whisper significantly:

"I will not say farewell, Katinka hugom, for I am coming back to tell you all about it." Then he took his place in the extra post-chaise, and bade the postilion drive directly to the neighboring castle. The Nameless Castle was built on a narrow tongue of land that extended into Lake Neusiedl. The road to the castle gate ran along a sort of causeway, which was protected from the water by a strong bulwark composed of fascines, and a row of willows with knotty crowns. A drawbridge at the farther end made it necessary for the person who wished to enter the gate to ask permission.

On ringing the bell, there appeared at the gate the servant who has already been described,—the groom, coachman, and man of all work in one person. He had on a handsome livery, white gloves, white stockings, and shoes without heels.

"Is the count at home?" inquired the vice-palatine.

"He is."

"Announce us. I am the vice-palatine of the county, and wish to pay an official visit."

"The Herr Count is already informed of the gentlemen's arrival, and bids them welcome."

This certainly was getting on smoothly enough! And the most convincing proof of a hearty welcome was that the stately groom himself hastened to remove the luggage from the chaise and carry it into the vestibule—a sign that the guests were expected to make a visit of some duration.

Now, however, something curious happened.

Before the groom opened the hall door, he produced three pairs of socks, woven of strands of cloth,—*mamuss* they are called in this region,—and respectfully requested the visitors to draw them over their boots.

"And why, pray?" demanded the astonished vice-palatine.

"Because in this house the clatter of boots is not considered pleasant; and because the socks prevent boots from leaving dusty marks on the carpets."

"This is exactly like visiting a powder-magazine." But they had to submit and draw their socks over their yellow boots, and, thus equipped, they ascended the staircase to the reception-room.

An air of almost painful neatness reigned in all parts of the castle. Stairs and corridors were covered with coarse white cloth, the sort used for peasants' clothing in Hungary. The walls were hung with glossy white paper. Every door-latch had been polished until it glistened. There were no cobwebs to be seen in the corners; nor would a spider have had anything to prey upon here, for there were no flies, either. The floor of the reception-room into which the visitors had been conducted shone like a mirror, and not a speck of dust was to be seen on the furniture.

"The Herr Count awaits your lordship in the salon," announced the groom, and conducted Herr Bernat into the adjoining chamber. Here, too, the furniture was white and gold. The oil-paintings in the rococo frames represented landscapes, fruit pieces, and game; there was not a portrait among them.

Beside the oval table with tigers' feet stood the mysterious occupant of the Nameless Castle. He was a tall man, with knightly bearing, expressive face, a high, broad forehead left uncovered by his natural hair, a straight Greek nose, gray eyes, a short mustache and pointed beard, which where a shade lighter than his hair.

"*Magnifice comes—*" the vice-palatine was beginning in Latin, when the count interposed:

"I speak Hungarian."

"Impossible!" exclaimed the visitor, whose astonishment was reflected in his face. "Hungarian? Why, where can your worship have learned it?"

"From the grammar."

"From the grammar?" For the vice-palatine this was the most astounding of all the strange things about the mysterious castle. Had he not always known that Hungarian could only be learned by beginning when a child and living in a Hungarian family? That any one had learned the language as one learns the *hic, hæc, hoc* was a marvel that deserved to be recorded. "From the grammar?" he repeated. "Well, that is wonderful! I certainly believed I should have to speak Latin to your worship. But allow me to introduce my humble self—"

"I already have the honor," quietly interrupted the count, "of knowing that you are Herr Vice-palatine Bernat Görömbölyi von Dravakeresztur."

He repeated the whole name without a single mistake!

The vice-palatine bowed, and began again:

"The object of my visit to-day is—"

Again he was interrupted.

"I know that also," said the count. "The Fertöszeg estate has passed into the hands of another proprietor, who has a legal right to withdraw the lease and revoke the conditions made and agreed to by her predecessor; and the Herr Vice-palatine is come, at the request of the baroness, to serve a notice to quit."

Herr Bernat did not like it when any one interrupted him or knew beforehand what he intended to say.

"On the contrary, I came because the baroness desires to renew the lease. She has learned how kind to the poor your worship is, and offers the castle and park at half the rent paid heretofore." He fancied this would melt the haughty lord of the castle, but it seemed to increase his hauteur.

"Thanks," frigidly responded the count. "If the baroness thinks the rent too high, she will find in her own neighborhood poor people whom she can assist. I shall continue to pay the same rent I paid to the former owner."

"Then my business will be easily settled. I have brought my clerk with me; he can write out the necessary papers, and the matter can be concluded at once."

"Thank you very much," returned the count, but without offering to shake hands. Instead, he kept his arms crossed behind his back.

"Before we proceed to business," resumed the vice-palatine, "I must tell your worship an anecdote. A professor once told his pupils that he knew everything. Shortly afterward he asked one of the lads what his name was. 'Why,' responded the youth, 'how does it come that you don't know my name—you who know everything?'"

"I cannot see why you thought it necessary to relate this anecdote to me," observed the count, without a smile.

"I introduce it because I am compelled to inquire your worship's name and title, in order to draw up the contracts properly."

This, then, was the strategem by which he proposed to learn the name which no one yet had been able to decipher on the count's letters?

The count gazed fixedly for several seconds at his questioner, then replied quietly:

"My name is Count Ludwig Vavel de Versay—with a *y* after the *a*."

"Thanks. I shall not forget it; I have a very good memory," said Herr Bernat, who was perfectly satisfied with his success. "Allow me, also, to inquire the family name of the worshipful Frau Countess?"

At this question the count at last removed his hands from his back, and with the sort of gesture a man makes who would tear asunder an adversary. At the same time he cast upon Herr Bernat a glance that reminded the valiant official of the royal commissioner, as well as of his energetic spouse at home. The angry man seemed to have increased a head in stature.

Instead of replying to the question, he turned on his heel and strode from the room, leaving his visitor standing in the middle of the floor. Herr Bernat was perplexed; he did not know what to do next. Was it not quite natural to ask the name of a man's wife when a legal contract was to be written? His question, therefore, had not been an insult.

At last, as the count did not return, there was nothing left for Herr Bernat to do but go to his room and wait there for further developments. The contracts would have to be renewed, else the count would have to vacate the castle; and one could easily see that a great deal of money had been expended in fitting it up. The count had transformed the old hunting-seat, which had been a filthy little nest, into a veritable fairy castle. Yes, undoubtedly the contracts would be renewed.

The vice-palatine was pacing the floor of his room in his noiseless cloth socks, when he suddenly heard the voices of his clerk and his servant outside the door.

"Well, Janos, we are not going to dine here to-day; from what I can learn, we are going to be eaten ourselves."

"What do you mean?"

"The groom told me his master was loading his pistols to shoot some one. The count challenges to a duel every one who inquires after the countess."

The voices ceased. The vice-palatine opened wide his eyes, and muttered:

"May the devil fly away with him! He wants to fight a duel, does he? I am not afraid of his pistols; I have one, too, and a sword into the bargain. But it 's a silly business altogether! I am to fight about a woman I have n't even seen! And what will my wife say? I wish I had n't come into this crazy castle! I wish I had n't sealed a compact of fraternity with the baroness! Why did not I leave this whole installation business to the second vice-palatine? If only I could think of an excuse to turn my back on this lunatic asylum! But I am not going to run away from a pistol. The Hungarian noble is a born soldier. If only I had my pipe! A man is only half a man without his pipe. A pipe inspires one with ideas. Where, I wonder, is that Audiat gadding?"

At this moment the clerk opened the door.

"Fetch our luggage, Audiat; we are going to leave this damned lunatic asylum. The Herr Count may see to it then how he renews his lease." Hereupon he kicked off the socks with such vigor that the very castle shook. Then, grasping his sword in his hand, he marched out of his room, and down the staircase, to prove that he was not fleeing like a coward, but was clearing his way by force.

When the clerk, who went to fetch the luggage, was about to enter the groom's apartment, the count came toward him and said:

"You are the vice-palatine's clerk?"

"That 's what they call me."

"When do you expect to become a lawyer?"

"When I have passed my examination."

"When will that be?"

"When I have served a year as jurat, and have paid a ducat for my diploma."

"I will give you the ducat, and when you have become a lawyer I will employ you as my attorney at six hundred guilders a year. I know that a Hungarian gentleman will not accept a gift without making some return; I ask you, therefore, to give me for this ducat some information."

"What is it you wish to know?"

"How can I obtain possession of a portion of Lake Neusiedl for my own use alone?"

"By becoming a naturalized citizen of the county, and by purchase of a portion of the shore. I dare say there are some landowners on the shore who would be glad to part with their possessions in exchange for solid cash. If you buy such an estate you will have sole right to that part of the water in front of your property, and to the middle of the lake."

"Thank you. One more question: if you were my attorney, what could you do to prevent me from being ejected from this castle, in case I did not sign a new contract with the present owner?"

"First, I should take advantage of the law of possession, and drag the case through a twelve years' process; then I should appeal, which would postpone a settlement for three years longer. Would that be long enough?"

"Quite!"

The count nodded a farewell to the youthful jurist without even inquiring his name; nor did Audiat venture to propound a like question to his future employer.

Bernat bácsi did not, as he had promised, return to the manor to tell the baroness the result of his visit. He drove direct to his home.

PART III
THE MISTRESS OF THE CATS

CHAPTER I

When they heard the call, "Puss, puss!" they scampered down the roof, leaped from the eaves, and vanished, one after the other, between the curtains of the open window. It was quite an ethnographic, so to speak, collection of cats; a panther-like French pussy from Dund, a Caucasian with long pointed ears, one from China with wavy silken fur and drooping ears. Then the window was closed, for the company were all assembled—four cats, two pug-dogs, and a sparrow, and the hostess, a young girl.

The girl, to judge from her figure, was perhaps fifteen years old; but her manner and speech were those of a much younger child. With her arched brow and rainbow-formed eyebrows, she might have served as a model for a saint, had not the roguish smile about the corners of her red lips betrayed an earthly origin. The sparkling dark eyes, delicately chiseled nostrils, and rounded chin gave to her face certain family characteristics which many persons would have recognized at a first glance.

Her clothing was richly adorned with lace and embroidery, which was not the fashion for girls of her age; at the same time, there was about her attire a peculiar negligence, as if she had no one to advise her what was proper to wear, or how to wear it.

Her room was furnished with luxurious elegance. Satin hangings covered the walls; the furniture was upholstered with rare gobelin tapestry. Gilded cabinets veneered with tortoise-shell held, behind glass doors, all sorts of costly toys, and dolls in full costume. On a Venetian table with mosaic top lay a pack of cards and three heaps of money—one of gold, one of silver, the third of copper. On a low, three-legged table was a something shaped like an organ, with a long row of metal and wooden pipes. Near the window stood a drawing-table, on which were sheets of drawing-board, and glasses containing pulverized colors. There was also a bookcase; on the shelves were volumes of Vertuch's "Orbis pictus," the "Portefeuille des enfants," the "History of Robinson Crusoe," and several numbers of a fashion magazine, the "Album des salons," the illustrations of which lay scattered about on tables and chairs.

The guests were all assembled; not one was missing. The little hostess inquired after the health of each one in turn, and how they had enjoyed their outing. They all had names. The cats were Hitz, Mitz, Pani, and Miura. They were introduced to the two pugs, Phryxus and Helle. Then the little maid fetched a porcelain basin, and with a sponge washed each nose and paw. Only after this operation had been thoroughly performed were the guests allowed to take their places at the breakfast-table—the four cats opposite the two pugs.

Then a clean napkin was tied about the neck of each guest,—that their jabots might not get soiled with milk,—and a cup of bread and milk placed in front of each one.

No complaints were allowed (the one that broke this rule was severely lectured), while all of them had patiently to submit when the sparrow helped himself from whichever cup he chose. The breakfast over, the guests bow-wowed and miaued their thanks, and were dismissed to their morning nap.

The musical clock now began to play its shepherd's song; the brass Cyclops standing on the dial struck the hour; the cuckoo called, and the halberdier saluted. Then the little maid changed her toilet. She had a whole wardrobe full of clothes; she might select what she chose to wear. There was no one to tell her what to put on, or to help her attire herself. When her toilet was completed, a bell outside rang once, whereupon she donned her hat and tied over her face a heavy lace veil that effectually concealed her features. After a few minutes the bell rang a second time, and the sound of wheels in the courtyard was heard. Then three taps sounded on the door, and in answer to the little maid's clear-voiced "Come in!" a gentleman in promenade toilet entered the room and bowed respectfully. First he satisfied himself that the veil was securely fastened around the young girl's hat; then, drawing her hand through his arm, he led her to the carriage.

On the box was seated the broad-shouldered groom, now clad in coachman's costume. The gentleman assisted the little maid into the carriage, took his seat by her side, and the black horses set off over the same road they had traversed a thousand times, in the regulation trot, avoiding the main thoroughfare of the village. Those persons whom they chanced to meet did not salute, for they knew that the occupants of the carriage from the Nameless Castle did not wish to be spoken to; and any of the villagers who were standing idly at their doors stepped inside until they had passed;

no inquisitive woman face peered after them. And thus the carriage passed on its way, as if it had been invisible. When it arrived at the forest, the horses knew just where they had to halt. Here the gentleman assisted his veiled companion to alight, gave her his left arm, because he held in his right hand a heavy walking-stick, in the center of which was concealed a long, three-edged poniard, an effective weapon in the hands of him who knew how to wield it.

In silence the man and the maid promenaded along the green sward in the shade of the trees. A campanula had just opened its blue eye at the foot of one of the trees, and pale-blue forget-me-nots grew along the path. Blue was the little maid's favorite color; but she was not permitted to pluck the flowers herself. She had never been told why she must not do this; perhaps it was because the flowers belonged to some one else.

Sometimes the little maid's steps were so light and elastic, as if a fairy were gliding over the dewy grass; and sometimes she walked so slowly, so wearily, as if a little old grandmother came limping along, hunting for lichens on the mossy ground.

After the promenade, they seated themselves again in the carriage, which returned to the Nameless Castle, and the gates were closed again.

The man conducted the maid to her room, and the serious occupation of the day began. Books were produced, and the man proceeded to explain the classics. They were his own favorites; he could not give her any others. She had not yet seen or heard of romances, and she was still too young to begin the study of history. The man could teach the maid only what he himself knew; a strange tutor or governess was not allowed to enter the castle.

Because her instructor could not play the piano, the little maid had not learned. But in order that she might enjoy listening to music, a hand-organ had been bought for her, and new melodies were inserted in it every four months.

When the little maid wearied of her organ and her picture-making, she seated herself at the card-table, and played *l'hombre*, or *tarok*, with two imaginary adversaries, enjoying the manner in which the copper coins won the gold ones.

At noon, when the bell rang a third time, the man tapped at the door again, offered his gloved hand to the maid, and conducted her to the dining-room. At either end of a large table was a plate. The maid took her place at the head; the man seated himself at the foot. They conversed during the meal. The maid talked about her cats and dogs; the man told her about his books. When the maid wanted anything, she called the man Ludwig; and when the man addressed his companion, he called her simply Marie.

After dinner, they went to the library to look at the late newspapers. Ludwig himself made the coffee, after which he read the papers, and dictated his comments and criticisms on certain articles to Marie, who wrote them out in her delicate hair-line chirography.

When Ludwig and Marie separated for the afternoon, he touched his lips to her hand and brow. Marie then returned to her own apartments, played the hand-organ for her pets, changed her dolls' toilets, counted her gains or losses at cards, colored with her paints a few of the illustrations in the magazines, looked through her "Orbis pictus," reading without difficulty the text which was printed in four languages, and read for the hundredth time her favorite "Robinson Crusoe."

And thus passed day after day, from spring until autumn, from autumn until spring.

Evenings, when Marie prepared for bed, before she undressed herself, she spread a heavy silken coverlet over the leather lounge which stood near the door. She knew very well that the some one she called Ludwig slept every night on the lounge, but he came in so late, and went away so early in the morning, that she never heard his coming or his going.

The little maid was a sound sleeper, and the pugs never barked at the master of the house, who gave them lumps of sugar.

Often the little maid had determined that she would not go to sleep until she heard Ludwig come into the room. But all her attempts to remain awake were in vain. Her eyelids closed the moment her head touched the pillow. Then she tried to waken early, in order to wish him good morning; but when she thrust her little head from between the bed-curtains, and called cheerily, "Good morning, dear Ludwig!" there was no one there.

Ludwig never slept more than four hours of the twenty-four, and his slumber was so light that he woke at the slightest noise. Then, too, he slept like a soldier in the field—always clothed, with his weapons beside him.

CHAPTER II

One day in the year formed an exception to all the rest. It was Marie's birthday. From her earliest childhood this one day had been entirely her own. On this day she addressed Ludwig with the familiar "thou," as she had been wont to do when he had taught her to walk. She always looked forward with great pleasure to this day, and made for it all sorts of plans whose accomplishment was extremely problematic.

And who came to congratulate her on her birthday? First of all, the solitary sparrow, whose name was David—surely because he, too, was a tireless singer! Already at early dawn, when the first faint rosy hues of morning glimmered through the jalousie, he would fly to the head of her bed. Then the cats would come with their gratulations, but not until their little mistress had leaped from the bed, run to the window, flung open the sash, and called, "Puss, puss!" Then the whole four would scamper into the room, one after the other, and wish her many happy returns of the day.

When the pugs had gone through their part of the program, the little maid proceeded to attire herself, a task she performed behind a tall folding screen. When she stepped forth again, she had on a gorgeous Chinese-silk wrapper, covered all over with gay-colored palms, and confined only at the waist with a heavy silk cord. Her hair was twisted into a single knot on the crown of her head.

Then she prepared breakfast for herself and her guests. The eight of them drank cold milk, and ate of the dainty little cakes which some one placed on her table every night while she slept. To-day Marie did not amuse herself with her guests, but turned over the leaves of her picture-book, thus passing the time until she should hear, after the bell had rung twice, the tap at her door.

"Come in!"

The man who entered was surprised.

"What? We are not yet ready for the drive?" he exclaimed.

The maid threw her book aside, ran toward him, and flung her arms with childish abandon around his neck.

"We are not going to drive to-day. Dost thou not know that this is my birthday—that I alone give orders in this house to-day? To-day everything must be done as *I* say; and *I* say that we will pass the time of the drive here in my room, and that thou shalt answer several silly questions which have come into my head. And forget not that we are to 'thou' each other to-day. And now, congratulate me nicely. Come, let us hear it!"

The count almost imperceptibly bent his knee and his head, but spoke not one word. There are gratulations which are expressed in this manner.

"Very good! Then I am a queen for to-day, and thou art my sole subject. Sit thou here at my feet on this taboret."

The man obeyed. Marie seated herself on the ottoman, and drew her feet underneath the wide skirt of her robe.

"Put that book away!" she commanded, when Ludwig stooped to lift from the floor the volume she had cast there. "I know every one of the four volumes by heart! Why dost not thou give me one of the books thou readest so often?"

"Because they are medical works."

"And why dost thou read such books?"

"In order that, should any one in the castle become ill, I may be able to cure him or her without a doctor."

"And must the person die who is ill and cannot be cured?"

"That is generally the end of a fatal illness."

"Does it hurt to die?"

"That I am unable to tell, as I have never tried it."

"Ha, ha, ha!" laughed the maid. "Thou canst not put me off that way! Thou knowest many things thou hast not yet tried. Thou hast read about them; thou knowest! What is death like? Is it more unpleasant than a disagreeable dream? Is the pain all over when one has died, or is there more to come afterward? If death is painful, why must we die? If it is pleasant, why must we live?"

Children ask such strange questions!

"Life is a gift from God that must be preserved as long as possible," returned Ludwig, evading the main question. "Through us the world exists—"

"What is the world?" interrupted Marie.

"The entire human race and their habitations—the earth."

"Then every person owns a plot of earth? Where is the plot which belongs to us? Answer me that!"

"By the way, that reminds me!" exclaimed Ludwig, relieved to find an opportunity to change the subject. "I have not yet told thee that I intend to buy a lovely plot of ground on the shore of the lake, which is to be made into a pretty flower-garden for thy use alone. Will not that be pleasant?"

"Thou art very kind; the garden will be lovely. That plot of ground, then, will be our home, will it not? What is one's home called?"

"It is called the fatherland."

"Then every country is not one's fatherland?"

"If our enemies live there, it is not."

"What are enemies?"

"Persons with whom we are angry."

"What is angry? I have never yet seen anything like it. Why art thou never angry?"

"Because I have no reason to be angry with thee, and I never associate with any one else."

"What do those persons do who become angry with one another?"

"They avoid each other. If they are very angry they fight; and if they are very, very angry they kill each other."

The maid was tortured with curiosity to-day. She drew a pin from her robe, and secretly thrust the point into Ludwig's hand.

"What art thou doing?" he asked, in surprise.

"I want to see what thou art like when thou art angry. Did it hurt thee?"

"Certainly it hurt me; see, the blood is flowing."

"Ah, heaven!" cried the maid, in terror, drew the young man's head toward her, and pressed a kiss on his face.

He sprang to his feet, his face pale as death, extreme horror depicted in his glance.

"There!" exclaimed the maid. "Thou dost not kill me, and yet I have made thee very angry."

"This is not anger," sighed the young man.

"What is it, then?"

"It has no name."

"Then I may not kiss thee? Thou lettest me kiss thee last year, and the year before, and every other year."

"But thou art fifteen years old to-day."

"Ah! Then what was allowed last year, and always before that, is not allowed now. Dost not thou love me any more?"

"All my thoughts are filled with thee."

"Thou knowest that I have always been allowed to make one wish on my birthday, and that it has always been granted. That is what some one accustomed me to—thou knowest very well who."

"Thy desires have always been fulfilled."

"Yes; and children understand how to desire what is impossible. But grown persons are clever enough to know how to impose on the children. Three years ago I asked thee to bring me some one with whom I could talk— some one who would be company for me. Thou broughtest me cats and dogs and a bird! Two years ago I wished I might learn how to make pictures; and I was given paper patterns to color with water-colors. One year ago to-day I wished I might learn how to make music; and a hand-organ was bought for me. Oh, yes; my wishes have always been fulfilled, but always in a way that cheated me. Children are always treated so. To-day thou sayest that I am fifteen years old, and that I am not any more to be treated as a child. Mark that! To-day, as heretofore, I ask something of thee which thou canst give me—and thou canst not cheat me, either!"

"Whatever it may be, thou shalt have it, Marie."

"Thy hand on it! Now, thou knowest that I asked thee not long ago to send to Paris for a 'Melusine costume' for me!"

"And has it not already arrived? I myself delivered the box into thy hands."

"Knowest thou what a Melusine costume is? See, this is it."

With these words she sprang from her seat, untied the cord about her waist, flung off the silken wrapper, and stood in front of the speechless young man in one of those costumes worn by Paris dames at the sea-shore when they disport themselves amid the waves of the ocean. The Melusine costume was a bathing-dress.

"To-day, Ludwig, I ask that thou wilt teach me how to swim. The lake is just out yonder below the garden."

The maid, in her pale-blue bathing-dress, looked like one of those fairy-like creatures in Shakspere's "Midsummer Night's Dream," innocent and alluring, child and siren.

Disconcerted and embarrassed, Ludwig raised his hand.

"Art thou going to strike me?" inquired the child, half crying, half laughing.

"Pray put on the wrapper again!" said Ludwig, taking the garment from the sofa and with it veiling the model for a Naiad. "What sort of a caprice is this?"

"I have had the thought in my head for a long, long time, and I beg that thou wilt grant my request. Thou canst not say that thou canst not swim; for once, when we were traveling in great haste, I know not why, we came to a river, and found that the boat was on the farther shore. Thou swammest across, and broughtest back the boat in which the four of us then crossed to the other side. Already then the desire to swim arose in me. What a delicious sensation to swim through the water—to make wings of one's arms and fly like a bird! Since we live in this castle the wish has become stronger. Night after night I dream that I am cleaving through the waves. I never see God's sky when I go out, because I have to cover my face. It is just like looking at creation through a grating! I should love dearly to sing and shout for joy; but I dare not, for I am afraid the trees, the walls, the people, might hear me and betray me. But out yonder I could float on the green waves, where I should meet no one, where no one would see me. I could look up at the shining sky, and about in chorus with the fish-hawks, surrounded by the darting fishes, that would tell no one what they had seen or heard. That would be supreme happiness for me; wilt not thou help me to secure it?"

The child's wish was so true, so earnest, and Ludwig himself had experienced the proud delights of which she had spoken. Perhaps, too, he had related to Marie the story of Clelia and her companions, who swam the Tiber to preserve the Roman maidens' reputation for virtue.

"Whatever gives pleasure to thee pleases me," he said, extending his hand to take hers.

"And thou wilt grant my wish? Oh, how kind, how dear thou art!" And in vain the young man sought to withdraw the hand she covered with kisses. "What!" she exclaimed reproachfully, "may I not kiss thy hand either?"

"How canst thou behave so, Marie? Thou art fifteen years old! A grown-up girl does not kiss a man's hand."

He passed his hand across his brow and sighed heavily; then he rose to his feet.

"Where art thou going? Knowest thou not that to-day thou dost not belong to thy horrid books nor to thy telescope, but that thou art my subject?"

"I go to execute the commands of my little queen. If she desires to learn to swim, I must have a bath-house built on the shore, and look about for a suitable spot in the little cove."

"When I have learned to swim all by myself, may not I go beyond the little cove—away out into the open lake?"

"Yes, on two conditions. One is that I may follow in my canoe—"

"But not keep very near to me?"

"Of course not. The second condition is that in daylight thou wilt not swim beyond those willows which conceal the cove. Only on moonlight evenings mayest thou venture into the open lake."

"But why may not I venture by daylight?"

"Because a telescope does not enable one to distinguish features after night. Other people may have a telescope, like myself."

"Who would have one in this village?"

"The manor has a new occupant. A lady has taken possession there."

"A lady? Is she pretty?"

"She is young."

"Didst thou see her through the telescope? What kind of hair has she got?"

"Blonde."

"Then she must be very pretty. May I take a look at her some time?"

"I am afraid thou mightest fall in love with her; for she is very beautiful, and very good."

"How dost thou know she is good?"

"Because she visits the sick and the poor, and because she goes regularly to church."

"Why do we never go to church?"

"Because we profess a different belief from that acknowledged by those persons who attend this church."

"Do they pray to a different God from ours?"

"No; they pray to the same God."

"Then why should n't we all go to the same church?"

Unable longer to control himself, Ludwig took the shrewd little child-head between his hands, and said tenderly:

"My darling! my little queen! not all the synods of the four quarters of the globe could answer thy questions—let alone this poor forgotten soldier!"

"There! thou always pretendest to be stupid when I want to borrow a little bit of thy wisdom. Thou art like the rich man who tells the beggar that he has no money. By the way, I must not forget that I always send money to the poor children on my birthday. Come, tell me which of the heaps I shall send to-day—these small coins, or these large ones? If thou thinkest I ought to send these little yellow ones, I have no objections. I think I prefer to keep the white coins, they have such a musical sound; besides, they have the image of the Virgin. If thou thinkest I ought to send some of the large red ones, too, I will do so."

The "little yellow ones" were gold sovereigns; the "white coins" were silver *Zwanziger*; and the "large red ones" were copper medals of the Austrian minister of finance, worth half a guilder.

"We will send some of the small coins and some of the large ones," decided Ludwig, smiling at the little maid's ignorance of the value of the money.

CHAPTER III

Tradition maintained that many years before, during the preceding century, the tongue of land now occupied by the Nameless Castle was part of the lake; and it may have been true, for Neusiedl Lake is a very capricious body of water. During the past two decades we ourselves have seen a greater portion of the lake suddenly recede, leaving dry land where once had been several feet of water. The owners of what had once been the shore took possession of the dry lake bottom; they used it for meadows and pastures; leased it, and the lessees built farm-houses and steam-mills on the "new ground." They cultivated wheat and maize, and for many years harvested two crops a year. Suddenly the lake took a notion to occupy its old bed again; and when the water had resumed its former level, fields and farms had vanished beneath the green flood; only here and there the top of a chimney indicated where a steam-mill had been. Magic tricks like this Neusiedl Lake has played more than once on trusting mortals.

On either side of the peninsula on which stood the Nameless Castle was a little cove. One of these the count had spoken of to Marie; the other separated the castle from the village of Fertöszeg.

The manor, the habitation of the owner of the Fertöszeg estate, stood on the slope of a hill at the eastern end of the village, and fronted, as did the neighboring castle, on the lake.

In the second half of the month of August, in the year 1806, one might have seen from the veranda of the manor, after the sun had gone down and the marvelous tints of the evening sky were reflected in the water, a small boat speed out from the cove on the farther side of the Nameless Castle, trailing after it a long silvery streak on the parti-colored surface of the lake. A solitary man sat in the boat.

But what could not be seen from the veranda of the manor was that a girlish form swam a little in advance of the boat.

Marie had proved an excellent scholar in the school of the hydriads. Already after the fourth lesson she could swim alone, and sped over the waves as lightly and gracefully as a swan.

She did not need to wear a hat on these evening swimming excursions; her long hair floated unbound after her on the waves. When the twilight shadows deepened, the swimmer would speed far ahead of the accompanying canoe. She had lost all fear of the water. The waves were her friends—they knew each other well. When she wished to rest, she would turn her face to the sky, fold her arms across her breast, and lie on the waves as among swelling cushions like a child in a rocking cradle. And here she was allowed the full privileges of a child. She shouted; called to the startled wild geese; teased the night-swallows, and the bats skimming along the surface of the lake in quest of water-spiders. Here she even ventured to sing, and gave voice to charming melodies, which floated over the water like the sounds of an Æolian harp.

Many hours were spent thus on the lake. The little maid never wearied of the water. The protecting element restored to her nerves the strength which the stepmotherly earth had taken from them. A promenade of a hundred steps would tire her so that she would have to stop and rest. She had become unused to walking. But here in the water she moved about like a Naiad; her whole being was transformed; she lived! Then, when her guardian would call her, she would swim back to the canoe, clamber into it, and spread her long hair over his knees to dry while they rowed back to the shore. Poor little maid! She declared she had found happiness in the water.

One evening, after the waning moon had risen, Ludwig's canoe, as usual, followed Marie, who was swimming a considerable distance ahead. Among the peculiarities of Neusiedl Lake are its numerous islets, the shores of which are thickly grown with rushes, and covered with broom and tall trees. Such an island lay not far from the shore in front of the Nameless Castle; it had frequently aroused Marie's curiosity.

The little maid was now permitted to swim as far out into the open world of waves as she desired, only now and again signaling her whereabouts through a clear-toned "Ho, ho!"

During this time Ludwig reclined in his boat, and while the waves gently rocked him, he gazed dreamily into the depths of the starry sky, and listened to the mysterious voices of the night—the moaning, murmuring, echoing voices floating across the surface of the water.

Suddenly a piercing scream mingled with the mysterious voices of the night. It was Marie's voice.

Frantic with terror, Ludwig seized his oars, and the canoe shot through the water in the direction of the scream.

The trail of light left behind her by the swimmer was visible on the calm surface of the lake. Suddenly it made an abrupt turn, and began to form a gigantic V. Evidently the little maid was impelled by desperate terror to reach the protecting canoe. When she came abreast of it she uttered a second cry, convulsively grasped the edge of the boat, and cast a terrified glance backward.

"Marie!" cried the count, greatly alarmed, seizing the girdle about her waist and lifting her into the canoe. "What has happened? Who is following you?"

The child trembled violently; her teeth chattered, and she gasped for breath, unable to speak; only her large eyes were still fixed with an expression of horror on the water.

Ludwig looked searchingly around, but could see nothing. And yet, after a few seconds, something rose before him.

What was it? Man or beast?

The head, the face, were head and face of a human being—a man, perhaps. The cheeks and head were covered with short reddish hair like the fur of an otter. The long, pointed ears stood upright. The mouth was closed so tightly that the lips were invisible. The nose was flat. The eyes, like those of a fish, were round and staring. There was no expression whatever in the features.

The mysterious monster had risen quite close to the boat.

Ludwig seized an oar with both hands to crush the monster's head; but the heavy blow fell on the water. The creature had vanished underneath the boat, and only the motion of the water on the other side indicated the direction it had taken. Terror and rage had benumbed Ludwig's nerves.

What was it? Who had sent this nameless monster after his carefully guarded treasure? Even the bottom of the lake concealed her enemies! He could think of nothing but intrigues and malignant persecutions. Rage boiled in his veins.

He enveloped the maid in her bath-mantle, and took up his oars.

"I will come back here to-morrow," he muttered to himself, "hunt up this creature, and shoot it—be it man or beast."

Marie murmured something which sounded like a remonstrance.

"I will shoot the creature!" repeated Ludwig, savagely.

The young girl withdrew trembling to the stern of the boat, and said nothing further; she even strove to suppress her nervous terror, like a child that has behaved naughtily.

When the boat reached the shore, Ludwig bade Marie in a stern voice to make haste and change her bathing-dress, and became very impatient when she lingered longer than usual in the bath-house. Then he took her arm and walked rapidly with her to the castle.

"Are you really going to shoot that creature?" asked Marie, still trembling.

"Yes."

"But suppose it is a human being?"

"Then I shall certainly shoot him."

"I will never, never again venture into the lake."

"I am certain of that! If you once become frightened in the water, you will always have a dread of it."

"My dear, beautiful lake!" sighed Marie, casting backward a sorrowful glance at the glittering expanse of water, at the paradise of her dreams, which the rising wind was curling into wavelets.

"Go at once to bed," said Ludwig, when he had conducted his charge to the door of her room. "Cover yourself up well, and if you feel chilly I will make you a cup of camomile tea."

All children have such a distaste for this herb tea that it was not to be wondered at if Marie declared she did not feel in the least chilly, and that she would go at once to bed.

But she did not sleep well. She dreamed all night long of the water-monster. She saw it pursuing her. The staring fish-eyes rose before her in the darkness. Then she saw Ludwig with his gun searching for the monster—saw him shoot at it, but without effect. The hideous creature leaped merrily away.

More than once she awoke from her restless slumber and called softly:

"Ludwig, are you there?"

But no one answered the question. Since her last birthday Ludwig had not occupied the lounge in her room. Marie had discovered this. She had placed a rose-leaf on the silken coverlet every evening, and found it still there in the morning. If any one had slept on the lounge, the rose-leaf would have fallen to the floor.

The following day Ludwig was more silent than usual. He did not speak once during their drive, and ate hardly anything at meals.

One could easily see how impatiently he waited for evening, when he might go down to the lake and search for the monster—a sorry object for a fury such as his! An otter, most likely, or a beaver—mayhap an abortion of the Dead Sea, which had survived the ages since the days of Sodom! All the same, it was a living creature, and must become food for fishes. Marie, however, prayed so fervently that nothing might come of Ludwig's fury that Heaven heard the prayer. The weather changed suddenly in the afternoon. A cold west wind succeeded to the warm August sunshine; clouds of dust arose; then came a heavy downpour of rain. Ludwig was obliged to forego his intention to row about on the lake in the evening. He spent the entire evening in his room, leaving Marie to complain to her cats; but they were sleepy, and paid no attention to what she said.

The little maid had no desire to go to bed; she was afraid she might dream again of horrible things. The heavy rain beat against the windows; thunder rumbled in the distance.

"I should not like to venture out of the house in such weather," said Marie to her favorite cat, who was dozing on her knee. "Ugh-h! just think of crossing the lonely court, or going through the dark woods! Ugh-h! how horrible it must be there now! And then, to pass the graveyard at the end of the village! When the lightning flashes, the crosses lift their heads from the darkness—ugh-h!"

The clock struck eleven; directly afterward there came a hesitating knock at her door.

"Come in! You may come in!" she called joyfully. She thought it was Ludwig.

The door opened slowly, only half-way, and the voice which began to speak was not Ludwig's; it was the groom.

"Beg pardon, madame!" (thus he addressed the little maid).

"Is it you, Henry? What do you want? You may come in. I am still up."

The groom entered, and closed the door behind him. He was a tall, gray-haired man, with an honest face and enormously large hands.

"What is it, Henry? Did the count send you?"

"No, madame; I only wish he were able."

"Why? What is the matter with him?"

"I don't know, indeed! I believe he is dying."

"Who? Ludwig?"

"Yes, madame; my master."

"For God's sake, tell me what you mean!"

"He is lying on his bed, quite out of his mind. His face is flushed, his eyes gleam like hot coals, and he is talking wildly. I have never seen him in such a condition."

"Oh, heaven! what shall we do?"

"I don't know, madame. When any of us gets sick the count knows what to do; but he does n't seem able to cure himself now; the contents of the medicine-chest are scattered all over the floor."

"Is there no doctor in the village?"

"Yes, madame; the county physician."

"Then he must be sent for."

"I thought of that, but I did not like to venture to do so."

"Why not?"

"Because the count has declared that he will shoot me if I attempt to bring a stranger into his room, or into madame's. He told me I must never admit within the castle gate a doctor, a preacher, or a woman; and I should not think of disobeying him."

"But now that he is so ill? and you say he may die? Merciful God! Ludwig die! It cannot—must not—happen!"

"But how will madame hinder it?"

"If you will not venture to fetch the doctor, then I will go myself."

"Oh, madame! you must not even think of doing this!"

"I think of nothing else but that he is ill unto death. I am going, and you are coming with me."

"Holy Father! The count will kill me if I do that."

"And if you don't do it you will kill the count."

"That is true, too, madame."

"Then don't you do anything. *I* shall do what is necessary. I will put on my veil, and let no one see my face."

"But in this storm? Just listen, madame, how it thunders."

"I am not afraid of thunder, you stupid Henry. Light a lantern, and arm yourself with a stout cudgel, while I am putting on my pattens. If Ludwig should get angry, I shall be on hand to pacify him. If only the dear Lord will spare his life! Oh, hasten, hasten, my good Henry!"

"He will shoot me dead; I know it. But let him, in God's name! I do it at your command, madame. If madame is really determined to go herself for the doctor, then we will take the carriage."

"No, indeed! Ludwig would hear the sound of wheels, and know what we were doing. Then he would jump out of bed, run into the court, and take a cold that would certainly be his death. No; we must go on foot, as noiselessly as possible. It is not so very far to the village. Go now, and fetch the lantern."

Several minutes afterward, the gates of the Nameless Castle opened, and there came forth a veiled lady, who clung with one hand to the arm of a tall man, and carried a lantern in the other. Her companion held over her, to protect her from the pouring rain, a large red umbrella, and steadied his steps in the slippery mud with a stout walking-stick. The lady walked so rapidly that her companion with difficulty kept pace with her.

CHAPTER IV

Dr. Tromfszky had just returned from a *visum repertum* in a criminal case, and had concluded that he would go to bed so soon as he had finished his supper. The rain fell in torrents on the roof, and rushed through the gutters with a roaring noise.

"Now just let any one send again for me this night!" he exclaimed, when his housekeeper came to remove the remnants of cheese from the supper-table. "I would n't go—not if the primate himself got a fish-bone fast in his throat; no, not for a hundred ducats. I swear it!"

At that moment there came a knock at the street door, and a very peremptory one, too.

"There! did n't I know some one would take it into his head to let the devil fetch him to-night? Go to the door, Zsuzsa, and tell them that I have a pain in my foot—that I have just applied a poultice, and can't walk."

Frau Zsuzsa, with the kitchen lamp in her hand, waddled into the corridor. After inquiring the second time through the door, "Who is it?" and the one outside had answered: "It is I," she became convinced, from the musical feminine tone, that it was not the notorious robber, Satan Laczi, who was seeking admittance.

Then she opened the door a few inches, and said:

"The Herr Doctor can't go out any more to-night;-he has gone to bed, and is poulticing his foot."

The door was open wide enough to admit a delicate feminine hand, which pressed into the housekeeper's palm a little heap of money. By the light of the lamp Frau Zsuzsa recognized the shining silver coins, and the door was opened its full width.

When she saw before her the veiled lady she became quite complaisant. Curiosity is a powerful lever.

"I humbly beg your ladyship to enter."

"Please tell the doctor the lady from the Nameless Castle wishes to see him."

Frau Zsuzsa placed the lamp on the kitchen table, and left the visitors standing in the middle of the floor.

"Well, what were you talking about so long out yonder?" demanded the doctor, when she burst into his study.

"Make haste and put on your coat again; the veiled lady from the Nameless Castle is here."

"What? Well, that is an event!" exclaimed the doctor, hurriedly thrusting his arms into the sleeves of his coat. "Is the count with her?"

"No; the groom accompanied her."

These magic words, "the veiled lady," had more influence on the doctor than any imaginable number of ducats.

At last he was to behold the mythological appearance—yes, and even hear her voice!

"Show her ladyship into the guest-chamber, and take a lamp in there," he ordered, following quickly, after he had adjusted his cravat in front of the looking-glass.

Then she stood before him—the mysterious woman. Her face was veiled as usual. Behind her stood the groom, with whose appearance every child in the village was familiar.

"Herr Doctor," stammered the young girl, so faintly that it was difficult to tell whether it was the voice of a child, a young or an old woman, "I beg that you will come with me at once to the castle; the gentleman is very seriously ill."

"Certainly; I am delighted!—that is, I am not delighted to hear of the worshipful gentleman's illness, but glad that I am fortunate enough to be of service to him. I shall be ready in a few moments."

"Oh, pray make haste."

"The carriage will take us to the castle in five minutes, your ladyship."

"But we did not come in a carriage; we walked."

Only now the doctor noticed that the lady's gown was thickly spattered with mud.

"What? Came on foot in such weather—all the way from the Nameless Castle? and your ladyship has a carriage and horses?"

"Cannot you come with us on foot, Herr Doctor?"

"I should like very much to accompany your ladyship; but really, I have *rheumatismus acutus* in my foot, and were I to get wet I should certainly have an *ischias*."

Marie lifted her clasped hands in despair to her lips, but the beseeching expression on her face was hidden by the heavy veil. Could the doctor have seen the tearful eyes, the trembling lips!

Seeing that her voiceless petition was in vain, Marie drew from her bosom a silken purse, and emptied the contents, gold, silver, and copper coins, on the table.

"Here," she exclaimed proudly. "I have much more money like this, and will reward you richly if you will come with me."

The doctor was amazed. There on the table lay more gold than the whole county could have mustered in these days of paper notes. Truly these people were not to be despised.

"If only it did not rain so heavily—"

"I will let you take my umbrella."

"Thanks, your ladyship; I have one of my own."

"Then let us start at once."

"But my foot—it pains dreadfully."

"We can easily arrange that. Henry, here, is a very strong man; he will take you on his shoulders, and bring you back from the castle in the carriage."

There were no further objections to be offered when Henry, with great willingness, placed his broad shoulders at the doctor's service.

The doctor hastily thrust what was necessary into a bag, locked the money Marie had given him in a drawer, bade Frau Zsuzsa remain awake until he returned, and clambered on Henry's back. In one hand he held his umbrella, in the other the lantern; and thus the little company took their way to the castle—the "double man" in advance, the little maid following with her umbrella.

The doctor had sufficient cause to be excited. What usurious gossip-interest might be collected from such a capitol! Dr. Tromfszky already had an enviable reputation in the county, but what would it become when it became known that he was physician in ordinary to the Nameless Castle?

The rain was not falling so heavily when they arrived at the castle.

Marie and Henry at once conducted the doctor to Ludwig's chamber. Henry first thrust his head cautiously through the partly open door, then whispered that his master was still tossing deliriously about on the bed; whereupon the doctor summoned courage to enter the room. His first act was to snuff the candle, the wick having become so charred it scarcely gave any light. He could now examine the invalid's face, which was covered with a burning flush. His eyes rolled wildly. He had not removed his clothes, but had torn them away from his breast.

"H'm! h'm!" muttered the doctor, searching in his bag for his bloodletting instruments. Then he approached the bed, and laid his fingers on the invalid's pulse.

At the touch of his cold hand the patient suddenly sat upright and uttered a cry of terror:

"Who are you?"

"I am the doctor—the county physician—Dr. Tromfszky. Pray, Herr Count, let me see your tongue."

Instead of his tongue, the count exhibited a powerful fist.

"What do you want here? Who brought you here?" he demanded.

"Pray, pray be calm, Herr Count," soothingly responded the doctor, who was inclined to look upon this aggressive exhibition as a result of the fever. "Allow me to examine your pulse. We have here a slight paroxysm that requires medical aid. Come, let me feel your pulse; one, two—"

The count snatched his wrist from the doctor's grasp, and cried angrily:

"But I don't need a doctor, or any medicine. There is nothing at all the matter with me. I don't want anything from you, but to know who brought you here."

"Beg pardon," retorted the offended doctor. "I was summoned, and came through this dreadful storm. I was told that the Herr Count was seriously ill."

"Who said so? Henry?" demanded the count, rising on one knee.

Henry did not venture to move or speak.

"Did you fetch this doctor, Henry?" again demanded the invalid, with expanded nostrils, panting with fury.

The doctor, fancying that it would be well to tell the truth, now interposed politely:

"Allow me, Herr Count! Herr Henry did not come alone to fetch me, but he came with the gracious countess; and on foot, too, in this weather."

"What? Marie?" gasped the invalid; and at that moment his face looked as if he had become suddenly insane. An involuntary epileptic convulsion shook his limbs. He fell from the bed, but sprang at the same instant to his feet again, flung himself like an angry lion upon Henry, caught him by the throat, and cried with the voice of a demon:

"Wretch! Betrayer! What have you dared to do? I will kill you!"

The doctor required nothing further. He did not stop to see the friendly promise fulfilled, but, leaving his lances, elixirs, and plasters behind him, he flew down the staircase, four steps at a time, and into the pouring rain, totally forgetting the ischias which threatened his leg. Nor did he once think of a carriage, or of a human dromedary,—not even of a lantern, or an umbrella,—as he galloped down the dark road through the thickest of the mud.

When the count seized Henry by the throat and began to shake him, as a lion does the captured buffalo, Marie stepped suddenly to his side, and in a clear, commanding tone cried:

"Louis!"

At this word he released Henry, fell on his knees at Marie's feet, clasped both arms around her, and, sobbing convulsively, pressed kiss after kiss on the little maid's wet and muddy gown.

"Why—why did you do this for me?" he exclaimed, in a choking voice.

The doctor's visit had, after all, benefited the invalid. The spontaneous reaction which followed the violent fit of passion caused a sudden turn in his illness. The salutary crisis came of its own accord during the outburst of rage, which threw him into a profuse perspiration. The brain gradually returned to its normal condition.

"You will get well again, will you not?" stammered the little maid shyly, laying her hand on the invalid's brow.

"If you really want me to get well," returned Ludwig, "then you must comply with my request. Go to your room, take off these wet clothes, and go to bed. And you must promise never again to go on another errand like the one you performed this evening. I hope you may sleep soundly."

"I will do whatever you wish, Ludwig—anything to prevent your getting angry again."

The little maid returned to her room, took off her wet clothes, and lay down on the bed; but she could not sleep. Every hour she rose, threw on her wrapper, thrust her feet into her slippers, and stole to the door of Ludwig's room to whisper: "How is he now, Henry?"

"He is sleeping quietly," Henry would answer encouragingly. The faithful fellow had forgotten his master's anger, and was watching over him as tenderly as a mother over her child.

"He did not hurt you very much, did he, Henry?"

"No; it did not hurt, and I deserved what I got."

The little maid pressed the old servant's hand, whereupon he sank to his knees at her feet, and, kissing her pretty fingers, whispered:

"This fully repays me."

The next morning Ludwig was entirely recovered. He rose, and, as was his wont, drank six tumblerfuls of water—his usual breakfast.

Of the events of the past night he spoke not one word.

At ten o'clock the occupants of the Nameless Castle were to be seen out driving as usual—the white-haired groom, the stern-visaged gentleman, and the veiled lady.

That same morning Dr. Tromfszky received from the castle a packet containing his medical belongings, and an envelop in which he found a hundred-guilder bank-note, but not a single written word.

Meanwhile the days passed with their usual monotony for the occupants of the Nameless Castle, and September, with its delightfully warm weather drew on apace. In Hungary the long autumn makes ample amends for the brief spring—like the frugal mother who stores away in May gifts with which to surprise her children later in the season.

Down at the lake, a merry crowd of naked children disported in the water; their shouts and laughter could be heard at the castle. Ludwig fully understood the deep melancholy which had settled on Marie's countenance. Her sole amusement, her greatest happiness, had been taken from her. Other high-born maidens had so many ways of enjoying themselves; she had none. No train of admirers paid court to her. No strains of merry dance-music entranced her ear. Celebrated actors came and went; she did not delight in their performances—she had never even seen a theater. She had no girl friends with whom to exchange confidences—with whom to make merry over the silly flatterers who paid court to them; no acquaintances whose envy she could arouse by the magnificence of her toilets—one of the greatest pleasures in life!

She had no other flatterers but her cats; no other confidantes but her cats; no other actors but her cats. The world of waves had been her sole enjoyment. The water had been her theater, balls, concert—the great world. It was her freedom. The land was a prison.

Again it was the full of the moon, and quite warm. The tulip-formed blossoms of the luxuriant water-lilies were in bloom along the lake shore. Ludwig's heart ached with pity for the little maid when he saw how sorrowfully she gazed from her window on the glittering lake.

"Come, Marie," he said, "fetch your bathing-dress, and let us try the lake again. I will stay close by you, and take good care that nothing frightens you. We will not go out of the cove."

How delighted the child was to hear these words! She danced and skipped for joy; she called him her dear Ludwig. Then she hunted up the discarded Melusine costume, and hastened with such speed toward the shore that Ludwig was obliged to run to keep up with her. But the nearer she approached to the bath-house, the less quickly she walked; and when she stood in the doorway she said:

"Oh, how my heart beats!"

When Ludwig appeared with the canoe from behind the willows, the charming Naiad stepped from the bath-house. The rippling waves bore the moonlight to her feet, where she stood on the narrow platform which projected into the lake. She knelt and, bending forward, kissed the water; it was her beloved! After a moment's hesitation she dropped gently from the platform, as she had been wont to do; but when she felt the waves about her shoulders, she uttered a cry of terror, and grasped the edge of the canoe with both hands.

"Lift me out, Ludwig! I cannot bear it; I am afraid!"

With a sorrowful heart the little maid took leave of her favorite element. The hot tears gushed from her eyes, and fell into the water; it was as if she were bidding an eternal, farewell to her beloved. From that hour the child became a silent and thoughtful woman.

Then followed the stormy days of autumn, the long evenings, the weeks and months when nothing could be done but stay in doors and amuse one's self with books—Dante, Shakspere, Horace. To these were occasionally added learned folios sent from Stuttgart to Count Ludwig, who seemed to find his greatest enjoyment in perusing works on philosophy and science. Meanwhile the communication by letter between the count and the erudite shepherd of souls in the village was continued.

One day Herr Mercatoris sent to the castle a brochure on which he had proudly written, "With the compliments of the author." The booklet was written in Latin, and was an account of the natural wonder which is, to this day, reckoned among the numerous memorable peculiarities of Lake Neusiedl,—a human being that lived in the water and ate live fishes.

A little boy who had lost both parents, and had no one to care for him, had strayed into the morass of the Hansag, and, living there among the wild animals, had become a wild animal himself, an inhabitant of the water like the otters, a dumb creature from whose lips issued no human sound.

The decade of years he had existed in the water had changed his skin to a thick hide covered with a heavy growth of hair. The phenomenon would doubtless be accepted by many as a convincing proof that the human being was really evolved from the wild animal.

Accompanying the description was an engraved portrait of the natural wonder.

The new owner of Fertöszeg, Baroness Katharina Landsknechtsschild, had been told that a strange creature was frightening the village children who bathed in the lake. She had given orders to some fishermen to catch the monster, which they had been fortunate enough to do while fishing for sturgeon. The boy-fish had been taken to the manor, where he had been properly clothed, and placed in the care of a servant whose task it was to teach the poor lad to speak, and walk upright instead of on all fours, as had been his habit. Success had so far attended the efforts to tame the wild boy that he would eat bread and keep on his clothes. He had also learned to say "Ham-ham" when he wanted something to eat; and he had been taught to turn the spit in the kitchen. The kind-hearted baroness was sparing no pains to restore the lad to his original condition. No one was allowed to strike or abuse him in any way. ¬

This brochure had a twofold effect upon the count. He became convinced that the monster which had frightened Marie was not an assassin hired by her enemies, not an expert diver, but a natural abnormity that had acted innocently when he pursued the swimming maid. Second, the count could not help but reproach himself when he remembered that *he* would have destroyed the irresponsible creature whom his neighbor was endeavoring to transform again into a human being.

How much nobler was this woman's heart than his own! His fair neighbor began to interest him.

He took the pamphlet to Marie, who shuddered when her eyes fell on the engraving.

"The creature is really a harmless human being, Marie, and I am sorry we became so excited over it. Our neighbor, the lovely baroness, is trying to restore the poor lad to his original condition. Next summer you will not need to be afraid to venture into the lake again."

The little maid gazed thoughtfully into Ludwig's eyes for several moments; evidently she was pondering over something.

There had risen in her mind a suspicion that Ludwig himself had written the pamphlet, and had had the monster's portrait engraved, in order to quiet her fears and restore her confidence in the water.

"Will you take me sometime to visit the baroness?" she asked suddenly.

"And why?" inquired Ludwig, in turn, rising from his seat.

"That I, too, may see the wonderful improvement in the monster."

"No," he returned shortly, and taking up the pamphlet, he quitted the room. "No!"

"But why 'No'?"

PART IV
SATAN LACZI

CHAPTER I

Count Vavel (thus he was addressed on his letters) had arranged an observatory in the tower of the Nameless Castle. Here was his telescope, by the aid of which he viewed the heavens by night, and by day observed the doings of his fellow-men. He noticed everything that went on about him. He peered into the neighboring farm-yards and cottages, was a spectator of the community's disputes as well as its diversions. Of late, the chief object of his telescopic observations during the day were the doings at the neighboring manor. He was the "Lion-head" and the "Council of Ten" in one person. The question was, whether the new mistress of the manor, the unmarried baroness, should "cross the Bridge of Sighs"? His telescope told him that this woman was young and very fair; and it told him also that she lived a very secluded life. She never went beyond the village, nor did she receive any visitors.

In the neighborhood of Neusiedl Lake one village was joined to another, and these were populated by pleasure-loving and sociable families of distinction. It was therefore a difficult matter for the well-born man or woman who took up a residence in the neighborhood to avoid the jovial sociability which reigned in those aristocratic circles.

Count Vavel himself had been overwhelmed with hospitable attentions the first year of his occupancy of the Nameless Castle; but his refusals to accept the numerous invitations had been so decided that they were not repeated.

He frequently saw through his telescope the same four-horse equipages which had once stopped in front of his own gates drive into the court at the manor; and he recognized in the occupants the same jovial blades, the eligible young nobles, who had honored him with their visits. He noticed, too, that none of the visitors spent a night at the manor. Very often the baroness did not leave her room when a caller came; it may have been that she had refused to receive him on the plea of illness. During the winter Count Vavel frequently saw his fair neighbor skating on the frozen cove; while a servant propelled her companion over the ice in a chair-sledge.

On these occasions the count would admire the baroness's graceful figure, her intrepid movements, and her beautiful face, which was flushed with the exercise and by the cutting wind.

But what pleased him most of all was that the baroness never once during her skating exercises cast an inquiring glance toward the windows of the Nameless Castle—not even when she came quite close to it.

On Christmas eve she, like Count Vavel, arranged a Christmas tree for the village children. The little ones hastened from the manor to the castle, and repeated wonderful tales of the gifts they had received from the baroness's own hands.

Every Sunday the count saw the lady from the manor take her way to church, on foot if the roads were good; and on her homeward way he could see her distribute alms among the beggars who were ranged along either side of the road. This the count did not approve. He, too, gave plenteously to the poor, but through the village pastor, and only to those needy ones who were too modest to beg openly. The street beggars he repulsed with great harshness—with one exception. This was a one-legged man, who had lost his limb at Marengo, and who stationed himself regularly beside the cross at the end of the village. Here he would stand, leaning on his crutches, and the count, in driving past, would always drop a coin into the maimed warrior's hat.

One day when the carriage drew near the cross, Count Vavel saw the old soldier, as usual, but without his crutches. Instead, he leaned on a walking-stick, and stood on two legs.

The count stopped the carriage, and asked: "Are not you the one-legged soldier?"

"I am, your lordship," replied the man; "but that angel, the baroness, has had a wooden leg made for me,—I could dance with it if I wished,—so I don't need to beg any more, for I can cut wood now, and thus earn my living. May God bless her who has done this for me!"

The count was dissatisfied with himself. This woman understood everything better than he did. He felt that she was his rival, and from this feeling sprang the desire to compete with her.

An opportunity very soon offered. One day the count received from the reverend Herr Mercatoris a gracefully worded appeal for charity. The new owner of Fertöszeg had interested herself in the fate of the destitute children whose fathers had gone to the war, and, in order to render their condition more comfortable, had undertaken to found a home for them. She had already given the necessary buildings, and had furnished them. She now applied to the sympathies of the well-to-do residents of the county for assistance to educate the children. In addition to food and shelter, they required teachers. Such sums as were necessary for this purpose must be raised by a general subscription from the charitably inclined.

The count promptly responded to this request. He sent the pastor fifty louis d'or. But in the letter which accompanied the gift he stipulated that the boy whose mother was in prison should not be removed from Frau Schmidt's care to the children's asylum.

It was quite in the order of things that the baroness should acknowledge the munificent gift by a letter of thanks.

This missive was beautifully written. The orthography was singularly faultless. The expressions were gracefully worded and artless; nothing of flattery or sentimentality—merely courteous gratefulness. The letter concluded thus:

"You will pardon me, I trust, if I add that the stipulation which you append to your generous gift surprises me; for it means either that you disapprove the principle of my undertaking, or you do not wish to transfer to another the burden you have taken upon yourself. If the latter be the reason, I am perfectly willing to agree to the stipulation; if it be the former, then I should like very much to hear your objection, in order that I may justify my action."

This was a challenge that could-not be ignored. The count, of course, would have to convince his fair neighbor that he was in perfect sympathy with the principle of her philanthropic project, and he wrote accordingly; but he added that he disapproved the prison-like system of children's asylums, the convict-like regulations of such institutions. He thought the little ones would be better cared for, and much happier, were they placed in private homes, to grow up as useful men and women amid scenes and in the sphere of life to which they belonged.

The count's polemic reply was not without effect. The baroness, who had her own views on the matter, was quite as ready to take the field, with as many theoretic and empiric data and recognized authorities as had been her opponent. The count one day would despatch a letter to the manor, and Baroness Katharina would send her reply the next—each determined not to remain the other's debtor. The count's epistles were dictated to Marie; he added only the letter V to the signature.

This battle on paper was not without practical results. The baroness paid daily visits to her "Children's Home"; and on mild spring days the count very often saw her sitting on the open veranda, with her companion and one or two maid-servants, sewing at children's garments until late in the evening. The count, on his part, sent every day for his little protégé, and spent several hours patiently teaching the lad, in order that he might compete favorably with the baroness's charges. The task was by no means an easy one, as the lad possessed a very dull brain. This was, it must be confessed, an excellent thing for the orphans. If the motherly care which the baroness lavished on her charges were to be given to all destitute orphans in children's asylums, then the "convict system" certainly was a perfect one; while, on the other hand, if a preceptor like Count Vavel took it upon himself to instruct a forsaken lad, then one might certainly expect a genius to evolve from the little dullard growing up in a peasant's cottage.

Ultimately, however, the victory fell to the lady. It happened as follows:

One day the count was again the recipient of a letter from his neighbor at the manor (they had not yet exchanged verbal communication).

The letter ran thus:

"HERR COUNT: I dare say you know that the father of your little protégé is no other than the notorious robber, Satan Laczi, whom it is impossible to capture. The mother of the lad was arrested on suspicion. She lived in the village under her own honest family name—Satan Laczi being only a thief's appellation. As nothing could be proved against her, the woman has been set at liberty, and has returned to the village. Here she found every door closed against her—for who would care to shelter the wife of a robber? At last the poor woman came to me, and begged me to give her work. My servants are greatly excited because I have taken her into my employ; but I am convinced that the woman is innocent and honest. Were I to cast her adrift, she might become what she has been accused of being— the accomplice of thieves. I know she will conduct herself properly with me. I tell you all this because, if you approve what I have done, you will permit the lad you have taken under your protection to come to the manor, where he would be with his mother. If, however, you condemn my action, you will refuse to grant my request, and generously continue to care for the lad in your own way. The decision I leave to you."

Count Vavel was forced to capitulate. The baroness's action—taking into her household the woman who had been repulsed by all the world— was so praiseworthy, so sublime, that nothing could approach it. That same day he sent the lad with Frau Schmidt to the manor, and herewith the correspondence between himself and the baroness ceased. There was no further subject for argument.

And yet, Count Vavel could not help but think of this woman. Who was she?

He had sought to learn from his foreign correspondents something concerning the Baroness Katharina, but could gain no information save that which we have already heard from the county physician: disappointed love and shame at her rejection had driven the youthful baroness to this secluded neighborhood.

This reason, however, did not altogether satisfy Count Vavel. Women, especially young women, rarely quit the pleasures of the gay world because of one single disappointment.

And for Count Vavel mistrust was a duty; for the reader must, ere this, have suspected that the count and the mysterious man of the Rue Mouffetard were identical, and that Marie was none other than the child he had rescued from her enemies. Here in this land, where order prevailed, but where there were no police, he was guarding the treasure intrusted to his care, and he would continue to guard her until relieved of the duty.

But when would the relief come?

One year after another passed, and the hour he dreamed of seemed still further away. When he had accepted the responsible mission he had said to himself: "In a year we shall gain our object, and I shall be released."

But hope had deceived him; and as the years passed onward, he began to realize how vast, how enormous, was the task he had undertaken. It was within the possibilities that he, a young man in the flower of his youth, should be able to bury himself in an unknown corner of the world, to give up all his friends, to renounce everything that made life worth living, but that he should bury with himself in his silk-lined tomb a young girl to whom he had become everything, who yet might not even dream of becoming anything to him—that was beyond human might.

More and more he realized that his old friend's prophetic words were approaching fulfilment: "The child will grow to be a lovely woman. Already she is fond of you; she will love you then. Then what?"

"I shall look upon myself as the inhabitant of a different planet," he had replied; and he had kept his promise.

But the little maid had not promised anything; and if, perchance, she guessed the weighty secret of her destiny, whence could she have taken the strength of mind to battle against what threatened to drive even the strong man to madness?

Ludwig was thirty-one years old, the fourth year in this house of voluntary madmen. With extreme solicitude he saw the child grow to womanhood, blessed with all the magic charms of her sex. Gladly would he have kept her a child had it been in his power. He treated her as a child— gave her dolls and the toys of a child; but this could not go on forever. Deeply concerned, Ludwig observed that Marie's countenance became more and more melancholy, and that now it rarely expressed childlike naïveté. A dreamy melancholy had settled upon it. And of what did she dream? Why was she so sad? Why did she start? Why did the blood rush to her cheeks when he came suddenly into her presence?

CHAPTER II

Count Vavel had made his fair neighbor at the manor the object of study. He had ample time for the task; he had nothing else to do. And, as he was debarred from making direct inquiries concerning her, or from hearing the current gossip of the neighborhood, he learned only that about her which his telescope revealed; and from this, with the aid of his imagination, he formed a conclusion—and an erroneous one, very probably.

His neighbor lived in strict seclusion, and was a man-hater. But, for all that, she was neither a nun nor an Amazon. She was a true woman, neither inconsolably melancholy nor wantonly merry. She proved herself an excellent housewife. She rose betimes mornings, sent her workmen about their various tasks, saw that everything was properly attended to. Very often she rode on horseback, or drove in a light wagon, to look about her estate. She had arranged an extensive dairy, and paid daily visits to her stables. She did not seem aware that an attentive observer constantly watched her with his telescope from the tower of the Nameless Castle. So, at least, it might be assumed; for the lady very often assisted in the labor of the garden, when, in transplanting tulip bulbs, she would so soil her pretty white hands to the wrists with black mold that it would be quite distressing to see them. Certainly this was sufficient proof that her labor was without design.

And, what was more to the purpose, she acted as if perfectly unaware of the fact that a lady lived in the Nameless Castle who possibly might be the wife of her tenant. Common courtesy and the conventional usages of society demanded that the lady who took up a residence anywhere should call on the ladies of the neighborhood—if only to leave a card with the servant at the door. The baroness had omitted this ceremony, which proved that she either did not know of Marie's hiding-place, or that she possessed enough delicacy of feeling to understand that it would be inconvenient to the one concerned were she to take any notice of the circumstance. Either reason was satisfactory to Count Vavel.

But a woman without curiosity!

Meanwhile the count had learned something about her which might be of some use to Marie.

He had received, during the winter, a letter from the young law student with whom he had become acquainted on the occasion of the vice-palatine's unpleasant visit to the castle. The young man wrote to say that he had passed his examination, and that when he should receive the necessary authority from the count he would be ready to proceed to the business they had talked about.

The count replied that a renewal of his lease was not necessary. The new owner of the castle having neglected to serve a notice to quit within the proper time, the old contracts were still valid. Therefore, it was only necessary to secure the naturalization documents, and to purchase a plot of ground on the shore of the lake. The young lawyer arranged these matters satisfactorily, and the count had nothing further to do than to appoint an *absentium ablegatus* to the Diet, and to take possession of his new purchase, which lay adjacent to the Nameless Castle.

The count at once had the plot of ground inclosed with a high fence of stout planks, engaged a gardener, and had it transformed into a beautiful flower-garden.

Then, when the first spring blossoms began to open, he said to Marie, one balmy, sunshiny afternoon: "Come, we will take a promenade."

He conducted the veiled maiden through the park, along the freshly graveled path to the inclosed plot of ground.

"Here is your garden," he said, opening the gate. "Now you, too, own a plot of ground."

Count Vavel had expected to see the little maid clap her hands with delight, and hasten to pluck the flowers for a nosegay.

Instead, however, she clung to his arm and sighed heavily.

"Why do you sigh, Marie? Are you not pleased with your garden?"

"Yes; I think it beautiful."

"Then why do you sigh?"

"Because I cannot thank you as I wish."

"But you have already thanked me."

"That was only with words. Tell me, can any one see us here?"

"No one; we are alone."

At these words the little maid tore the veil from her face, and for the first time in many years God's free sunlight illumined her lovely features.

What those features expressed, what those eyes flashed through their tears, that was her gratitude.

When she had illumined the heart of her guardian with this expressive glance, she was about to draw the veil over her face again; but Ludwig laid a gently restraining hand on hers, and said: "Leave your face uncovered, Marie; no one can see it here; and every day for one hour you may walk thus here, without fear of being seen, for I shall send the gardener elsewhere during that time."

When they were leaving the garden, Marie plucked two forget-me-nots, and gave one of them to Ludwig. From that day she had one more pleasure: the garden, a free sight of the sky, the warmth of the sunlight—enjoyments hitherto denied her; but, all the same, the childlike cheerfulness faded more and more from her countenance.

Ludwig, who was distressed to see this continued melancholy in the child's face, searched among his pedagogic remedies for a cure for such moods. A sixteen-year-old girl might begin the study of history. At this age she would already become interested in descriptions of national customs, in archaeological study, in travels. He therefore collected for Marie's edification quite a library, and became a zealous expounder of the various works.

In a short time, however, he became aware that his pupil was not so studious as she had been formerly. She paid little heed to his learned discourses, and even neglected to learn her lessons. For this he was frequently obliged to reprove her. This was a sort of refrigerating process. For an instructor to scold a youthful pupil is the best proof that he is a being from a different planet!

One day the tutor was delineating with great eloquence to his scholar— who, he imagined, was listening with special interest—the glorious deeds of heroism performed by St. Louis, and was tracing on the map the heroic king's memorable crusade. The scholar, however, was writing something on a sheet of paper which lay on the table in front of her.

"What are you writing, Marie?"

The little maid handed him the sheet of paper. On it were the words:

"Dear Ludwig, love me."

Map and book dropped from the count's hands. The little maid's frank, sincere gaze met his own. She was not ashamed of what she had written, or that she had let him read it. She thought it quite in the order of things.

"And don't I love you?" exclaimed Ludwig, with sudden sharpness. "Don't I love you as the fakir loves his Brahma—as the Carthusian loves his Virgin Mary? Don't I love you quite as dearly?"

"Then don't love me—quite so dearly," responded Marie, rising and going to her own room, where she began to play with her cats. From that hour she would not learn anything more from Ludwig.

The young man, however, placed the slip of paper containing the words, "Dear Ludwig, love me," among his relics.

Since the new mistress's advent in the neighboring manor Count Vavel had spent more time than usual in his observatory. At first suspicion had been his motive. Now, however, there was a certain fascination in bringing near to him with his telescope the woman with whom he had exchanged only written communication. If he was so eager to behold her, why did he not go to the manor? Why did he look at her only through his telescope? She would certainly receive his visits; and what then?

This "what then?" was the fetter which bound him hand and foot, was the lock upon his lips. He must make no acquaintances. Results might follow; and what then?

The entombed man must not quit his grave. He might only seat himself at the window of his tomb, and thence look out on the beautiful, forbidden world.

What a stately appearance the lady makes as she strolls in her long white gown across the green sward over yonder! Her long golden hair falls in glittering masses from beneath her wide-rimmed straw hat. Now she stops; she seems to be looking for some one. Now her lips open; she is calling some one. Her form is quite near, but her voice stops over yonder, a thousand paces distant. The person she calls does not appear in the field of vision. Now she calls louder, and the listening ear hears the words, "Dear Ludwig!"

He starts. These words have not come from the phantom of the object-glass, but from a living being that stands by his side—Marie.

The count sprang to his feet, surprised and embarrassed, unable to say a word. Marie, however, did not wait for him to speak, but said with eager inquisitiveness:

"What are you looking at through that great pipe?"

Before Ludwig could turn the glass in another direction, the little maid had taken his seat, and was gazing, with a wilful smile on her lips, through the "great pipe."

The smile gradually faded from her lips as she viewed the world revealed by the telescope—the beautiful woman over yonder amid her flowers, her form encircled by the nimbus of rainbow hues.

When she withdrew her eye from the glass, her face betrayed the new emotion which had taken possession of her. The lengthened features, the half-opened lips, the contracted brows, the half-closed eyes, all these betrayed—Ludwig was perfectly familiar with the expression—jealousy.

Marie had discovered that there was an enchantingly beautiful woman upon whose phenomenal charms *her* Ludwig came up here to feast his eyes. The faithless one!

Ludwig was going to speak, but Marie laid her hand against his lips, and turned again to the telescope. The "green-eyed monster" wanted to see some more!

Suddenly her face brightened; a joyful smile wreathed her lips. She seized Ludwig's hand, and exclaimed, in a voice that sounded like a sigh of relief:

"What you told me was true, after all! You did not want to deceive me."

"What do you see?" asked Ludwig.

"I see the water-monster that frightened me. I believed that you invented a fable and had it printed in that book in order to deceive me. And now I see the creature over yonder with the beautiful lady. She called to him, and he came walking on his hands and feet. Now he is standing upright. How ridiculous the poor thing looks in his red clothes! He does n't want to keep on his hat, and persists in wanting to walk on all fours like a poodle. Dear heaven! what a kind lady she must be to have so much patience with him!"

Then she rose suddenly from the telescope, flung her arms around Ludwig's neck, and began to sob. Her warm tears moistened the young man's face; but they were not tears of grief.

Very soon she ceased sobbing, and smiled through her tears.

"I am so thankful I came up here! You will let me come again, won't you, Ludwig? I will come only when you ask me. And to-morrow we will resume our swimming excursions. You will come with me in the canoe, won't you?"

Ludwig assented, and the child skipped, humming cheerily, down the tower stairs; and the whole day long the old castle echoed with her merry singing.

CHAPTER III

And why should not Baroness Landsknechtsschild take observations with a telescope, as well as her neighbor at the Nameless Castle?

She could very easily do so unnoticed. From the outside of a house, when it is light, one cannot see what is going on in a dark room.

This question Count Vavel was given an opportunity to decide.

The astronomical calendar had announced a total eclipse of the moon on a certain night in July. The moon would enter the shadow at ten o'clock, and reach full obscuration toward midnight.

Ludwig had persuaded Marie to observe the phenomenon with him; and the young girl was astonished beyond measure when she beheld for the first time the full moon through the telescope.

Ludwig explained to her that the large, brilliant circles were extinct craters; the dark blotches, seas. At that time scientists still accepted the theory of oceans on the moon. What interested Marie most of all, however, was the question, "Were there people on the moon?" Ludwig promised to procure for her the fanciful descriptions of a supposed journey made to the moon by some naturalists in the preceding century. Innocent enough reading for a girl of sixteen!

"I wonder what the people are like who live on the moon?"

And Ludwig's mental reply was: "One of them stands here by your side!"

After a while Marie wearied of the heavenly phenomena, and when the hour came at which she usually went to bed she was overcome by sleep.

In vain Ludwig sought to keep her awake by telling her about the Imbrian Ocean, and relating the wonders of Mount Aristarchus. Marie could not keep from nodding, and several times she caught herself dreaming.

"I shall not wait to see the end of the eclipse," she said to Ludwig. "It is very pretty and interesting, but I am sleepy."

She was yet so much a child that she would not have given up her sweet slumbers for an eclipse of all the planets of the universe.

Ludwig accompanied her to the door of her apartments, bade her good night, and returned to the observatory.

Already the disk of the moon was half obscured. Ludwig removed the astronomical eye-piece from the telescope, and inserted the tellurian glass instead; then he turned the object-glass toward the neighboring manor instead of toward the moon. Now, if ever, was the time to find out if his fair neighbor possessed a telescope. If she had one, she would certainly be using it now.

It was sufficiently light to enable him to see quite distinctly the baroness sitting, with two other women, on the veranda. She was observing the eclipse, but with an opera-glass—a magnifier that certainly could not reveal very much.

Of this Count Ludwig might rest satisfied. And yet, in spite of the satisfaction this decision had given him, he continued to observe the disappearance of the moonlight from the veranda of the manor with far more attention than he bestowed upon the gradual darkening of the heavenly luminary itself. Then there happened to the baroness's companions what had happened to Marie: the women began to nod, whereupon the baroness sent them to bed. There remained now only the count and his fair neighbor to continue the astronomical observations. The lady looked at the moon; the count looked at the lady.

The baroness, as was evident, was thorough in whatever she undertook. She waited for the full obscuration—until the last vestige of moonlight had vanished, and only a strange-looking, dull, copper-hued ball hung in the sky.

The baroness now rose and went into the house. The astronomer on the castle tower observed that she neglected to close the veranda door.

It was now quite dark; the silence of midnight reigned over everything.

Count Vavel waited in his observatory until the moon emerged from shadow.

Instead of the moon, something quite different came within the field of vision.

From the shrubbery in the rear of the manor there emerged a man. He looked cautiously about him, then signaled backward with his hand, whereupon a second man, then a third and a fourth, appeared.

Dark as it was, the count could distinguish that the men wore masks, and carried hatchets in their hands. He could not see what sort of clothes they wore.

They were robbers.

One of the men swung himself over the iron trellis of the veranda; his companions waited below, in the shadow of the gate.

The count hastened from his observatory.

First he wakened Henry.

"Robbers have broken into the manor, Henry!"

"The rascals certainly chose a good time to do it; now that the moon is in shadow, no one will see them," sleepily returned Henry.

"I saw them, and I am going to scare them away."

"We can fire off our guns from here; that will scare them," suggested Henry.

"Are you out of your senses, Henry? We should frighten Marie; and were she to learn that there are robbers in the neighborhood, she would want to go away from here, and you know we are chained to this place."

"Yes; then I don't know what we can do. Shall I go down and rouse the village?"

"So that you may be called on to testify before a court, and be compelled to tell who you are, what you are, and how you came here?" impatiently interposed the count.

"That is true. Then I can't raise an alarm?"

"Certainly not. Do as I tell you. Stop here in the castle, take your station in front of Marie's door, and I will go over to the manor. Give me your walking-stick."

"What? You are going after the robbers with a walking-stick?"

"They are only petty thieves; they are not real robbers. Men of this sort will run when they hear a footstep. Besides, there are only four of them."

"Four against one who has nothing but a cudgel!"

"In which is concealed a sharp poniard—a very effective weapon at close quarters," supplemented the count. "But don't stop here talking, Henry. Fetch the stick, and my driving-coat, into the pocket of which put my bloodletting instruments. Some one might faint over yonder, and I should need them."

Henry brought the stick and coat. Only after he had gone some distance from the castle did Count Vavel notice that some heavy object kept thumping against his side. The faithful Henry had smuggled a double-barreled pistol into the pocket of his coat, in addition to the bloodletting instruments.

The count did not take the road which ran around the cove to the manor, but hurried to the shore, where he sprang into his canoe, and with a few powerful strokes of the oars reached the opposite shore. A few steps took him to the manor. His heart beat rapidly. He had a certain dread of the coming meeting—not the meeting with the robbers, but with the baroness.

The gates of the manor were open, as was usual in Hungarian manors day and night. The count crossed the court, and as he turned the corner of the house there happened what he had predicted: the masked man who was on watch at the door gave a shrill whistle, then dashed into the shrubbery. Count Vavel did not give chase to the fleeing thief, but, swinging his cudgel around his head, ran through the open door into the hall. Here a lamp was burning. He hurried into the salon, and saw, as he entered, two more of the robbers jump from the window into the garden.

Count Ludwig hurried on toward the adjoining room, whence came the faint light of a lamp. The light came from another room still farther on. It was the sleeping-chamber of the lady of the house. There were no robbers here, but on the table lay jewelry and articles of silver which had been emptied from the cases lying about the floor. In an arm-chair which stood near the bed-alcove reclined a female form, the arms and hands firmly bound with cords to the chair.

What a beautiful creature! The clinging folds of her dressing-robe revealed the perfect proportions of her figure. Her hair fell like a golden cataract to the floor. Modest blushes and joy at her deliverance made the lovely face even more enchanting when the knightly deliverer entered the room—a hero who came with a cudgel to do battle against a band of robbers, and conquered!

"I am Count Vavel," he hastened to explain, cudgel in hand, that the lady might not think him another robber and fall into a faint.

"Pray release me," in a low tone begged the lady, her cheeks crimsoning with modest shame when he bent over her to untie the cords.

The task was quickly performed; the count took a knife from his pocket and cut the cords; then he turned to look for a bell.

"Please don't ring," hastily interposed the baroness. "Don't rouse my people from their slumbers. The robbers are gone, and have taken nothing. You came in good time to help me."

"Did the rascals ill-treat you, baroness?"

"They only tied me to this chair; but they threatened to kill me if I refused to give them money—they were not content to take only my jewelry. I was about to give them an order to the steward, who has charge of my money, when your arrival suddenly ended the agreement we had made."

"Agreement?" repeated the count. "A pretty business, truly!"

"Pray don't speak so loudly; I don't want any one to be alarmed—and please go into the next room, where you will find my maid, who is also bound."

Count Vavel went into the small chamber which communicated with that of the baroness, and saw lying on the bed a woman whose hands and feet were bound; a handkerchief had been thrust into her mouth. He quickly released her from the cords and handkerchief; but she did not stir: she had evidently lost consciousness.

By this time the baroness had followed with a lighted candle. She had flung a silken shawl about her shoulders, thrust her feet into Turkish slippers, and tucked her hair underneath a becoming lace cap.

"Is she dead?" she asked, lifting an anxious glance to Ludwig's face.

"No, she is not dead," replied the count, who was attentively scanning the unconscious woman's face.

"What is the matter with her?" pursued the baroness, with evident distress.

The count now recognized the woman's face. He had seen her with the lad who had been his protégé, and who was now a member of the baroness's household. It was the wife of Satan Laczi.

"No, she is not dead," he repeated; "she has only fainted."

The baroness hastily fetched her smelling-salts, and held them to the unconscious woman's nostrils.

"Peasant women have strong constitutions," observed the count. "When such a one loses consciousness a perfume like that will not restore her; she needs to be bled."

"But good heavens! What are we to do? I can't think of sending for the doctor now! I don't want him to hear of what has happened here to-night."

"I understand bloodletting," observed Vavel.

"You, Herr Count?"

"Yes; I have studied medicine and surgery."

"But you have no lance."

"I brought my chirurgic instruments with me."

"Then you thought you might find here some one who had fainted?" exclaimed the baroness, wonderingly.

"Yes. I shall require the assistance of a maid to hold the woman's arm while I perform the operation."

"I don't want any of the servants wakened. Can't I—help you?" she suggested hesitatingly.

"Are not you afraid of the sight of blood, baroness?"

"Of course I am; but I will endure that rather than have one of my maids see you here at this hour."

"But this one will see me when she recovers consciousness."

"Oh, I can trust this one; she will be silent."

"Then let us make an attempt."

The result of the attempt was, the fainting maid was restored to consciousness by the skilfully applied lance, while the face of the assisting lady became deathly pale. Her eyes closed, her lips became blue. Fortunately, she had a more susceptible nature than her maid. A few drops of cold water sprinkled on her face, and the smelling-salts, quickly restored her to consciousness. During these few moments her head had rested on the young man's shoulder, her form had been supported on his arm.

"Don't trouble any further about me," she murmured, when she opened her eyes and saw herself in Vavel's arms; "but attend to that poor woman"; and she hastily rose from her recumbent position.

The woman was shivering with a chill—or was it the result of extreme terror? If the former, then a little medicine would soon help her; but if it was terror, there was no remedy for it.

To all questions she returned but the one answer: "Oh, my God! my God!"

The baroness and Count Vavel now returned to the outer room.

"I regret very much, baroness, that you have had an unpleasant experience like this—here in our peaceful neighborhood, where every one is so honest that you might leave your purse lying out in the court; no one would take it."

The baroness laughingly interrupted him:

"The robber adventure amused more than it frightened me. All my life I have wanted to see a real Hungarian robber, of whom the Viennese tell such wonderful tales. My wish has been gratified, and I have had a real adventure—the sort one reads in romances."

"Your romance might have had a sorrowful conclusion," responded Count Ludwig, seriously.

"Yes—if Heaven had not sent a brave deliverer to my rescue."

"You may well say Heaven sent him," smilingly returned the count; "for if there had not been an eclipse of the moon to-night, which I was observing through my telescope, and at the same time taking a look about the neighborhood, I should not have seen the masked men enter the manor."

"What!" in astonishment exclaimed the baroness; "you saw the men through a telescope? Truly, I shall have to be on my guard in future! But," she added more seriously, lifting from the table the count's walking-stick, toward which he had extended his hand, "before you go I want to beg a favor. Please do not mention the occurrence of this night to any one. I don't want the authorities to make any inquiries concerning the attempted robbery."

"That favor I grant most willingly," replied Count Vavel, who had not the least desire for a legal examination which would require him to tell who he was, what he was, whence he came, and what he was doing here.

"I can tell you why I don't want the affair known," continued the baroness. "The woman in yonder is the one of whom I wrote you some time ago—the wife of Ladislaus Satan, or, as he is called, Satan Laczi. Should it become known that a robbery was attempted here, the villagers will say at once, 'It was the wife of the robber Satan Laczi who helped the men to rob her mistress,' and the poor woman will be sent back to prison."

"And do you really believe her innocent?"

"I can assure you that she knew-nothing about this matter. I shall not send her away, but, as a proof that I trust her entirely, shall let her sleep in the room next to mine, and let her carry all my keys!" To emphasize her declaration, she thumped the floor vigorously with Vavel's iron-ferruled stick.

Involuntarily the count extended his hand to her. She grasped it cordially, and, shaking it, added: "Don't speak of our meeting to-night to any one; I shall not mention it, I can promise you! And now, I will give you your stick; I am certain some one at home is anxious about you. God be with you!"

At home Count Vavel found Henry on guard at the door of Marie's room, his musket cocked, ready for action.

"Did anything happen here?" asked the count. "Did Marie waken?"

"No; but she called out several times in her sleep, and once I heard her say quite distinctly: 'Ludwig, take care; she will bite!'"

Count Vavel could not deny that his fair neighbor had made a very favorable impression on him. In astronomy she had taken the place of the moon, in classic literature that of an ideal, and in metaphysics that of the absolutely good.

He had sufficient command of himself, however, to suppress the desire to see her again. From that day he did not again turn his telescope toward the neighboring manor. But to prevent his thoughts from straying there was beyond his power. These straying thoughts after a while began to betray themselves in his countenance and in his eyes; and there are persons who understand how to read faces and eyes.

"Are you troubled about anything, Ludwig?" one day inquired Marie, after they had been sitting in silence together for a long while.

Ludwig started guiltily.

"Ye-es; I have bad news from abroad."

Such a reply, however, cannot deceive those who understand the language of the face and eyes.

One afternoon Marie stole noiselessly up to the observatory, and surprised Ludwig at the telescope.

"Let me see, too, Ludwig. Are you looking at something pretty?"

"Very pretty," answered Ludwig, giving place to the young girl.

Marie looked through the glass, and saw a farm-yard overgrown with weeds. On an inverted tub near the door of the cottage sat a little old grandmother teaching her grandchildren how to knit a stocking.

"Then you were not looking at our lovely neighbor," said Marie. "Why don't you look at her?"

"Because it is not necessary for me to know what she is doing."

Marie turned the telescope toward the manor, and persisted until she had found what she was looking for.

"How sad she looks!" she said to Ludwig.

But he paid no attention to her words.

"Now it seems as though she were looking straight into my eyes; now she clasps her hands as if she were praying."

Ludwig said, with pedagogic calmness:

"If you continue to gaze with such intensity through the telescope your face will become distorted."

Marie laughed. "If I had a crooked mouth, and kept one eye shut, people would say, 'There goes that ugly little Marie!' Then I should not have to wear a veil any more."

She distorted her face as she had described, and turned it toward Ludwig, who said hastily: "Don't—don't do that, Marie."

"Is it not all the same to you whether I am ugly or pretty?" she retorted. Then, as if to soften the harshness of her words, she added: "Even if I were ugly, would you love me—as the fakir loves his Brahma?"

Ludwig continued his correspondence with the learned Herr Mercatoris. He always dictated his letters to Marie. No one in the neighborhood had yet seen his own writing. Therefore, it would have been impossible for him to ask the pastor anything relating to the baroness without Marie knowing it. In one of his letters, however, he inquired how the mother of the lad he had once had in his care was conducting herself at the manor, and was informed that the woman had disappeared—and without leaving any explanation for her conduct—a few days after the eclipse of the moon. The baroness had been greatly troubled by the woman's going, but would not consent to having a search made for her, as she had taken nothing from the manor.

This incident made Count Vavel believe that the woman had secretly joined the band of robbers, and that there would be another attempt made sometime to break into the manor.

From that time the count slept more frequently in his observatory than he did in his bedchamber, where an entire arsenal of muskets and other firearms were always kept in readiness.

One evening, when he approached the door of his room, he was surprised to see a light through the keyhole; some one was in the room.

He entered hastily. On the table was a lighted candle, and standing with his back toward the table was a strange man, clad in a costume unlike that worn by the dwellers in that neighborhood.

For an instant Count Vavel surveyed the stranger, who was standing between him and his weapons; then he demanded imperiously:

"Who are you? How came you here, and what do you want?"

"I am Satan Laczi," coolly replied the man.

On hearing the name, Count Vavel sprang suddenly toward the robber, and seized him by the arms. The fellow's arms were like the legs of a vulture—nothing but bone and sinew. Count Vavel was an athletic man, strong and powerful; but had the room been filled with men as strong and powerful as he, and had they every one hurled themselves upon Satan Laczi, he would have had no difficulty in defending himself. He had performed such a feat more than once. This evening, however, he made no move to defend himself, but looked calmly at his assailant, and said: "The Herr Count can see that I have no weapons; and yet, there are enough here, had I wanted to arm myself against an attack. I am not here for an evil purpose."

The count released his hold on the man's arms, and looked at him in surprise.

"Why are you here?" he asked.

"First, because I want to tell the Herr Count that it was not I who attempted to rob the baroness, nor were those thieves comrades of mine. I know that the people around here say it was Satan Laczi; but it was n't, and I came to tell you so. I confess I have robbed churches; but the house which has given shelter and food to my poor little lad is more sacred to me than a church. The people insist that I was guilty of such baseness because I am Satan Laczi; but the Herr Count, who has doubtless read a description of my person, can say whether or no it was I he saw at the manor."

With these words he turned his face toward the light. It was a very repulsive countenance.

"Do you think there is another face that the description of mine would fit, Herr Count?" he asked, a certain melancholy softening the repulsiveness of his features. "But what is the use of such senseless chatter?" he added hastily. "I am not silly enough to come here seeking honor and respect—though it does vex me when people say that one man with a cudgel put to flight Satan Laczi and three of his comrades. I came here to-night because the Herr Count rescued my poor little lad from the morass, gave him shelter and food, and even condescended to teach him. For all this I owe you, Herr Count, and I am come to return favor for favor. You are thinking: 'How can this robber repay me what he owes?' I will tell you: by giving you a robber's information. I want to prove to the Herr Count that the robber—the true robber who understands his trade—can enter this securely barred castle whenever he is so minded. The locks on the doors, the bolts on the windows, are no hindrance to the man who understands his business, and the way I came in another can come as well. It is said that the Herr Count guards a great treasure here in this castle. I don't know, and I don't ask, what this treasure is. If I should find it, I would n't take it from the Herr

Count, and if any one else took it I should try to get it back for him. But some one may steal in here, as I did, while the Herr Count is looking at the stars up in the tower, and carry off his carefully guarded treasure."

Count Vavel gave utterance to a groan of terror; his knees gave way beneath him; a chill shook his entire frame.

"Marie!" he gasped, forgetting himself.

Then, hastily snatching the candle from the table, he rushed frantically toward the young girl's sleeping-chamber, leaving Satan Laczi alone in his room.

Since he had ceased guarding Marie's door at night by sleeping on the lounge in her room, he had cautioned her to lock the door before retiring. Now he found the door open.

Breathless with fear, the count sprang toward the alcove and flung back the bed-curtains. The little maid was sleeping peacefully, her face resting against her arm. Her favorite cat was lying at her feet, and on the floor by the bedside lay the two pugs. But the door of the wall-cupboard in which was hidden the steel casket stood wide open, and on the casket was a singular toy—a miniature human figure turning a spinning-wheel.

For an instant Count Vavel's heart ceased beating. Here was sufficient proof that the maid, together with the steel casket, might have been carried away during his absence.

He took the curious image, which was molded of black bread, and returned to his room.

As he crossed the threshold, Satan Laczi pointed to the toy and said:

"I left it on the casket as a remembrance in exchange for the little stockings some one in this house knit for my little lad. We learn to make such things in prison, where time hangs heavily on one's hands."

"But how did you manage to open the door when it was locked and the key inside?" inquired the count.

Satan Laczi showed him the tools which he used to turn keys from the outside.

"Any burglar can open a door from the outside if the key is left in the lock, Herr Count. Only those doors can be securely locked which have no keyholes outside."

"I have no idea how that could be arranged," said Count Vavel.

"I am acquainted with a jack of all trades here in the neighborhood who could make such a door for you if I told him how to make it. He is a carpenter, locksmith, and clock-maker, all in one person."

The count shook his head wonderingly. The robber was to direct the locksmith how to fashion a lock that no one could open!

"Shall I send the man to the castle?" asked Satan Laczi.

"Yes; if the fellow is sensible, and does not chatter."

"But he is a fool that never knows when to stop talking. But he talks only on one subject, so you need not be afraid to employ him. He understands everything you tell him, will do just as you say, but will not talk about what he is doing for you. There is only one subject on which he will chatter, and that is, how Napoleon might be beaten. He is continually talking about stratagems, infernal machines, and how to win a battle. On this subject he is crazy. He will make doors for the Herr Count that can't be opened, and tell everybody else only how to make infernal machines, and how to build fortifications."

"Very good; then send him to me."

"But—I must say something else, Herr Count—no matter how secure your locks may be, that treasure is best guarded against robbers which is kept in the room you sleep in. A man of courage is worth a hundred locks. I am not talking without a purpose when I say the Herr Count must look after his treasure. I know more than I say, and Satan Laczi is not the greatest robber in the world. Be on your guard!"

"I thank you."

"Does the Herr Count still believe that it was I and my comrades who broke into the manor?"

"No; I am convinced that it was not you."

"Then my mission here is accomplished—"

"Not yet," interposed the count, stepping to a cupboard, and taking from it a straw-covered bottle and a goblet. "Here," —filling the goblet and handing it to the robber, —"he who comes to my house as a guest must not quit it without a parting glass."

"A strange guest, indeed!" responded the robber, taking the proffered glass. "I came without knocking for admittance. But I performed a masterpiece to-day; the Herr Count will find it out soon enough! I do not drink to your welfare Herr Count, for my good wishes don't go for much in heaven!"

The count seated himself at the table, and said: "Don't go just yet, my friend; I want to give you a few words of advice. I believe you are a good man at heart. Quit your present mode of life, which will ultimately lead you—"

"Yes, I know—to the gallows and to hell," interposed the robber.

"Take up some trade," pursued the count. "I will gladly assist you to become an honest man. I will lend you the money necessary to begin work, and you can pay me when you have succeeded. Surely honest labor is the best."

"I thank you for the good advice, Herr Count, but it is too late. I know very well what would be best for me; but, as I said, it is too late now. There was a time when I would gladly have labored at my trade,—for I have one,—but no one would tolerate me because of my repulsive face. From my childhood I have been an object of ridicule and abuse. My father was well-born, but he died in a political prison, and I was left destitute with this hideous face. No one would employ me for anything but swine-herd; and even then luck was against me, for if anything went wrong with a litter of pigs, I was always blamed for the mishap, and sent about my business. Count Jharose gave me a job once; it was a ridiculous task, but I was glad to get any kind of honest work. I had to exercise the count's two tame bears— promenade with them through the village. The bears' fore paws were tied about their necks, so that they were obliged to walk on their hind feet, and I had to walk between them, my hands resting on a fore leg of each animal, as if I were escorting two young women. When we promenaded thus along the village street, the people would laugh and shout: 'There go Count Jharose's three tame bears.' At last I got out of the way of doing hard work, and got used to being ridiculed by all the world. But I had not yet learned to steal. The bears grew fat under my care. I was given every day two loaves of bread to feed to them. One day I saw, in a wretched hut at the end of the village, a poor woman and her daughter who were starving. From that day the bears began to grow thin; for I stole one of the loaves of bread and gave it to the poor women, who were glad enough to get it, I can tell you! But the steward found out my theft, and I was dismissed from the count's service. The poor women were turned out of their miserable hut. The mother froze to death,—for it was winter then,—and the daughter was left on my hands. We got a Franciscan monk, whom we met in the forest, to marry us—which was a bad move for the girl, for no one would employ her, because she was my wife. So the forest became our home, hollow trees our shelter; and what a friend an old tree can become! Well, to make a long story short, necessity very soon taught me how to take what belonged to others. I got used to the vagrant life. I could not sleep under a roof any more. I could n't live among men, and pull off my hat to my betters. When the little lad came into the world, I said to my wife: 'Do you quit the forest, and look for work in some village. Don't let the little one grow up to become a thief.' She did as I bade her; but the people who hired her always found out that she was the wife of Satan Laczi, and then they would not keep her, and she would have to come back to me in the forest. And that is where I shall end my days—in the forest. I am not good for anything any more; I could n't even plow a furrow any more. I shall end on the gallows—I feel it. I should have liked the life of a soldier, but they never would take me; they always said I would disgrace any regiment to which I might belong. Yes, I would rather have been a soldier than anything else; but what is not to be will not be! I shall keep to my forest. I am obliged to the Herr Count for his good wishes and this delicious brandy."

The robber placed the empty glass on the table, took up his hat, and walked with heavy steps toward the door. Here he halted to say:

"I must tell you that the touch-holes of all your firearms are filled with wax. Have them cleaned, or you will not be able to shoot with them."

The count rose, and hastened to convince himself that this statement was true. He found that his firearms had indeed been rendered useless; the robber had taken good care to protect himself from an attack. When Vavel looked around again, Satan Laczi had disappeared.

CHAPTER IV

The afternoon of the following day, Henry entered the count's study to announce that a crazy person was below, who insisted on speaking to the lord of the castle. The stranger said he had invented a cannon that would at one shot destroy fifteen hundred men. He would take no denial, but insisted that Henry should tell the Herr Count that Master Matyas had arrived.

"Yes; I sent for him to come here," answered the count. "Show him up."

The appearance of the man whom Henry conducted to his master's presence was certainly original. He wore a costume unlike any prevailing fashion. His upper garment was so made that it might be worn either as a coat or a mantle; if sleeves were desired there were sleeves, and none if none were required. Even his shoes were inventions of his own, for no regular shoemaker could have fashioned them. He held between the fingers of his right hand a bit of lead-pencil, with which he would illustrate what he described on the palm of his left hand.

"You come in good time, Master Matyas," said the count.

"Yes—yes. If only I had been in good time at the battle of Marengo!" sighed the singular man.

"Too late now for regrets of that sort, Master Matyas," smilingly responded Count Vavel. "Facts cannot be changed! I have a task for you which I desire to have completed as quickly as possible. Come, and I will show you what I want you to do."

It was the hour Marie spent in her garden; consequently the count was at liberty to conduct the jack of all trades to the young girl's apartment, and explain what he wished to have done.

Master Matyas listened attentively to what the count said, and took the necessary measurements. When he had done so, he turned toward his patron, and said in a serious tone:

"Do you know why we lost the battle of Marengo? Because General Gvozdanovics, when Napoleon's cavalry made that famous assault, was not clever enough to order three men into every tree on that long avenue—two of the men to load the muskets, while the third kept up a continual fire. The

French horsemen could not have ridden up the trees, and the entire troop of cavalry would have dropped under the continuous fire! The general certainly should have commanded: 'Half battalion—half left! Up the trees— forward!'"

"That is true, Master Matyas," assented Count Vavel; "but I should like to know if you fully understand what I want you to do, and if you can do it?"

Master Matyas's face brightened suddenly. "I 'll tell you what, Herr Count; if I succeed in doing what you want, I shall be able, if ever Napoleon makes another attack on us, to pen him up, with his entire army, so securely that he won't be able to stir!"

"I have no doubt of that!" again assented the count. "What I want, however, is a secure barrier that cannot be opened from the outside. Pray understand me. I want this barrier made in such a manner that the person within the barricade will have sufficient light and air, but be invisible to any one outside, and be perfectly secure from intruders. Could not you let me have a little drawing of what you propose to do?"

"Certainly"; and taking a small sketch-book from his pocket, Master Matyas proceeded to do as he was requested—first, however, explaining to the count a drawing of the cannon which would mow down at one shot fifteen hundred men. "You see," he explained, "here are two cannon welded together at the breech, with their muzzles ten degrees apart. But one touch-hole suffices for both. The balls are connected by a long chain, and when the cannon are fired off, the balls naturally fly in opposite directions and forward at the same time, and, stretching the chain, mow off the heads of every man jack with whom it comes in contact! Fire! Boom! Heads off!"

The count was perfectly satisfied with Master Matyas. He had found a man who fully understood his business, and who knew how to hold his tongue on all subjects but on that of his infernal machines, and of his stratagems to defeat Napoleon. For two weeks Master Matyas labored diligently at his task in the Nameless Castle, during which time Henry heard so much about warlike stratagems that his sides ached from the continued laughter. But when the villagers questioned Master Matyas about his work at the castle, they could learn nothing from him but schemes to capture the ever-victorious Corsican.

"Herr Count," one day observed Henry, toward the close of the second week, "if I hear much more of Master Matyas's wonderful battles, I shall become as crazy as he is!"

And the count replied:

"You are crazy already, my good Henry—and so am I!"

At last the task was completed. Count Vavel was satisfied with the work Master Matyas had performed, and it only remained for Marie to express herself satisfied with the arrangement which would barricade her every night as securely as were the treasures of the "green vault" in Dresden.

A few days afterward was Marie's sixteenth birthday. Count Vavel had come to her apartments, as usual, to congratulate her, and to hear what her birthday wish might be. But the young girl, whose sparkling eyes had become veiled with melancholy, whose red lips had already learned to express sadness, had no commands to give to-day.

After dinner the count, on some pretence, detained Marie in the library while Master Matyas completed his task in her room.

This masterpiece was a peculiar curtain composed of small squares of steel so joined together that light and air could easily penetrate the screen. It was fitted between the two marble columns which supported the arch of the bed-alcove. When the metal curtain was lowered, by means of a cord, two springs in the floor caught and held it so securely that it could not be lifted from the outside. To raise the screen the person in the alcove had only to touch a secret spring near the bed, when the screen would roll up of itself.

"And hast thou no wish this year, Marie?" asked the count, adopting, as usual on this anniversary, the familiar "thou."

"Yes, I have one, dear Ludwig," replied the young girl, but with no brightening of the melancholy features. "I have lost something, but thou canst not give it back to me."

"And what may this something be? What hast thou lost, Marie? Tell me."

"My former sweet, sound sleep! and thou canst not buy me another in Vienna or Paris. I used to sleep so soundly. I used to be so fond of my sweet slumber that I could hardly wait to say my prayers, and often I would be in dreamland long before I got to the 'Amen.' And if by any chance I awoke in the night and heard the clock strike, I would beg of it not to hurry along the hours so fast—I did not want morning to come so soon! But now that I have to sleep with locked doors, I lie awake often until midnight—terrified by I know not what. I dread to be so entirely alone when everything is so quiet; and when it is dark I feel as if some one were stealthily creeping about my room. When I hear a noise I wonder what it can be, and my heart beats so rapidly! Then I draw the covers over my head to shut out all sound, and if I fall asleep thus I have such disagreeable dreams that I am glad when I waken again."

Count Vavel gently took the young girl's hand in his.

"Suppose I could restore to thee thy former sweet slumber, Marie? Suppose I take up my old quarters on the lounge by the door?"

The young girl gazed into his eyes as if she would penetrate his very soul. Then she said sorrowfully: "No, dear Ludwig; that would not restore my slumber."

"Then suppose I have thought of something that will? Come with me, and see."

She laid her hand on his arm, and went with him to her room.

Ludwig conducted her into the alcove, and stepped outside.

"Draw the cord which hangs at the head of the bed," he said, smiling at her wondering face.

Marie did as he bade her, and the metal screen unrolled, and was caught in the springs in the floor.

"Oh, how wonderful!" she exclaimed in amazement. "I am a prisoner in my own alcove."

"Only so long as you care to remain in your prison," returned Count Vavel. "No one can lift the screen from this side; but if you will press your foot on the little brass button in the floor at the foot of the column to your left, you will be at liberty again."

The next instant Master Matyas's handiwork was rolled up to the ceiling.

Marie was filled with delight and astonishment.

"There is another work of art connected with this wonderful mechanism," said the count, after Marie had rolled and unrolled the screen several times. "The cord which releases the screen rings a bell in my room. When I hear the bell I shall know that you have retired; then I shall bring my books and papers into your room out yonder, and continue my work there. Only enough light will penetrate the screen to the alcove to prevent utter darkness. You will not need to be afraid hereafter, and perhaps the sweet, sound sleep will return to you."

Marie did not offer to kiss her guardian for this birthday gift. She merely held out both hands, and gave his a clasp that was so close and warm that it said more than words or kisses. She waited impatiently for evening to test the working of her wonderful screen. She did not amuse herself with her cards, as usual, but went to bed at ten o'clock. At the same moment that the screen unrolled and was caught by the springs in the floor, Count Ludwig's footsteps were heard in the corridor. In one hand he carried a two-branched candlestick, in the other his pistol-case and ink-horn. His pen was between his lips; his books and papers were held under his arm. He seated himself at a table, and resumed his studies.

Marie would have been untrue to her sex had she not watched him for several minutes through her metal screen—watched and admired the superb head, supported on one hand as he bent intently over his book, the broad brow, the classical nose, the chin and lips of an Achilles—all as motionless as if they had been molded in bronze. A true hero—a hero who battled with the most powerful demons of earth, the human passions, and conquered. From that day Marie found her old sweet sleep again.

The second day Marie's curiosity prompted her to signal to Ludwig half an hour earlier. He heard, and came as readily at half-past nine o'clock. And then the little maid (like all indulged children) abused her privileges: she signaled at nine o'clock, and at last at eight o'clock—retiring with the birds in order to test if Ludwig would obey the signal.

He always came promptly when the falling screen summoned him.

And then Marie said to herself:

"He loves me. He loves me very much—as the fakir loves his Brahma, as the Carthusian loves his sainted Virgin. That is how he loves me!"

PART V
ANGE BARTHELMY

CHAPTER I

So far as Marie's safety from robbers was concerned, Count Vavel might now rest content. Satan Laczi's advice had been obeyed to the letter. But how about Baroness Landsknechtsschild? Danger still threatened her.

Count Vavel was seriously concerned about his fair neighbor, and wondered how he might communicate his extraordinary discovery to her. What could he do to warn her of the danger which still threatened her? Should he call in person at the manor, and tell her of his interview with Satan Laczi?

A propitious chance came to Count Vavel's aid in his perplexity.

One afternoon the sound of a trumpet drew him to his window. On looking out, he beheld a division of cavalry riding along the highway toward the village. They were dragoons, as their glistening helmets indicated.

When the troop drew near to the village, the band struck up a lively mazurka, and to this spirited march the soldiers made their entry into Fertöszeg. Ludwig could see through his telescope how the men were quartered in the houses in the village; and in the evening, after the retreat had been sounded, he also saw that the windows of the hitherto unused wing of the manor were brilliantly illuminated. Evidently the officers in command of the troop had taken up their quarters there, which was proper. The armed guard on duty at the manor gates verified this supposition.

Count Vavel might now feel perfectly sure that no robbers would attempt to break into the manor; they were too cunning to come prowling about a place where cavalry officers were quartered.

And with the arrival of the troop another danger had been averted. Now Baroness Katharina would not break into the Nameless Castle and despoil Count Vavel of something which Satan Laczi could not, with all his cunning, have restored to him—his heart!

Count Ludwig did not trouble himself further about the manor. He was convinced that enough gallant cavalrymen were over yonder to entertain the fair mistress, so that she would no longer wait for any more tiresome philosophizing from him.

Every evening he could hear the band playing on the veranda of the manor, and very often, too, the merry dance-music, which floated from the open windows until a late hour of the night. They were enjoying themselves over yonder, and they were right in so doing.

How did all this concern him?

In one respect, however, the soldiers taking up their quarters in Fertöszeg concerned him: they exercised daily on the same road over which it was his custom to take his daily drive with Marie. In order to avoid meeting them, he was obliged to change the hour to noon, when the soldiers would be at dinner.

Several days after the arrival of the troop at Fertöszeg, the officer in command paid a visit at the Nameless Castle—a courtesy required from one who was familiar with the usages of good society. At the door, however, he was told by the groom that Count Vavel was not at home. He left his card, which Henry at once delivered to his master, who was in his study.

The card bore the name:

"Vicomte Leon Barthelmy, K. K., Colonel of Cavalry."

Count Vavel tried to remember where he had heard the name before, but without success. He quieted his dread which this act of ceremony had aroused in him by the thought that it contained no further significance than the conventional courtesy which a stranger felt himself called upon to pay to a resident.

The call would, of course, have to be returned. From his observatory Count Vavel informed himself at what hour the colonel betook himself to the exercise-ground, and chose that time to make his visit. Naturally he found the colonel absent, and left a card for him. A few days afterward Colonel Barthelmy again alighted from his horse at the door of the Nameless Castle, and again met with a disappointment—the Herr Count was not at home to visitors; he was engaged, and had given orders not to be disturbed.

Again the troop's commander left his card, determining to remain indoors at the manor until the return visit had been paid, which would have to be done within twenty-four hours if no rudeness were intended.

He was not a little astonished to find, on returning to the manor, that Count Vavel had left a card for him with the porter. Such promptness perplexed the colonel. How had the count managed to reach the manor before he did? The porter informed him that the gentleman from the Nameless Castle had rowed across the cove, which was a much shorter way than by the carriage-road around the shore.

The colonel now determined to prove that he was an obstinate and persistent admirer of the occupant of the Nameless Castle. He paid a third visit at eight o'clock the next evening. This time Henry informed the visitor that the count had gone to bed.

"Is he ill?" inquired the colonel.

"No; this is his usual hour for retiring."

"But how can a man who is not ill go to bed at eight o'clock?"

And again he handed Henry a card.

This visit Count Vavel returned the next morning at three o'clock. At this hour, as may be supposed, every soul in the manor was still sound asleep. Only the guards on watch at the gate demanded: "Halt! Who comes there?"

On learning that the intruder was a "friend," they allowed him to waken the porter, who thrust his frowzy head from the half-open door to ask, in surprise, what was wanted.

"Is the Herr Colonel at home?" inquired Count Vavel.

"Yes, your lordship; but he is in bed."

"Is he ill?"

"No, your lordship; but he is in bed, of course, at this hour."

"Why, how can a man who is not ill stay in bed until three o'clock?"

The count turned over a corner of his card, and handed it to the porter.

This, at last, the colonel understood, and left no more cards at the Nameless Castle.

The officers quartered at the manor were agreeable companions. Vicomte Leon Barthelmy was a true courtier, a brave soldier, an entertaining comrade, and a generous master. Even his enemies would have admitted that his manners were irresistible in the salon, as well as on the battle-field. Every one knew that Colonel Barthelmy was a married man—that he had a wife with whom, however, he did not live, but from whom he had not been divorced.

Susceptible feminine hearts did not risk a flirtation with the fascinating soldier, being forewarned by the canonical laws of the church, which forbade more intimate relations. There was no need to fear for so prudent and discreet a woman as the Baroness Katharina Landsknechtsschild. Her principles were very sound, and firmly grounded. She permitted no familiarities beyond a certain limit, but made no coy pretence of avoiding innocent amusements. Her affable treatment of the officers was easily explained. She had not received the gentlemen residing in the neighborhood, because they would very soon have visited the manor with a special object—they would have come as suitors for her hand. She would have been compelled to reject such offers, and would have given rise to all sorts of gossip. Moreover, these country magnates were tiresome persons; for, when they were once gathered about a gaming-table, the four ladies in a pack of cards engrossed so much of their attention that they had no thought for any of the living women about them.

The sons of Mars, on the contrary, were devoted entirely to the service of the fair sex. Many of the officers' wives accompanied the regiment, and these helped to make up the quadrille, the mazurka, the redowa,—at that time the latest dance,—and every day saw a merry gathering of revelers.

One day there would be a series of entertaining games; another day there would be a play on a hastily improvised stage, in which the baroness herself would take a part, and win well-deserved applause by her graceful and artistic acting.

There were several skilled amateur jugglers among the merry company, who would give performances *à la* Bosko and Philadelphia; and others would delight the audience with the wonderful scenes of a magic lantern.

Once the baroness arranged a chase, and herself joined in the hunt after the pheasants and deer on her estate, proving herself a skilled Amazon in the saddle and in the management of her rifle. Then, the officers improvised a horse-race; and once they even got up a circus, in which all look part.

Count Vavel, in his tower, was an interested spectator of many of these amusements. There had been a time when he, too, had taken part in and enjoyed just such sports. He was a lover of the chase and of horse-racing. No one knew better than he the keen delights of a clean vault over ditches and hedges. If only he might join the merry company down yonder, *he* could show them some riding!

And as for hunting? He could spend whole days on the mountains, clambering after the fleet-footed chamois, following the larger game through morass and forest. He had grown up amid exhilarating sports such as these.

And the dance-music! How alluring were the strains! and how often through the day he found himself humming the melodies which had floated to him from the open windows of the manor! Once he, too, had taken pleasure in jesting with fair women until their white shoulders would shake with merry laughter. And all this he must look upon and hear at a distance, since he had made himself his own jailer!

During these weeks Marie was very restless. The sound of the trumpets startled her; the unusual noises terrified her. She whose nightly slumbers had been guarded from the barking of dogs and the crowing of fowls now was obliged to listen half the night to clarionet, horn, and piccolo, and to wonder what these people could be doing that they kept their music going until such late hours.

One circumstance, however, reconciled Marie to the excitement of these days: Ludwig spent more time with her; and though his face was as stern as ever, she could not detect in it the melancholy which cannot be concealed from the eyes of the woman who can look into the depths, of the soul.

CHAPTER II

At last, one day late in the autumn, Count Vavel received from his correspondent, Herr Mercatoris, the information that the dragoon regiment was going to change its quarters, and that the departure from Fertöszeg would be celebrated by various amusements, among them a regatta with colored lanterns on the lake and magnificent fireworks on the shore.

"We shall manage somehow to live through it," was the count's mental comment on the news. He knew Marie's horror of fire—how she suffered with terror when she saw a conflagration, no matter how distant. She was even afraid of the rockets and paper dragons which were used at the celebration at the conclusion of the grape harvest every year. On the evening of the merrymaking Marie was afraid to go to bed. She begged Ludwig to close the blinds and to read to her in a loud voice, so that she might not see the light of the fireworks or hear the tumult on the lake shore. That which amused the revellers at the manor was a terror for this timid child.

And that they were amusing themselves over at the manor was beyond a doubt. The program for the evening's entertainment was a varied one. Colonel Barthelmy was in the gayest of humors. The surprise of the evening was to conclude the entertainment, and was called on the program "The Militiaman." Every one in the audience expected that Colonel Barthelmy, who had arranged this part of the entertainment, would produce something extremely amusing. The reality surpassed all expectations.

The figure conducted on to the stage by the colonel was no other than the little water-monster, Baroness Katharina's protégé. He was clad in the uniform of a soldier, with a wooden sword and gun, a hat decorated with crane-feathers, a canteen at his side, and a knapsack on his back. An enormous false mustache extended from ear to ear, and a short-stemmed pipe was thrust between his lips.

"This, gentlemen and ladies, is a militiaman." The colonel was interrupted by a burst of merriment from his audience. Even the baroness laughed immoderately, but suppressed it hastily when she remembered the telescope on the tower of the Nameless Castle.

"Poor little fellow!" she murmured, with difficulty keeping her face straight.

"Attention!" called the colonel, snapping the whip he held in his hand. "What does the militiaman do when he is in a good humor?"

A bagpipe behind the curtain now began to play a familiar air, whereupon the little monster first touched his finger to his hat, then slapped his thighs with both hands, and lifted first one foot, then the other.

The baroness hid with her fan that side of her face which was toward the neighboring castle, and joined in the uproarious laughter.

"You see, gracious baroness," continued the colonel, "that I have accomplished what I determined I would do—made quite a man of the little fellow."

He snapped his whip again, and called sharply:

"Now let the militiaman show us what he does when he is in an ill humor."

The bagpipe struck up a different air. The dwarf muttered something unintelligible into his mustache, and grimaced hideously. Then he took from his tobacco-pouch flint, tinder, and steel, and struck fire in the proper manner; he thrust the burning tinder into his pipe, and pressed it down with his finger.

Tremendous applause rewarded this exhibition.

"Do you see, gracious baroness, what a complete man he is become? He can even strike fire and light a pipe!"

By this time the gnome began to understand that his antics amused the audience, and he, too, enjoyed them. For the first time an emotion was expressed on his stolid countenance; but it was not an agreeable transformation. The corners of his mouth widened until they reached his ears, which stood still farther out from his head; he closed one eye, and opened the other to its farthest extent; and pressing the stem of his pipe more firmly between his teeth, he blew the smoke and fire from the bowl like a miniature volcano. The thicker the smoke and sparks came from the pipe, the more furious became the strange creature's glee, while the entire company shouted and clasped their hands. Even the colonel himself was amazed at the performance of his dull pupil.

"Why have we not a Hogarth among us to perpetuate this caricature?" he exclaimed delightedly.

"Horrible! I cannot bear to look at him," said the baroness, holding her fan in front of her face. "Pray take him away, Herr Colonel—take him away."

"Presently. Ho, there, my little man! What does the militiaman do when he sees the enemy?"

The whip snapped, and the bagpipe set up a discordant shriek, upon which the actor sprang with one bound from the stage, and vanished behind the curtain, wooden sword and gun clattering after him, while the audience showered applause on the successful instructor.

"Herr Colonel," observed the baroness, when quiet had been restored, "I am very much afraid that your instructions will cause me some trouble in the future."

"Why, how so?" in surprise questioned the colonel.

"You have taught a wild creature to kindle a fire, and thus aroused in him a dangerous passion. His desire to amuse himself with the dangerous element will develop into a mania, and he will end by setting fire to houses and other buildings."

"I will tell you what to do, baroness. In order that the little monster may not play his tricks about here, give him to me; I will take him with me."

"No; I had rather keep him here. I shall take good care, however, that he does not get hold of tinder and flint, and have him constantly watched. You have quite ruined my system of education. *I* taught him to kneel and fold his hands to the music of the organ; *you* taught him to dance and grimace to the drone of the bagpipe. You have even accustomed him to drink wine, which is unchristian."

The company laughed at this harmless anger.

Then came the fireworks.

When the Roman candles and the fire-wheels illumined the darkness, it became impossible to control the little monster. He rushed into the thickest of the rain of fire, and tried to catch the red and blue stars in his hands. The sparks burned holes in his clothes, and he would not have escaped a severe burning himself had not some one thrown a pail of water over him. It was impossible to restrain him. He struck out with hands and feet, and bit at any one who attempted to prevent him from running into the fire. Suddenly a rocket shot in an oblique direction, and dropped into the lake. When the human beast saw this he uttered a yell, and dashed into the water. He thought that the beautiful fire belonged to him because it had fallen into his lake, and he went to hunt for it. He did not return. The baroness had search made for him; but he knew so well how to escape his pursuers that he was not seen again at the manor.

The next morning, while yet the stars were glittering in the sky, the trumpets sounded the departure of the regiment.

The sounds were familiar to Count Vavel. Even yet, when the blare of trumpets roused him from sleep, he felt as if he must hasten to the stable, saddle his horse, and buckle on his sword. But those days were past. His trusty war-horse had become used to the carriage-pole, and the keen Toledo blades were drawn from their scabbards only when they were to be oiled to prevent the rust from corroding them.

The departure of the troops removed one care from Count Ludwig's mind: the noise and turmoil would cease, and peace would again return to the silent neighborhood.

One morning when Frau Schmidt brought her basket, as usual, to the castle, there was a letter in it for the count. He recognized the hand at once; it was from his fair neighbor at the manor.

> "HERR COUNT: As I have something of the utmost importance to communicate to you, I beg that you will receive a call from me this morning before you take your usual drive. Answer when it will be convenient for you to see me."

What did it mean? Something of the utmost importance? Why could she not have asked him to come to the manor? The count was puzzled. And how was he to answer this most singular request? He could not write it himself; was it not said that he was unable to hold a pen? He could not dictate the letter to Marie appointing a meeting with the baroness. Henry was a very shrewd fellow, but he had never learned to write.

At last Count Vavel bethought him of an expedient. He marked on the back of his card the Roman numerals XI, and trusted that the baroness would understand that she was expected at eleven o'clock. When the appointed hour drew near, curiosity began to torture the count. He could not wait indoors, but hurried into the park, where he paced restlessly to and fro amid the fallen leaves.

He listened anxiously to every sound, and consulted his watch every few minutes. At last the gate bell rang. He hastened to admit the visitor, and found that the baroness had understood his reply. He recognized her figure, for the face was closely veiled. She wore a pale-blue silk gown with wide sleeves—Marie's favorite costume.

"It is I, Herr Count," she said in a low tone, looking anxiously about her.

"How did you come? I did not hear the carriage," said Count Vavel.

"I rowed across the cove—alone, because no one must know that I came. Can any one see us here?"

"No one."

"We need not go into the house," she continued; "I can tell you here why I came."

Ludwig was more and more perplexed. He had believed the baroness wished to enter the Nameless Castle out of curiosity.

"My visit," pursued the lady, "has as little conventionality about it as had yours. The magnitude of the danger which prompted yours must also excuse mine; I am come to repay the debt I owe you."

"Danger?" repeated the count.

"Yes; danger threatens you—and some one else! Let us come farther into the park, that no one may by a possible chance overhear me."

When they had reached a sheltered spot the lady again spoke:

"Do you know anything about Colonel Barthelmy?"

"I received the cards he left here when he called," indifferently replied Count Vavel.

"You certainly have heard more about him," returned the baroness, a trifle impatiently. "His domestic troubles were in all the newspapers—it was a *cause célèbre*. He was a major in the French army, under the Directory, but entered our service when the Empire was established. The domestic troubles I referred to occurred while he was still in France. His young and beautiful wife ran away with another man—a man who is unknown to Barthelmy, who is pursuing the fugitives over the whole world—"

"Ah! I remember now reading something about it. That is why his name seemed familiar to me."

"I thought you must have heard something about him," responded the baroness, in a peculiar tone. Then, with a sudden movement, she seized his hand and whispered:

"And you are the unknown who abducted Colonel Barthelmy's wife."

"I?" in boundless amazement ejaculated the count. Then he laughed heartily.

"Yes, you; and you are living here in seclusion with the lovely woman whose face no one is permitted to see."

Ludwig ceased laughing, and replied very seriously; "Gracious baroness, were I the person you believe me to be, I should have been glad to meet the man who compelled me to live here in seclusion. A skilful sword-thrust or a well-aimed bullet would have released me from this prison."

"And yet, everybody believes Count Vavel to be Ange Barthelmy's lover," responded the baroness.

"Do *you* believe it, baroness?"

"I? Perhaps—not. But Colonel Barthelmy believes it all the more firmly because you refused to see him."

"And suppose he had seen me?"

"He would have asked you to introduce him to your—family."

"Then he would have learned that I have no family."

"But you could not have refused to tell him what relation you bear to the lady at the castle."

"My answer would have been very brief had he asked the question," was the count's grim response.

"I know what men mean by a 'brief' answer; the result is usually fatal."

"And does your ladyship imagine that I fear such a result?"

"So far as courage is concerned, I should not give any one precedence to Count Vavel. A regular duel, however, requires more than courage. Colonel Barthelmy is a soldier by profession; you are a philosopher who lives amid his studies, and whose right hand is unable to hold a pen, let alone a sword or a pistol!"

Count Vavel was touched on the spot where men are most susceptible.

"Who can tell whether I have always been a studious hermit?" he demanded proudly. "Besides, might it not be that my hand is unable only when I don't want to use it?"

"That may be," retorted the lady. "But Barthelmy, who is perfectly insane on the subject of his wife's infamy, would have the advantage of you. He is suspicious of every stranger; and of all the gossip which environs you, the legend of that elopement is the mildest."

"Indeed? This is very flattering! Probably I am also said to be a counterfeiter?"

"I am not jesting, Herr Count. While Colonel Barthelmy was my guest I was able to prevent him from taking any aggressive steps toward you; this is why you did not hear from him again after his last call on you—"

"I certainly am greatly indebted to you," interrupted Count Vavel, with visible irony.

"You owe me no thanks, Herr Count. When a woman tries to prevent a quarrel between two men, she does so, believe me, out of pure self-love. The emotions which electrify your nerves torment ours. I could not have continued to live here had a tragic occurrence made the place memorable. That is why I prevented an encounter between you and the colonel; so you need not thank me. However, the evening before the regiment took its departure the colonel said to me: 'I have kept my word to you, baroness; but to-morrow I cease to be your guest. I shall take steps then to learn if the mysterious lady at the Nameless Castle be Ange Barthelmy or some one else.'"

At these words a deep flush crimsoned Count Vavel's face. "I should like to know how he proposes to settle that question?" he said, in a voice that trembled with suppressed rage.

"I will tell you. Just listen to the ridiculous plan which the man betrayed in his fury. He is quartered in the neighboring village to the edge of which you and a certain person drive every day. He is going to rise, with several friends, along the road; and when he meets your carriage, he is going to stop it, introduce himself, and demand if the lady by your side be Mme. Ange Barthelmy."

Count Vavel clenched his hands and closed his lips tightly. After a brief struggle he regained command of himself, and said quietly:

"I shall, of course, reply: 'On my word as a man of honor, this lady is not Ange Barthelmy.'"

"But if that does not satisfy him? Suppose he should insist on seeing the lady? Suppose he even attempts to lift the lady's veil?"

"Then he dies!" The count gave utterance to these words in a tone that sounded more like the growl of a lion that has the neck of his prey between his teeth.

"He is capable, in his present mood, of doing anything rash," murmured the baroness, with an expression of terror in her eyes.

"And I am capable of an equally rash act," responded the count.

"I believe it; I have heard of such courage before. But *you* must not forget that you do not belong to yourself; there is some one else you must think of before you risk your life."

Count Vavel started violently; he opened his lips as if to speak, but the baroness quickly raised her hand and interposed.

"I am not trying to pry into your secret, Herr Count; I am no spy—you must have seen that ere this. All I know is that there is under your protection a woman to whom you are everything, and who will have no one should she lose you."

"But what can I do?" in desperation exclaimed Count Vavel. "I cannot hide in my castle until Colonel Barthelmy leaves the neighborhood. Would you have me confess to all the world that I am a coward?"

"Let me advise you, Herr Count," with sudden resolution responded the baroness. "Turn this matter, which you look upon as a tragedy, into a capital jest. Take *me* to drive with you to-day instead of your—friend."

Count Vavel suddenly burst into a loud laugh—from extreme anger to unrestrained merriment.

But the baroness did not laugh with him.

"I am in earnest, Count Vavel. Now you will understand why I came here this morning." She drew her veil over her face, and asked: "Am I enough like her to take her place in the carriage?"

Count Vavel was astounded. The likeness to Marie was perfect. The gown, the hat, and veil were exactly like those Marie was wont to wear when she drove out with him. The daring suggestion, however, amazed him more than anything else.

"What! You, baroness? You would really venture to drive with me? Have you thought of the risk—the danger to yourself?"

"I have given it as much thought as did you when you risked coming to the manor with nothing but a walking-stick to battle with four thieves. One ought not stop to think of the risk when a danger is to be averted. This adventure may end as harmlessly as the other."

"And suppose the colonel should by any chance see your face? No, no, baroness; there is no comparison between my venture and this plan you propose. If I had had an encounter with those thieves I might have received a wound that would soon have healed; but your pure reputation as a woman might receive a wound that would never heal."

A bitter smile wreathed the lady's lips as she replied: "Could any wound that I might receive increase the burden on my heart?" She laughed harshly, then asked suddenly: "Perhaps you are afraid the colonel will think I am the mysterious lady of the Nameless Castle?"

Count Vavel's face reddened to the roots of his hair.

Again the lady laughed, then said apologetically: "Pardon me, but the idea amused me. But, to return to Colonel Barthelmy, he is going very shortly to Italy with his regiment; therefore, I need not care what fables he thinks of me—or repeats. The few persons whose opinion I care for will not believe him; as for the others—pah! Come, your hand on it! Let us perpetrate this joke. If I am willing to run the risk, you surely need not hesitate."

And yet he hesitated.

"Don't speak of this plan of yours as a mischievous trick, baroness," he said earnestly. "It is a great, a noble sacrifice—so great, indeed, that living woman could not perform a greater—to be willing to blush with shame while innocent. She who blushes for her love does not suffer; but to flush with shame out of friendship must be a torture like that endured by martyrs."

"Very well, then; let it be a sacrifice—as you will! I am a willing victim! I owe you a debt of gratitude; I want to pay it. Now go and order the carriage; I will wait here for you."

Every drop of blood in his body rebelled against his accepting this offer. A woman rescue a strong man from a threatened danger! And at what a risk!

"Well," a trifle impatiently exclaimed the baroness, as he still lingered, "are n't you going to fetch your cloak? I am ready for the drive."

Without another word the count turned and strode toward the castle.

Marie was satisfied with the excuse he made for not taking her with him as usual: he said he had urgent business in the neighboring village, and would have to drive there alone.

Then he ordered Henry to harness the horses to the carriage, and drive down to the gate, where he would await him.

He found the baroness waiting for him where he had left her.

"Well," she began, when he came near enough to hear her, "have you decided to take me with you?"

"No."

"Then you are going to take the lady?"

"No."

"Not? Then who is going with you?"

"These two pistols," replied the count, flinging back his cloak and revealing the weapons thrust into his pocket. "With these two companions I am going to meet the gentleman who is so determined to see the face of the veiled lady. I shall show him a lady whose face is not a subject of gossip."

The baroness uttered a cry of terror, and seized Count Vavel's hand.

"No, no; you shall not go alone. Listen. I was prepared for just such a decision on your part, so I wrote this letter. If you persist in going alone to meet the colonel, I shall hurry back to the manor, send my groom on the swiftest horse I own with this letter to Colonel Barthelmy. Read it."

She unfolded the letter she had taken from her pocket, and held it so that Count Vavel might read, without taking it in his hands:

"HERR COLONEL: You need not seek Mme. Ange Barthelmy at the Nameless Castle. The veiled lady seen in company with Count Vavel is

"B.KATHARINA LANDSKNECHTSSCHILD."

In speechless amazement Count Vavel looked down at the baroness, who calmly folded the letter and returned it to her pocket.

"Now you may go if you like," she said coolly, "and I, too, shall do as *I* like! The colonel will then have written proof to justify him in dragging my name in the dust!"

The count gazed long and earnestly into the lovely face turned defiantly toward him. What was said by those glowing eyes, what was expressed by those lips trembling with excitement, could not be mere sport. There is only one name for the emotion which urges a woman to risk so much for a man; and if Count Vavel guessed the name, then there was nothing for him to do but offer his arm to the lady and say:

"Come, baroness, we will go together."

When the count assisted his veiled companion into the carriage, and took his seat by her side, not even Henry could have told that it was not his young mistress from the castle who was going to drive, as usual, with her guardian.

It was with a singular feeling that Count Vavel looked at the woman beside him, to whom he was bound for one hour by the strongest, most dangerous of ties. Only for one hour! For this one hour the woman belonged to him as wholly, as entirely as the soul belongs to the living human being. And afterward? Afterward she would be no more to him than is the vanished soul to the dead human being.

The carriage had arrived at the boundary of the neighboring village, where the usual turn was made for the homeward drive, and they had not yet seen any one. Had Colonel Barthelmy's words been merely an idle threat?

Henry knew that he was not to drive beyond this point; he mechanically turned the horses' heads in the homeward direction, as he had done every day for years.

On the return drive the carriage always stopped at the edge of the forest, where a shaded path led through the dense shrubbery to a cleared space some distance from the highway. This was the spot for their daily promenade.

The count and his companion had gone but a short distance along the path when they saw coming toward them three men in uniform. They were cavalry officers. The two in the rear had on white cloaks; the one in front was without, an outer garment—merely his close-fitting uniform coal.

"That is Barthelmy," whispered the baroness, pressing the arm on which she was leaning.

The count's expression of calm indifference did not change. He walked with a firm step toward the approaching officers.

Very soon they stood face to face.

The colonel was a tall, distinguished-looking man; he carried his head well upright, and every movement spoke of haughty self-confidence and pride.

"Herr Count Vavel, I believe?" he began, halting in front of Ludwig and his companion. "Allow me to introduce myself; I am Colonel Vicomte Leon Barthelmy."

Count Vavel murmured something which gave the colonel to understand that he (the count) was very glad to learn the gentleman's name.

"I have long desired to make your acquaintance," continued the colonel (his companions had halted several paces distant). "I was so unfortunate as not to find you at home the three calls I made at your castle. Now, however, I shall take this opportunity to say to you what I wanted to say then. First, however, let me introduce my friends,"—waving his hand toward the two officers,—"Captain Kriegeisen and Lieutenant Zagodics, of Emperor Alexander's dragoons."

Count Vavel again gave utterance to his pleasure on making the acquaintance of the colonel's friends. Then he said courteously:

"In what way can I serve you, Herr Colonel?"

"In a very simple manner, Herr Count," responded the colonel. "I have had the peculiar misfortune which sometimes overtakes a married man; my wife deceived me, and ran away with her lover, whom I do not even know. As mine is not one of those phlegmatic natures which can meekly tolerate such an indignity, I am searching for the fugitives—for what purpose I fancy you can guess. For four years my quest has been fruitless; I have been unable to find a trace of the guilty pair. A lucky chance at last led me to this secluded corner of the earth, and here I learned that—but, to be brief, Herr Count, I owe it to my heart and to my honor to ask you this question: Is not this lady by your side, who is always closely veiled, Ange Barthelmy, my wife?"

"Herr Vicomte Leon de Barthelmy," calmly replied Count Vavel, "I give you my word of honor as a cavalier that this lady never was your wife."

The colonel laughed in a peculiar manner.

"Your word of honor, Herr Count, would be entirely satisfactory in all other questions save those relating to the fair sex—and to war. You will excuse me, therefore, if I take the liberty to doubt your assertion in this case, and request you to prove that my suspicions are at fault. Without this proof I will not move from this spot."

"Then I am very sorry for you, Herr Colonel," returned Count Vavel, "but I shall be compelled to leave you and your suspicions in possession of this spot."

He made as if he would pass onward; but the colonel politely but with decision barred the path.

"I must request that you wait a little longer, Herr Count," he said, his face darkening.

"And why should I?" demanded the count.

"To convince me that the lady on your arm is not my wife," was the reply, in an excited tone.

"You will have to remain unconvinced," in an equally excited tone retorted Count Vavel; and for a brief instant it was a question which of the two enraged men would strike the first blow.

The threatening scene was suddenly concluded by the baroness, who flung back her veil, exclaiming: "Here, Colonel Barthelmy, you may convince yourself that I am *not* your wife."

Leon Barthelmy started in amazement, and hastily laid his hand against his lips as if to repress the words which had rushed to them. Then he bowed with exaggerated courtesy, and said: "I most humbly beg your pardon,

Herr Count Vavel. This lady is *not* Ange Barthelmy. These gentlemen are witnesses that I have asked your pardon in the proper form."

The colonel's companions, who had come hastily forward at the threatened conflict between their superior and the count, were gazing in a peculiar manner at the lady whose hospitality they had so lately enjoyed. Colonel Barthelmy also, although he bowed with elaborate courtesy before the baroness, cast upon her a glance that was full of insulting scorn.

The situation had changed so rapidly—as when a sudden flash of lightning illumines the darkness of night; and like the electric flash a light sped into Vavel's heart and illumined it with a delicious, a heavenly warmth that made it throb madly. But only for an instant. Then he realized that this woman who had dared everything for his sake had been insulted by the glance of scorn and derision.

He had now lost all control of himself. He snatched a pistol from his pocket, directed the muzzle toward Colonel Barthelmy's sneering face, and said in a voice that quivered with savage fury:

"I demand that you beg this lady's pardon."

"You do?" coolly returned the colonel, still smiling, and gazing calmly into the muzzle of the pistol.

"Yes—or I will blow out your brains!"

The two officers accompanying the colonel drew their swords. The baroness uttered a cry of terror, and flung herself on Vavel's breast.

"I presume you will allow me to inquire, first, what relation this lady bears to you?"

Colonel Barthelmy asked the question in measured tones; and without an instant's hesitation came Count Vavel's reply:

"The lady is my betrothed wife."

The sneer vanished from the colonel's lips, and the swords of his companions were returned to their scabbards.

"I hasten to apologize," said the colonel. "Accept, madame, my deepest reverence, and do not refuse to forgive the insulting scorn my ignorance caused me to express. Permit me to convince you of my sincere homage, by this salute."

He bent his head and pressed his lips to one of the lady's hands, which were clasped about Count Vavel's arm. Then, with his helmet still in his hand, he turned to Count Vavel, and added: "Are you satisfied?"

"Yes," was the curt reply.

"Then let us shake hands—without malice. Accept my sincerest congratulations. To you, baroness, I give thanks for the lesson you have taught me this morning."

He bowed once more, then stepped to one side, indicating that the way was clear.

The baroness drew her veil over her face, and, clinging tremblingly to the arm of her escort, walked by his side back to the highway, the three officers following at a respectful distance.

When they emerged from the forest they saw the three horses which had been left by the colonel and his companions in charge of the grooms. Henry must have told the gentlemen where to find his master.

With what different emotions Count Vavel returned to the castle! The dreamer in his slumbers had given utterance to words which betrayed what he had been dreaming, and he compelled the vision to abide with him even after he had wakened. He felt that he had the right to do what he had done. This woman loved him as only a woman can love; and what he had done had only been his duty, for he loved her! What he had said was no falsehood—the words had not been forced from him merely to preserve her honor; they were the truth.

Count Vavel stopped the carriage at the park gate, assisted his companion to alight, and sent Henry on to the castle with the horses.

"What have you done?" in a deeply agitated voice exclaimed the baroness, when they were alone in the park.

"I gave expression to the feeling which is in my heart."

"And do you realize what that has done?"

"What has it done?"

"It has made it impossible for us to meet again—for us ever to speak again to each other."

"I cannot see it in that light."

"You could were you to give it but a moment's serious thought. I do not ask what the mysterious lady at the castle is to you; I know, however, that you must be everything to her. Pray don't believe me cruel enough to rob her of her whole world. I cannot ask you to believe a lie—I cannot pretend that you are nothing to me. I have allowed you to look too deeply into my heart to deny my feelings. But there is something besides love in my heart! it is pride. I am too proud to take you from the woman to whom you are bound—no matter by what ties. Therefore, we must not meet again in this life; we may meet again in another world! Pray do not come any farther with me; I can easily find the way to my boat. No one at the manor knows of my absence. I must be careful to return as I came—unseen. And now, one request: Do not try to see me again. Should you do so, it will compel me to flee from the neighborhood. Adieu!"

She drew her veil closer over her face, and passed swiftly with noiseless steps through the gateway.

Ludwig Vavel stood where she had left him, and looked after her until she vanished from his sight amid the trees. Then he turned and walked slowly toward the castle.

CHAPTER III

Count Vavel did not see Marie, after his return from the drive with the baroness, until dinner. He had not ventured into her presence until then, when he fancied he had sufficiently mastered his emotions so that his countenance would not betray him. The consciousness of his disloyalty to the young girl troubled him, and he could not help but tremble when he came into her presence. It was not permitted to him to bestow his heart on any one. Did he not belong, soul and body, to this innocent creature, whom he had sworn to defend with his life?

From that hour, however, Marie's behavior toward him was changed. He could see that she strove to be attentive and obedient, but she was shy and reserved. Did she suspect the change in him? or could it be possible that she had seen the baroness driving with him? It was very late when her bell signaled that she had retired, and when Ludwig entered the outer room, as usual, he found a number of books lying about on the table. Evidently the young girl had been studying.

The next morning Ludwig came at the usual hour to conduct her to the carriage.

"Thank you, but I don't care to drive to-day," she said.

"Why not?"

"Riding out in a carriage does not benefit me."

"When did you discover this?"

"Some time ago."

Ludwig looked at her in astonishment. What was the meaning of this? Could she know that some one else had occupied her place in the carriage yesterday?

"And will you not go with me to-morrow?"

"If you will allow me, I shall stay at home."

"Is anything the matter with you, Marie?"

"Nothing. I don't like the jolting of the carriage."

"Then I shall sell the horses."

"It might be well to do so—if you don't want them for your own use. I shall take my exercise in the garden."

"And in the winter?"

"Then I will promenade in the court, and make snow images, as the farmers' children do."

And the end of the matter was that Ludwig sold the horses, and Marie's outdoor exercises were restricted to the garden. Moreover, she studied and wrote all day long.

When she went into the garden, Josef, the gardener's boy, was sent elsewhere so long as she chose to remain among the flowers.

One afternoon Josef had been sent, as usual, to perform some task in the park while Marie promenaded in the garden. He was busily engaged raking together the fallen leaves, when Marie suddenly appeared by his side, and said breathlessly:

"Please take this letter."

The youth, who was speechless with astonishment and confusion at sight of the lady he had been forbidden to look at, slowly extended his hand to comply with her request when Count Vavel, who had swiftly approached, unseen by either the youth or Marie, with one hand seized the letter, and with the other sent Josef flying across the sward so rapidly that he fell head over heels into some shrubbery.

Then the count thrust the letter into his pocket, and without a word drew the young girl's hand through his arm, and walked swiftly with her into the castle. The count conducted his charge into the library. He had not yet spoken a word. His face was startlingly pale with anger and terror.

When they two were alone within the four walls of the library, he said, fixing a reproachful glance on her:

"You were going to send a letter to some one?"

The young girl calmly returned his glance, but did not open her lips.

"To whom are you writing, Marie?"

Marie smiled sadly, and drooped her head.

Vavel then drew the letter from his pocket, and read the address:

"To our beautiful and kind-hearted neighbor."

The count looked up in surprise.

"You are writing to Baroness Landsknechtsschild!" he exclaimed, not without some confusion.

"I did not know her name; that is why I addressed it so."

Vavel turned the letter in his hands, and saw that the seal had been stamped with the crest which was familiar to all the world.

He hurriedly crushed it into bits, and, unfolding the letter, read:

> "DEAR, BEAUTIFUL, AND GOOD LADY: I want you to love my Ludwig. Make him happy. He is a good man. I am nothing at all to him.
> "MARIE."

When he had read the touching epistle, he buried his face in his hands, and a bitter sob burst from his tortured heart.

Marie looked sorrowfully at his quivering frame, and sighed heavily.

"Oh, Marie! To think you should write this! Nothing at all to me!" murmured the young man, in a choking voice.

"'Nothing at all,'" in a low tone repeated Marie.

Vavel moved swiftly to her side, and, looking down upon her with his burning eyes still filled with tears, asked in an unsteady voice:

"What do you want, Marie? Tell me what you wish me to do."

Marie softly took his hand in both her own, and said tremulously:

"I want you to give me a companion—a mother. I want some one to love,—a woman that I can love,—one who will love me and command me. I will be an obedient and dutiful daughter to such a woman. I will never grieve her, never disobey her. I am so very, very lonely!"

"And am not I, too, alone and lonely, Marie?" sadly responded Vavel.

"Yes, yes. I know that, Ludwig. It is your pale, melancholy face that oppresses me and makes me sad. Day after day I see the pale face which my cruel, curse-laden destiny has buried here with me. I know that you are unhappy, and that I am the cause of it."

"For heaven's sake, Marie! who has given you such fancies?"

"The long, weary nights! Oh, how much I have learned from the darkness! It was not merely caprice that prompted me to ask you once what death meant. Had you questioned me more fully then, I should have confessed something to you. That time, when you rescued me from death, you gave my name to Sophie Botta, who also took upon herself my fate. I don't know what became of her. If she died in my stead, may God comfort her! If she still lives, may God bless and help her to reign in my stead! But give me the name of Sophie Botta; give me the clothes of a working-girl; give me God's free world, which she enjoyed. Let me become Sophie Botta in reality, and let me wash clothes with the washerwomen at the brook. If Sophie and I exchanged lives, let the exchange become real. Let me learn what it is to live, or—let me learn what it is to die."

In speechless astonishment Count Vavel had listened to this passionate outburst. It was the first time he had ever heard the gentle girl speak so excitedly.

"Madame," he said with peculiar intonation, when she had ceased speaking, "I am now convinced that I am the guardian of the most precious treasure on this terrestrial ball. Henceforward I shall watch over you with redoubled care."

"That will be unnecessary," proudly returned the young girl. "If you wish to feel certain that I will patiently continue to abide in this Nameless Castle, then make a home here for me—bring some happiness into these rooms. If I see that you are happy I shall be content."

"Marie, Marie, the day of my perfect happiness only awaits the dawn of your own! And that yours will come I firmly believe. But don't look for it here, Marie. Don't ask for impossibilities. Marie, were my own mother, whom I worshiped, still living, I could not bring her within these walls to learn our secret."

"The woman who loves will not betray a secret."

For an instant Ludwig did not reply; then he said:

"And if it were true that some one loves me as you fancy, could I ask her to bury herself here—here where there is no intercourse with the outside world? No, no, Marie; we cannot expect any one else to become an occupant of this tomb—the gates of which will not open until the trump of deliverance sounds."

"And will it be long before that trump sounds, Ludwig?"

"I believe—nay, I know it must come very soon. The signs of the times are not deceptive. Our resurrection may be nearer than we imagine; and until then, Marie, let us endure with patience."

Marie pressed her guardian's hand, and drew a long sigh.

"Yes; we will endure—and wait," she repeated. "And now, give me back my letter."

"Why do you want it, Marie?"

"I shall keep it, and sometime send it to the proper address—when the angel of deliverance sounds his trump."

"May God hasten his coming!" fervently appended the count.

But he did not give her the letter.

Count Vavel now rarely ventured beyond the gate of the Nameless Castle. The weather had become stormy, and a severe frost had robbed the garden of its beauties. The very elements seemed to have combined against the dwellers in the castle. Even the lake suddenly began to extend its limits, overflowing its banks, and inundating meadows and gardens. Marie's little pleasure-garden suffered with the rest of the flooded lands, and threatened to become an unsightly swamp.

Count Vavel, knowing how Marie delighted to ramble amid her flowers, determined to protect the garden from further destruction. Laborers were easily secured. The numerous families of working-people who had been rendered homeless by the inundation besieged the castle for assistance and work, and none were turned empty-handed away. A small army was put to work to construct an embankment that would prevent further encroachment upon the garden by the water, while to Herr Mercatoris the count sent a liberal sum of money to be distributed among the sufferers by the flood.

This gift renewed the correspondence between the castle and the parsonage, which had been dropped for several months.

The pastor, in acknowledging the receipt of the money, wrote:

"The flood has made a new survey of the lake necessary, as the evil cannot be remedied until it has been determined what obstructs the outlet. Our surveyor made a calculation as to the probable cost of the work, and found that it would require an enormous sum of money—almost five thousand guilders! Where was all this money to come from? The puzzling question was answered by that angel from heaven, Baroness Landsknechtsschild. When she heard of the sufferings of the poor people who had been driven from their homes by the inundation, she offered to supply the entire sum necessary. Now, it seems, something besides the money is required for the undertaking.

"The surveyor, in order to calculate the distances which cannot be measured by the chain, needs a superior telescope, and such a glass would cost two or three thousand guilders more. As your lordship is the owner of a telescope, I take it upon myself to beg the loan of it—if your lordship can spare it to the surveyor for a short time."

The next day Count Vavel sent his telescope to the parsonage, with the message that it was a present to the surveyor. Then, that he might not be again tempted to look out upon the world and its people, the count closed the tower windows.

PART VI
DEATH AND NEW LIFE IN THE NAMELESS CASTLE

CHAPTER I

Since Count Vavel had ceased to take outdoor exercise, he had renewed his fencing practice with Henry, who was also an expert swordsman.

In a room on the ground floor of the castle, whence the clashing of steel could not penetrate to Marie's apartments, the two men, master and man, would fight their friendly battles twice daily, and with such vigor that their bodies (as they wore no plastrons) were covered with scratches and bruises.

One morning the count waited in vain for Henry to make his appearance in the fencing-hall. It was long past the usual hour for their practice, and the count, becoming impatient, went in search of the old servant.

The groom's apartment was on the same floor with the kitchen, adjoining the room occupied by his wife Lisette, the cook.

The door of Henry's room which opened into the corridor was locked; the count, therefore, passed into the kitchen, where Lisette was preparing dinner.

"Where is Henry?" he asked of the unwieldy mountain of flesh, topped by a face as broad and round as the full moon.

"He is in bed," replied Lisette, without looking up from her work.

"Is he ill?"

"I believe he has had a stroke of apoplexy."

She said it with as little emotion as if she had spoken of an underdone pasty.

The count hastened through Lisette's room to Henry's bedside.

The poor fellow was lying among the pillows; his mouth and one eye were painfully distorted.

"Henry!" ejaculated the count, in a tone of alarm; "my poor Henry, you are very ill."

"Ye-es—your—lord-ship," he answered slowly, and with difficulty; "but—but—I shall soon—soon be—all right—again."

Ludwig lifted the sick man's hand from the coverlet, and felt the pulse.

"Yes, you are very ill indeed, Henry—so ill that I would not attempt to treat you. We must have a doctor."

"He—he won't come—here; he is—afraid. Besides, there is nothing—the matter with—any part of me but—but my—tongue. I can—can hardly—move—it."

"You must not die, Henry—you dare not!" in an agony of terror exclaimed Ludwig. "What would become of me—of Marie?"

"That—that is what—troubles—troubles me—most, Herr Count. Who will—take my—place? Perhaps—that old soldier—with the machine leg—"

"No! no! no! Oh, Henry, no one could take your place. You are to me what his arms are to a soldier. You are the guardian of all my thoughts—my only friend and comrade in this solitude."

The poor old servant tried to draw his distorted features into a smile.

"I am—not sorry for—myself—Herr Count; only for you two. I have earned—a rest; I have—lost everything—and have long ago—ceased to hope for—anything. I feel that—this is—the end. No doctor can—help me. I know—I am—dying." He paused to breathe heavily for several moments, then added: "There is—something—I should—like to have—before—before I—go."

"What is it, Henry?"

"I know you—will be—angry—Herr Count, but—I cannot—cannot die without—consolation."

"Consolation?" echoed Ludwig.

"Yes—the last consolation—for the—dying. I have not—confessed for—sixteen years; and the—multitude of my—sins—oppresses me. Pray—pray, Herr Count, send for—a priest."

"Impossible, Henry. Impossible!"

"I beseech you—in the name of God—let me see a priest. Have mercy—on your poor old servant, Herr Count. My soul feels—the torments of hell; I see the everlasting flames—and the sneering devils—"

"Henry, Henry," impatiently remonstrated his master, "don't be childish. You are only tormenting yourself with fancies. Does the soldier who falls in battle have time to confess his sins? Who grants him absolution?"

"Perhaps—were I in—the midst of the turmoil of battle—I should not feel this agony of mind. But here—there is so much time to think. Every sin that I have committed—rises before me like—like a troop of soldiers that—have been mustered for roll-call."

"Pray cease these idle fancies, Henry. Of what are you thinking? You want to tell a priest that you are living here under a false name—tell him that I, too, am an impostor? You would say to him: 'When the revolutionists imprisoned my royal master and his family, to behead them afterward, I clothed my own daughter in the garments belonging to my master's daughter, in order to save the royal child from death, I gave up my own child to danger, and carried my master's child to a place of safety. My own child I gave up to play the rôle of king's daughter, when kings and their offspring were hunted down like wild beasts; and made of the king's daughter a servant, that she might be allowed to go free. I counterfeited certificates of baptism, registers, passports, in order to save the king's daughter from her enemies. I bore false witness—committed perjury in order to hide her from her persecutors—'"

"Yes—yes," moaned the dying man, "all that have I done."

"And do you imagine that you will be allowed to breathe such a confession into a human ear?" sternly responded the count.

"I must—I must—to make my peace with God."

"Henry, if you knew God as He is you would not tremble before him. If you could realize the immeasurable greatness of His benevolence, His love, His mercy, you would not be afraid to appear before Him with the plea: 'Master, Thou sentest me forth; Thou hast summoned me to return. I came from Thee; to Thee I return. And all that which has happened to me between my going and my coming Thou knowest.'"

"Ah, yes, Herr Count, you have a great soul. It will know how to rise to its Creator. But what can my poor, ignorant little soul do when it leaves my body? It will not be able to find its way to God. I am afraid; I tremble. Oh, my sins, my sins!"

"Your sins are imaginary, Henry," almost irritably responded Count Vavel. "I swear to you, by the peace of my own soul, that the load beneath which you groan is not sin, but virtue. If it be true that human speech and thought are transmitted to the other world, and if there is a voice that questions us, and a countenance that looks upon us, then answer with confidence: 'Yes, I have transgressed many of Thy laws; but all my transgressions were committed to save one of Thy angels.'"

"Ah, yes, Herr Count, if I could talk like that; but I can't."

"And are not all your thoughts already known to Him who reads all hearts? It does not require the absolution of a priest to admit you to His paradise."

But Henry refused to be comforted; his eyes burned with the fire of terror as he moaned again and again:

"I shall be damned! I shall be damned!"

Count Vavel now lost all patience, and, forgetting himself in his anger, exclaimed:

"Henry, if you persist in your foolishness you will deserve damnation. Did not you say so yourself, when you pledged your word to me on that eventful day? Did you not say, 'The wretch who would become a traitor deserves to be damned'?"

With these words he rose and strode toward the door. But ere he reached it his feeling heart got the better of his anger. He turned and walked back to the bed, took the dying man's ice-cold hand in his, and said gently:

"My old comrade—my brave old companion in arms! we must not part in anger. Don't you trust me any more? Listen, my old friend, to what I say to you. You are going on before to arrange quarters; then I will follow. When I arrive at the gates of paradise, my first question to St. Peter will be, 'Is my good old comrade, the honest, virtuous Henry, within?' And should the sainted gatekeeper reply, 'No, he is not here; he is down below,' then I shall say to him, 'I am very much obliged to you, old fellow, for your friendliness, but a paradise from which my old friend Henry is excluded is no place for me. I am going down below to be with him.' That is what I shall say, so help me Heaven!"

The sufferer who stood on the threshold of death strove to smile. He could not return the pressure of his master's hand, but he slowly and with painful effort turned his head so that his cold lips rested against the count's hand.

"Yes—yes," he whispered, and his dim eyes brightened for an instant. "If we were down there together—you and I—we should not have to stop long there; some one with her prayers would very soon win our release."

Count Vavel suddenly beat his palm against his forehead, and exclaimed:

"I never once thought of her! Wait, my brave Henry. I will return immediately. I cannot allow you to have a priest, but I will bring an angel to your bedside."

He hastened to Marie's apartments.

"You have been weeping?" she exclaimed, looking up into his tear-stained eyes with deep concern.

"Yes, Marie; we are going to lose our poor old Henry."

"Oh, my God! How entirely alone we shall be then!"

"Will you come with me to his bedside? The sight of you will cheer his last moments."

"Yes, yes; come quickly."

A wonderful light brightened Henry's face when he saw his young mistress. She moved softly to the head of his bed, and with her delicate fingers gently stroked the cheeks of the trusty old servant.

He closed his eyes and sighed when her hand touched his face.

"Is he smiling?" whispered Marie to Ludwig, gazing with compassionate awe on the distorted countenance. Then she bent over him and said:

"Henry—my good Henry, would you like me to pray with you?"

She knelt beside the bed and in a feeling tone repeated the beautiful prayer which the good Père Lacordaire composed for those who journey to the other world, pausing from time to time to let the dying man repeat the words after her.

Henry's tongue became heavier and heavier as he repeated, with visible effort, the soul-inspiring words.

Then Marie repeated the Lord's Prayer. Even Ludwig could not do otherwise than bend his knee upon the chair by which he stood, and bow his skeptical head, while the innocent maid and his dying servant prayed together.

When Marie rose from her knees, the painful smile had vanished from Henry's lips; his face was calm and peaceful; the distortion had disappeared from his countenance.

After Henry's death, life for the occupants of the Nameless Castle became still more uncomfortable. Ludwig Vavel had lost his only friend—the only one who had shared his cares and his confidences. He was obliged to hire a servant to assist Lisette, and, remembering what Henry had advised, took the old soldier with the wooden leg into the castle. For the old invalid, the change from hard labor to comfortable quarters and easy work was certainly an improvement. Instead of cutting wood all day long for a mere pittance, he had now nothing to do but brush clothes which were never dusty, polish the furniture, receive the supplies from and deliver orders to Frau Schmidt every morning, to place the newspapers on the library table, and convey the victuals from the kitchen to the dining-room.

But two weeks of this easy work and good wages, and the comforts of the castle, were all that the old soldier could endure. Then he took off his handsome livery, and begged to be allowed to return to his former life of hardship and poverty. Afterward he was heard to aver that not for the whole castle would he consent to live in it an entire year—where not one word was spoken all day long; even the cook never opened her lips. No, he could not stand it; he would rather, a hundred times over, cut wood for five groats the day.

No sooner did Baroness Katharina learn that Count Vavel was again without a man-servant than she sent to the castle Satan Laczi's son, who was then twelve years old, and a useful lad.

Two leading ideas now filled Count Vavel's entire soul.

One was an enthusiastic admiration for a high ideal, whose embodiment he believed he had found in the lovely person of his young charge. All the emotions that a man of deep and profound nature lavishes on his faithful love, his only offspring, his queen, his guardian saint, Count Ludwig now bestowed on this one woman, who endured with patience, renounced with meekness, forgave and loved with her whole heart, and who, even in her banishment, adored her native land which had repulsed and cruelly persecuted her.

The second idea encompassed all the emotions of an opposing passion: a boundless hatred for the giant who, with strides that covered kingdoms and empires, was marching over the entire eastern hemisphere, marking his every step with graves and human skeletons; an enmity toward the Titan who was using thrones as footstools, and who had made himself a god over a greater portion of Europe,

Count Vavel was not the only one who cherished a hatred of this sort; it was felt all over Europe. What was happening in those days could be learned only through the English newspapers. Liberty of speech was prohibited throughout the entire continent. Only an indiscreet correspondent would trust his secret to the post; and Ludwig Vavel only by the exercise of extreme caution could learn from his banker in Holland what was necessary for him to know. Through this medium he learned of the general discontent with the methods of the all-powerful one. He learned of the plans of the Philadelphia Club, which counted among its members renowned officers in the army of France. He heard that a number of distinguished Frenchmen had offered their services and swords to the foreign imperial army against their own hated emperor. He heard of the dissatisfied murmuring among the French people against the frightful waste of human life, the never-ending intrigues, the approaching shadows of the coalition.

All this he heard there in the Nameless Castle, while he waited for his watchword, ready when it came to reply: "Here!"

And while he waited he interested himself also in what was going on in the land in which he sojourned. He had two sources for acquiring information on this subject—Herr Mercatoris in Fertöszeg, and the young attorney, who was now living in Pest. The count corresponded with both gentlemen,—personally he had never spoken to the pastor, and but once to his attorney,—and from their letters learned what was going on in that portion of the world in the vicinity of the Nameless Castle.

However, as there was a wide difference between the characters of his two correspondents, the count was often puzzled to which of them he should give credence. The pastor, who was a student and a philosopher, and a defender of the existing state of affairs, affirmed that there was not on the face of the globe a more contented and peace-loving folk than the Hungarians. The young lawyer, on the other hand, asserted that the existing system was all wrong; that general dissatisfaction prevailed throughout Hungary. His irony did not spare the great ones who swayed the destiny of the country. In a word, resentment against oppression, and discontent, might be read in every line of his epistles.

Count Vavel was rather inclined to believe that the younger man expressed the temper of the nation. In reality, however, it was only the discontent of a small social body, which found quite enough room for its meetings in the sleeping-chamber of one of the sympathizers. Within this circumscribed space, and amid a lively interchange of opinions, originated many a daring project that was never carried beyond the threshold of the hall of meeting.

Ludwig Vavel, on reading the young man's letters, had come to the conclusion that Hungary awaited his (Vavel's) enemy as its liberator.

The Diet, it is true, had authorized the "recruit contingent," but the recruits were not taken from those who were inspired with love for the fatherland, and who would do battle for an idea. The enlisted men were chiefly homeless wanderers. This "cannon-fodder" would go into battle without enthusiasm, would perform what was required of them like obedient machines.

Of what good would be such a crew against a host that had called into being a great national consciousness, a host that was made up of the best force of a vigorous people, a host whose every member was proud of his ensign with its eagle, and who held himself superior to every other soldier in the world?

Vavel well knew that the giant of the century could be conquered only by heroes and patriots. A hireling crew could not enter the field against him.

CHAPTER II

When a sacrifice is demanded by one's fatherland, it becomes the duty of every true patriot to offer himself as the victim.

Consequently, Herr Vice-palatine Bernat Görömbölyi von Dravakeresztur did not hesitate to immolate himself on the sacrificial altar when his attention was directed by his superior to Section 1 of Article II. in the laws enacted by the Diet in the year 1808. Said clause required the vice-palatine to call in person on those "high and mighty persons" who, instead of appearing with their horses at the *Lustrations,*—according to Section 17 of Article III.,—preferred to send the fine of fifty marks for non-attendance.

Among these absentees from the county meetings was Count Ludwig Vavel.

The Vice-palatine's task was to teach these refractories, through patriotic reasoning, to amend their ways. The sacrifice attendant upon the performance of this duty was that Herr Bernat would be obliged, during his official visit to the Nameless Castle, to abstain from smoking.

But duty is duty, and he decided to do it. He preceded his call at the castle by a letter to Count Vavel, in which he explained, with satisfaction to himself, the cause of his hasty retreat on the occasion of his former visit, and also announced his projected official attendance upon the Herr Count on the following day.

He arrived at the castle in due time; and Count Vavel, who wished to make amends for his former rudeness to so important a personage, greeted him with great cordiality.

"The Herr Count has been ill, I understand?" began Herr Bernat, when greetings had been exchanged.

"I have not been ill—at least, not to my knowledge," smilingly responded the count.

"Indeed? I fancied you must be ill because you did not attend the Lustrations, but sent the fine instead."

"May I ask if many persons attended the meeting?" asked Count Vavel.

"Quite a number of the lesser magnates were present; the more important nobles were conspicuous by their absence. I attributed this failure to appear at the Lustrations to Section I of Article III. of the militia law, which prohibits the noble militiaman from wearing gold or silver ornamentation on his uniform. This inhibition, you must know, is intended to prevent emulation in splendor of decoration among our own people, and also to restrain the rapacity of the enemy."

"Then you imagine, Herr Vice-palatine, that I do not attend the meetings because I am not permitted to wear gold buttons and cords on my coat?" smilingly queried the count.

"I confess I cannot think of any other reason, Herr Count."

"Then I will tell you the true one," rather haughtily rejoined Count Vavel, believing that his visitor was inclined to be sarcastic. "I do not attend your meetings because I look upon the entire law as a jest—mere child's play. It begins with the mental reservation, 'The Hungarian noble militia will be called into service *only* in case of imminent danger of an attack from a foreign enemy, and then only if the attacking army be so powerful that the regular imperial troops shall be unable to withstand it!' That the enemy is the more powerful no commander-in-chief finds out until he has been thoroughly whipped! The mission of the Hungarian noble militia, therefore, is to move into the field—untrained for service—when the regular troops find they cannot cope with a superior foe! This is utterly ridiculous! And, moreover, what sort of an organization must that be in which 'all nobles who have an income of more than three thousand guilders shall become cavalry soldiers, those having less shall become foot-soldiers'? The money-bag decides the question between cavalry and infantry! Again, 'every village selects its own trooper, and equips him.' A fine squadron they will make! And to think of sending such a crew into the field against soldiers who have won their epaulets under the baptismal fires of battle! Again, to wage war requires money first of all; and this fact has been entirely ignored by the authorities. You have no money, gentlemen; do you propose that the noble militia host shall march only so long as the supply of food in their knapsacks holds out? Are they to return home when the provisions shall have given out? Never fear, Herr Vice-palatine! when it becomes necessary to shoulder arms and march against the enemy, I shall be among the first to respond to the first call. But I have no desire to be even a spectator of a comedy, much less take part in one. But let us not discuss this farce any further. I fancy, Herr Vice-palatine, we may be able to find a more sensible subject for discussion. There is a quiet little nook in this old castle where are to be found some excellent wines, and some of the best latakia you—"

"What?" with lively interest interrupted the vice-palatine. "Latakia? Why, that is tobacco."

"Certainly—and Turkish tobacco, too, at that!" responded Count Vavel. "Come, we will retire to this nook, empty one glass after another, enjoy a smoke, and tell anecdotes without end!"

"Then you do smoke, Herr Count?"

"Certainly; but I never smoke anywhere but in the nook before mentioned, and never in the clothes I wear ordinarily."

"Aha!—that a certain person may not detect the fumes, eh?"

"You have guessed it."

"Then there is not an atom of truth in the reports malicious tongues have spread abroad about you, for I know very well that a certain lady has not the least objection to tobacco smoke. I do not refer to the Herr Count's donna who lives here in the castle—you may be sure I shall take good care not to ask any more questions about *her*. No; I am not talking about that one, but about the other one, who has puzzled me a good deal of late. She takes the Herr Count's part everywhere, and is always ready to defend you. Had she not assured me that I might with perfect safety venture to call here again, I should have sent my secretary to you with the *Sigillum compulsorium*. I tell you, Herr Count, ardent partizanship of that sort from the other donna looks a trifle suspicious!"

The count laughed, then said:

"Herr Vice-palatine, you remind me of the critic who, at the conclusion of a concert, said to a gentleman near whom he was standing: 'Who is that lady who sings so frightfully out of tune?' 'The lady is my wife.' 'Ah, I did not mean the one who sang, but the lady who accompanied her on the piano—the one who performs so execrably.' 'That lady is my sister.' 'I beg a thousand pardons! I made a mistake; it is the music, the composition, that is so horrible. I wonder who composed it?' 'I did.'"

Herr Bernat was charmed—completely vanquished. This count not only smoked: he could also relate an anecdote! Truly he was a man worth knowing—a gentleman from crown to sole.

Toward the conclusion of the excellent dinner, to which Herr Bernat did ample justice, he ventured to propose a toast:

"I cannot refrain, Herr Count, from drinking to the welfare of this castle's mistress; and since I do not know whether there be one or two, I lift a glass in each hand. Vivant!"

Without a word the count likewise raised two glasses, and drained first one, then the other, leaving not enough liquor in either to "wet his finger-nail."

By the time the meal was over Herr Bernat was in a most generous mood; and when he took leave of his agreeable host, he assured him that the occupants of the Nameless Castle might always depend on the protection and good will of the vice-palatine.

Count Vavel waited until his guest was out of sight; then he changed his clothes, and when the regular dinner-hour arrived joined Marie, as usual, in the dining-room, to enjoy with her the delicate snail-soup and other dainties.

CHAPTER III

At last war was declared; but it brought only days of increased unhappiness and discontent to the tiger imprisoned in his cage at the Nameless Castle—as if burning oil were being poured into his open wounds.

The snail-like movements of the Austrian army had put an end to the appearance of the apocalyptic destroying angel.

Ludwig Vavel waited like the tiger crouched in ambush, ready to spring forth at the sound of his watchword, and heard at last what he had least expected to hear.

The single-headed eagle had not hesitated to take possession of that which the double-headed eagle had hesitated to grasp.

Napoleon had issued his memorable call to the Hungarian people to assert their independence and choose their king from among themselves.

Count Ludwig received a copy of this proclamation still damp from the press, and at once decided that the cause to which he had sacrificed his best years was wholly lost.

He was acquainted with but a few of the people among whom he dwelt in seclusion, but he believed he knew them well enough to decide that the incendiary proclamation could have no other result than an enthusiastic and far-reaching response. All was at an end, and he might as well go to his rest!

In one of his gloomiest, most dissatisfied hours, he heard the sound of a spurred boot in the silent corridor.

It was an old acquaintance, the vice-palatine. He did not remove his hat, which was ornamented with an eagle's feather, when he entered the count's study, and ostentatiously clinked the sword in its sheath which hung at his side. A wolfskin was flung with elaborate care over his left shoulder.

"Well, Herr Count," he began in a cheery tone, "I come like the gypsy who broke into a house through the oven, and, finding the family assembled in the room, asked if they did not want to buy a flue-cleanser. At last the watchword has arrived: 'To horse, soldier! To cow, farmer.' The militia law is no longer a dead letter. We shall march, *cum gentibus*, to repulse the invading foe. Here is the royal order, and here is the call to the nation." [3]

[3] Written by Alexander Kisfalndy, by order of the palatine. A memorable document.

Count Vavel's face at these words became suddenly transfigured—like the features of a dead man who has been restored to life. His eyes sparkled, his lips parted, his cheeks glowed with color—his whole countenance was eloquent; his tongue alone was silent.

He could not speak. He rushed toward his sword, which was hanging on the wall, tore it from its sheath, and pressed his lips to the keen blade. Then he laid it on the table, and dashed like a madman from the room—down the corridor to Marie's apartment. Without knocking, he opened the door, rushed toward the young girl, raised her in his arms as if she were a little child, and, carrying her thus, returned to his guest. "Here—here she is!" he cried breathlessly. "Behold her! Now you may look on her face—now the whole world may behold her countenance and read in it her illustrious descent. This is my idol—my goddess, for whom I have lived, for whom I would die!"

He had placed the maid on a sort of throne between the two bookcases, and alternately kissed the hem of her gown and his sword.

"Can you imagine a more glorious queen?" he demanded, in a transport of ecstasy, flinging one arm over the vice-palatine's shoulder, and pointing with the other toward the confused and blushing girl. "Is there anywhere else on earth so much love, so much goodness and purity, a glance so benevolent—all the virtues God bestows upon his favorites? Is not this the angel who has been called to destroy the Leviathan of the Apocalypse?"

The vice-palatine gazed in perplexity at the young girl, then said in a low tone:

"She is the image of the unfortunate Queen, Marie Antoinette, who looked just like that when she was a bride."

Involuntarily Marie lifted her hands and hid her face behind them. She had grown accustomed to the piercing rays of the sun, but not to the questioning glances from strange eyes.

"What—what does—this mean, Ludwig?" she stammered, in bewilderment. "I don't understand you."

Count Vavel stepped to the opposite side of the room, where a large map concealed the wall. He drew a cord, and the map rolled up, revealing a long hall-like chamber, which, large as it was, was filled to the ceiling with swords, firearms, saddles, and harness.

"I will equip a company of cavalry, and command it myself. The entire equipment, to the last cartridge, is ready here."

He conducted the vice-palatine into the arsenal, and exhibited his terrible treasures.

"Are you satisfied with my preparations for war?" he asked.

"I can only reply as did the poor little Saros farmer when his neighbor, a wealthy landowner, told him he expected to harvest two thousand yoke of wheat: 'That is not so bad.'"

"Now *I* intend to hold a Lustration, Herr Vice-palatine," resumed the count. "Here are weapons. Are enough men and horses to be had for the asking?"

"I might answer as did the gypsy woman when her son asked for a piece of bread: 'You are always wanting what is not to be had.'"

"Do you mean that there are no men?"

"I mean," hastily interposed Herr Bernat, "that there are enough men, and horses, too; but the treasure-chest is empty, and the *Aerar* has not yet sent the promised subsidy."

"What care I about the Aerar and its money!" ejaculated Count Vavel, contemptuously. "*I* will supply the funds necessary to equip a company—and support them, into the bargain! And if the county needs money, my purse-strings are loose! I give everything that belongs to me—and myself, too—to this cause!"

He opened, as he spoke, a large iron chest that was fastened with iron bolts to the floor.

"Here, help yourself, Herr Vice-palatine!" he added, waving his hand toward the contents of the chest. It was a more wonderful sight than the arsenal itself. Rolls of gold coin, sacks of silver, filled the chest to the brim.

Herr Bernat could only stare in speechless amazement. He made no move to obey the behest to "help himself," whereupon Count Vavel himself thrust his hands into the chest, lifted what he could hold between them of gold and silver, and filled the vice-palatine's hat, which that worthy was holding in his hand.

"But—pray—I beg of you—" remonstrated Herr Bernat, "at least, let us count it."

"You can count it when you get home," interrupted Count Vavel.

"But I must give you a receipt for it."

"A receipt?" repeated his host. "A receipt between gentlemen? A receipt for money which is given for the defense of the fatherland?"

"But I certainly cannot take all this money without something to show from whom I received it, and for what purpose. Give me at least a few words with your signature, Herr Count."

"That I will gladly do," responded the count, turning toward his desk, and coming face to face with Marie, who had descended from her throne.

"What are you going to do?" she asked, laying her hand on his arm.

"Write."

"Are you going to let strangers see your writing, and perhaps betray who you are?"

"In a week the strokes from my hand will tell who I am," he replied, with double meaning.

"Oh, you are terrible!" murmured Marie, turning her face away.

"I am so for your sake, Marie."

"For my sake?" echoed the young girl, sorrowfully. "For my sake? Do you imagine that *I* shall take pleasure in seeing you go into battle? Suppose you should fall?"

"Have no fear on that score, Marie," returned the young man, confidently. "I shall have a guiding star to watch over me; and if there be a God in heaven—"

"Then may He take me to Himself!" interposed the young girl in a fervent tone, lifting a transfigured glance toward heaven. "And may He grant that there be not on earth one other Frenchwoman who is forced to pray for the defeat of her own nation! May He grant that there be not another woman in the world who is waiting until a pedestal is formed of her countrymen's and kinsmen's skeletons, that she may be elevated to it as an idol from which many, many of her brothers will turn with a curse! May God take me to Himself now—now, while yet my two hands are white, while yet I cherish toward my nation nothing but love and tenderness, now when I forgive and forget everything, and desire none of this world's splendor for myself!"

Ludwig Vavel was filled with admiration by this outburst from the innocent girl heart.

"Your words, Marie, only increase the brilliancy of the halo which encircles your head. They legalize the rights of my sword. I, too, adore my native land—no one more than I! I, too, bow before the infinite judge and submit my case to His wise decision. O God, Thou who protecteth France, look down and behold him who rides yonder, his horse ankle-deep in the blood of his countrymen, who looks without pity on the dying legions and says, 'It is well!' Then, O God, look Thou upon this saint here, who prays for her persecutors, and pass judgment between the two: which of the two is Thy image on earth?"

"Oh, pray understand me," in a pleading voice interposed Marie, passing her trembling fingers over Ludwig's cheek. "Not one drop of heroic blood flows in my veins. I am not the offspring of those great women who crowned with their own hands their knights to send them into battle. I dread to lose you, Ludwig; I have no one in this wide world but you. On this whole earth there is not another orphan so desolate as I am! When you go to war, and I am left here all alone, what will become of me? Who will care for me and love me then?"

Vavel gently drew the young girl to his breast.

"Marie, you said once to me: 'Give me a mother—a woman whom I can love, one that will love me.' When I leave you, Marie, I shall not leave you here without some one to care for you. I will give you a mother—a woman you will love, and who will love you in return."

A gleam of sunshine brightened the young girl's face; she flung her arms around Ludwig's neck, and laughed for very joy.

"You will really, really do this, Ludwig?" she cried happily. "You will really bring her here? or shall I go to her? Oh, I shall be so happy if you will do this for me!"

"I am in earnest," returned Ludwig, seriously. "This is no time for jesting. My superior here"—turning toward the vice-palatine—"will see that I keep the promise I made in his presence."

"That he will!" promptly assented Herr Bernat. "I am not only the vice-palatine of your county: I am also the colonel of your regiment."

"And I want you to add still another office to the two you fill so admirably: that of matrimonial emissary!" added Count Vavel. "In this patriarchal land I find that the custom still obtains of sending an emissary to the lady one desires to marry. Will you, Herr Vice-palatine and Colonel, undertake this mission for me?"

"Of all my missions this will be the most agreeable!" heartily responded Herr Bernat.

"You know to whom I would have you go," resumed the count. "It is not far from here. You know who the lady is without my repeating her name. Go to her, tell her what you have seen and heard here,—I send her my secret as a betrothal gift,—and then ask her to send me an answer to the words she heard me speak on a certain eventful occasion."

"You may trust me!" with alacrity responded Herr Bernat. "Within half an hour I shall return with a reply: *Veni, vidi, vici!*"

After he had shaken hands with his client, the worthy emissary remembered that it was becoming for even so important a personage as a Hungarian vice-palatine to show some respect to the distinguished young lady under Count Vavel's protection. He therefore turned toward her, brought his spurred heels together, and was on the point of making a suitable speech, accompanying it with a deep bow, when the young lady frustrated his ceremonious design by coming quickly toward him and saying in her frank, girlish manner:

"He who goes on a matrimonial mission must wear a nosegay." With these words she drew the violets from her corsage, and fastened them in Herr Bernat's buttonhole.

Hereupon the gallant vice-palatine forgot his ceremonious intentions. He seized the maid's hand, pressed it against his stiffly waxed mustache, and muttered, with a wary glance toward Count Vavel: "I am sorry this pretty little hand belongs to those messieurs Frenchmen!"

Then he quitted the room, and in descending the stairs had all he could do to transfer without dropping them the coins from his hat to the pockets of his dolman.

Marie skipped, singing joyously, into the dining-room, where the windows faced toward the neighboring manor. She did not ask if she might do so, but flung open the sash, leaned far out, and waved her handkerchief to the vice-palatine, who was driving swiftly across the causeway.

CHAPTER IV

When Herr Bernat Görömbölyi, in his character of emissary, arrived at the manor, he proceeded at once to state his errand:

"My lovely sister Katinka, I am come a-wooing—as this nosegay on my breast indicates. I ask your hand for a brave, handsome, and young cavalier."

"Thank you very much for the honor, my dear Bernat bácsi, but I intend to remain faithful to my vow never to marry."

"Then you send me out of your house with a mitten, Katinka hugom?"

"I should prefer to detain you as a welcome guest."

"Thanks; but I cannot stop to-day. I am invited to a betrothal feast over at the Nameless Castle. The count intends to wed in a few weeks."

He had been watching, while speaking, the effect of this announcement on the lovely face before him.

Baroness Katharina, however, acted as if nothing interested her so much as the letter she was embroidering with gold thread on a red streamer for a militia flag.

"The count is in a hurry," continued Herr Bernat, "for he may have to ride at the head of a company of militia to the war in less than three weeks."

Here the cruel needle thrust its point into the fair worker's rosy finger.

Herr Bernat smiled roguishly; and said:

"Would n't you like to hear the name of the bride, my pretty sister Katinka?"

"If it is no secret," was the indifferent response.

"It is no secret for me, and I am allowed to repeat it. The charming lady Count Vavel intends to wed is—Katharina Landsknechtsschild!"

The baroness suddenly dropped her embroidery, sprang to her feet, and surveyed the smiling emissary with her brows drawn into a frown.

"It is quite true," continued Herr Bernat. "Count Vavel sent me here to beg you to answer the words he spoke to you on an eventful occasion. Do you remember them?"

The lady's countenance did not brighten as she replied:

"Yes, I remember the words; but between them and my reply there is a veil that separates the two."

"The veil has been removed."

"Ah! Then you saw the lady of the castle without her veil? Is she pretty?"

"More than pretty!"

"And who is she? What is she to Count Vavel?"

"She is not your rival, my pretty sister Katinka; she is neither wife nor betrothed to Count Vavel—nor yet his secret love."

"Then she must be his sister—or daughter."

"No; she is neither sister nor daughter."

"Then what is she? Not a servant?"

"No; she is his mistress."

"His mistress?"

"Yes, his mistress—as my queen is my mistress."

"Ah!" There was a peculiar gleam in the lovely baroness's eyes. Then she came nearer to Herr Bernat, and asked with womanly shyness: "And you believe the count—loves *me?*"

"That I do not know, baroness, for he did not tell me; but I think you know that he loves you. That he deserves your love I can swear! No one can become thoroughly acquainted with Count Vavel and not love him. I went to the castle to ask him to join the noble militia, and he let me see the lady about whom so much has been said. She had excellent reasons, baroness, for veiling her lovely face, for whoever had seen her mother's pictures would have recognized her at once. When Count Vavel goes into battle to help defend our fatherland, he must leave the royal maid in a mother's hands. Will you fill that office? Will you take the desolate maid to your heart? And now, Katinka hugom, give me your answer to the Count's words."

With sudden impulsiveness the baroness extended both hands to Herr Bernat, and said earnestly:

"With all my heart I consent to be Count Vavel's betrothed wife!"

"And I may fly to him with this answer?"

"Yes—on condition that you take me with you."

"What, baroness? You wish to go to the castle—now?"

"Yes, now—this very moment—in these clothes! I have no one to ask what I should or should not do, and—*he* needs me."

When his emissary had departed, Count Vavel began to reflect whether he had not been rather hasty. Had he done right in giving to the world his zealously guarded secret?

But there lay the royal manifesto on the table; there was no doubting that. The venture must be made now or never. If only d'Avoncourt were free! How well he would know what to do in this emergency!

He seated himself at the table to write to his friends abroad; but he could accomplish nothing; his hand trembled so that he could hardly guide the pen. And why should he tremble? Was he afraid to hear Katharina's answer? It is by no means a wise move for a man to make on the same day a declaration of war and one of love.

His meditations were interrupted by Marie, who came running into his study, laughing and clapping her hands. She snatched the pen from his fingers, and flung it on the floor.

"She is coming! She is coming!" she cried in jubilant tones.

"Who is coming?" asked Ludwig, surveying the young girl in surprise.

"Who? Why, the lady who is to be my mother—the beautiful lady from the manor."

"What nonsense, Marie! How can you give voice to such impossible nonsense?"

"But the vice-palatine would not be returning to the castle in *two* carriages!" persisted the maid. "Come and see them for yourself!"

She drew him from his chair to the window in the dining-room, where his own eyes convinced him of the truth of Marie's announcement.

Already the two vehicles were crossing the causeway, and the baroness's rose-colored parasol gleamed among the trees. Deeply agitated, Count Vavel hastened to meet her.

"May I come with you?" shyly begged Marie, following him.

"I beg that you will come," was the reply; and the two, guardian and ward, hand in hand, descended to the entrance-hall.

Baroness Katharina's countenance beamed with a magical charm— the result of the union of opposite emotions; as when shame and courage, timidity and daring, love and heroism, meet and are blended together in a wonderful harmony—a miracle seen only in the magic mirror of a woman's face.

While yet several paces distant, she held out her hand toward Count Vavel, and, with a charming mixture of embarrassment and candor, said:

"Yes, I am."

This was her confirmation of the words Vavel had spoken in the forest in the presence of the three dragoon officers: "She is my betrothed."

Vavel lifted the white hand to his lips. Then Katharina quickly passed onward toward Marie, who had timidly held back.

The baroness grasped the young girl's hands in both her own, and looked long and earnestly into the fair face lifted shyly toward her. Then she said:

"It was not for his sake I came so precipitately. He could have waited. They told me your heart yearned for a mother's care, and it must not be kept waiting."

After this speech the two young women embraced. Which was the first to sob, which kiss was the warmer, cannot be known; but that Marie was the happier was certain. For the first time in years she was permitted to embrace a woman and tell her she loved her. Ludwig Vavel looked with delight on the meeting between the two, and gratefully pressed the hand of his successful emissary.

When the two young women had sobbed out their hearts to each other, they began to laugh and jest. Was not the mother still a girl, like the daughter?

"You must come with me to the manor?" said Katharina, as, with arms entwined about each other, they entered the castle. "I shall not allow you to stop longer in this lonely place."

"I wish you would take me with you," responded Marie. "I shall be very obedient and dutiful. If I do anything that displeases you, you must scold me, and praise me when I do what is right."

"And I am not to be asked if I consent to this abduction of my ward?" here smilingly interposed Count Vavel.

"Why can't you come with us?" innocently inquired Marie.

The other young woman laughed merrily.

"He may come for a brief visit; later we will let him come to stay always." Then she added in a more serious tone: "Count Vavel, you may rest perfectly content that your treasure will be safe with me. My house is prepared for assault. My people are brave and well armed. There is no possible chance of another attack from robbers like that from which you delivered me."

"Ludwig delivered you from robbers?" repeated Marie, in astonishment. "When? How?"

"Then he did not tell you about his adventure? What a singular man!"

Here the vice-palatine interposed with: "What is this I hear? Robbers? I heard nothing about robbers."

"The baroness herself asked me not to speak of the affair," explained the count.

"Yes, but I did not forbid you to tell Marie, Herr Count," responded Katharina.

"'Baroness'—'Herr Count'?" repeated Marie, turning questioningly from her guardian to their fair neighbor. "Why don't you call each other by your Christian names?"

They were spared an explanation by Herr Bernat, who again observed:

"Robbers? I confess I should like to hear about this robbery?"

"I will tell you all about it," returned the baroness; "but first, I must beg the vice-palatine not to make any arrests. For," she added, with an enchanting smile, "had it not been for those valiant knights of the road I should not have become acquainted with my brave Ludwig."

"That is better!" applauded Marie, hurrying her "little mother" into the reception-room, where the wonderful story of the robbery was repeated.

And what an attentive listener was the fair young girl! Her lips were pressed tightly together; her eyes were opened to their widest extent—like those of a child who hears a wonderful fairy tale. Even the vice-palatine from time to time ejaculated:

"*Darvalia!*" "*Beste karaffia!*"—which, doubtless, were the proper terms to apply to marauding rascals.

But when the baroness came to that part of her story where Count Vavel, with his walking-stick, put to flight the four robbers, Marie's face glowed with pride. Surely there was not another brave man like her Ludwig in the whole world!

"That was our first meeting," concluded Katharina laughingly, laying her hand on that of her betrothed husband, who was leaning against the arm of her chair.

"I should like to know why you both thought it best to keep this robbery a secret?" remarked Herr Bernat.

"The real reason," explained Count Vavel, "was because the baroness did not want her protégé, Satan Laczi's wife, persecuted."

"Hum! if everybody was as generous as you two, then robbery would become a lucrative business!"

"You must remember," Katharina made haste to protest, "that all this has been told to the matrimonial emissary, and not to the vice-palatine. On no account are any arrests to be made!"

"I will suggest a plan to the Herr Vice-palatine," said Count Vavel. "Grant an amnesty to the robbers; not to the four who broke into the manor,—for they are merely common thieves,—but to Satan Laczi and his comrades, who will cheerfully exchange their nefarious calling for the purifying fire of the battle-field. I myself will undertake to form them into a company of foot-soldiers."

"But how do you know that Satan Laczi and his comrades will join the army?" inquired Herr Bernat.

"Satan Laczi told me so himself—one night here in the castle. He opened all the doors and cupboards, while I was in the observatory, and waited for me in my study."

It was the ladies' turn now to exhibit the liveliest interest. Each seized a hand of the speaker, and listened attentively to his description of the robber's midnight visit to the castle.

"Good!" was Herr Bernat's comment, when the count had concluded. "An amnesty shall be granted to Satan Laczi and his crew if they will submit themselves to the Herr Count's military discipline."

CHAPTER V

The little servant, Satan Laczi, junior, interrupted the conversation. He came to announce dinner. Lisette had not needed any instructions. She knew what was expected of her when a visitor happened to be at the castle at meal-times. Besides, she wanted to show the lady from the manor what she could do. Not since the count's arrival at the Nameless Castle had there been so cheerful a meal as to-day. Marie sparkled with delight; the baroness was wit personified; and the vice-palatine bubbled over with anecdotes. When the roast appeared he raised his glass for a serious toast:

"To our beloved fatherland. Vivat! To our revered king. Vivat! To our adored queen. Vivat!"

Count Vavel promptly responded, as did also the ladies. Then the count refilled the glasses, and, raising his own above his head, cried:

"And now, another vivat to *my* queen! Long may she reign, and gloriously! And," he added, with sudden fierceness, "may all who are her enemies perish miserably!"

"Ludwig, for heaven's sake!" ejaculated Marie, in terror. "Look at Katharina; she is ill."

And, indeed, the baroness's lovely face was pallid as that of a corpse. Her eyes were closed; her head had fallen back against her chair.

Ludwig and Marie sprang to her side, the young girl exclaiming reproachfully:

"See how you have terrified her."

"Don't be frightened," returned Ludwig, assuringly; "it is only a passing illness, and will soon be over."

He had restored the fair woman to consciousness on another occasion; he knew, therefore, what to do now. After a few minutes the baroness opened her eyes again. She forced a smile to her lips, shivered once or twice, then whispered to Ludwig, who was bending over her with a glass of water:

"I don't need any water. We were going to drink a toast; wine is required for that ceremony."

She extended her trembling hand, clasped the stem of her glass, and, raising it, continued: "I drink to your toast, Count Vavel! And here is to my dear little daughter, my good little Marie. May God preserve her from all harm!"

"You may safely drink to Ludwig's toast," gaily assented Marie, "safely wish that the enemies of your Marie may 'perish miserably,' for she has no enemies."

"No; she has no enemies," repeated the baroness in a low tone, as she pressed the young girl closely to her breast.

A few minutes later, when Katharina had regained her usual self-command, she said:

"Marie, my dear little daughter, I know that our friend Ludwig is eager to discuss war plans with his emissary. Let us, therefore, give him the opportunity to do so, while we make our plans for quite a different sort of war!"

"What!" jestingly exclaimed Count Vavel, "my lovely betrothed speaks thus of her preparations for our wedding?"

"The task is not so easy as you imagine," retorted Katharina. "There will be a great deal to do, and I mean to take Marie with me."

"To-day?"

"Certainly; is she not my daughter? But seriously, Ludwig, Marie must not remain here if the recruiting-flag is to wave from the tower, and if the castle is to be open to every notorious bully in the county. You gentlemen may attend to your recruits here, while Marie and I, over at the manor, arrange a fitting ensign for your company. Before we bid adieu to the castle, however, we must pay a visit to the cook. If her mistress leaves here I fancy she will not want to stop."

"Lisette was very fond of me once," observed Marie; "and there was a time when she did everything for me."

"Then she must come with us to the manor to a well-deserved rest. I can send one of my servants over here to attend to the wants of the gentlemen."

The two ladies now took leave of Count Vavel and his visitor. Marie led the way to her own apartments, where she introduced the cats and dogs to Katharina. Then she drew her into the alcove, and secretly pulled the cord at the head of the bed.

"Now you are my prisoner," she said to the baroness, who was looking about her in a startled manner. "Were I your enemy—your rival—I should not need to do anything to gratify my enmity but refuse to reveal the secret of this screen, and you would have to die here alone with me."

"Good heavens, Marie! How can you frighten me so?" exclaimed Katharina, in alarm.

"Ha, ha!" merrily laughed the young girl, "then I have really frightened you? But don't be alarmed; directly some one will come who will not let you 'perish miserably.'"

The baroness's face grew suddenly pallid; but she quickly recovered herself as Count Vavel came hastily into the outer room.

"Did you summon me, Marie?" he called, when he saw that the screen was down.

"Yes, I summoned you," replied Marie. "I want you to repeat the good-night wish you give me every night."

"But it is not night."

"No; but you will not see me again to-day, so you must wish me good night now."

Ludwig came near to the screen, and said in a low, earnest tone:

"May God give you a good night, Marie! May angels watch over you! May Heaven receive your prayers, and may you dream of happiness and freedom. Good night!"

Then he turned and walked out of the room.

"That is his daily custom," whispered Marie. Then she pressed her foot on the spring in the floor, and the screen was lifted.

⌐

CHAPTER VI

Lisette had finished her tasks in the kitchen when the two ladies came to pay her a visit. She was sitting in a low, stoutly made chair which had been fashioned expressly for her huge frame, and was shuffling a pack of cards when the ladies entered.

She did not lay the cards to one side, nor did she rise from her chair when the baroness came toward her and said in a friendly tone:

"Well, Lisette, I dare say you do not know that I am your neighbor from the manor?"

"Oh, yes, I do. I used often to hear my poor old man talk about the beautiful lady over yonder, and of course you must be she."

"And do you know that I expect to be Count Vavel's wife?"

"I did not know it, your ladyship, but it is natural. A gallant gentleman and a beautiful lady—if they are thrown together then there follows either marriage or danger. A marriage is better than a danger."

"This time, Lisette, marriage and danger go hand in hand. The count is preparing for the war."

This announcement had no other effect on the impassive mountain of flesh than to make her shuffle her cards more rapidly.

"Then it is come at last!" she muttered, cutting the cards, and glancing at the under one. It was only a knave, not the queen!

"Yes," continued the baroness; "the recruiting-flag already floats from the tower of the castle, and to-morrow volunteers will begin to enroll their names."

"God help them!" again muttered the woman.

"I am going to take your young mistress home with me, Lisette," again remarked the baroness. "It would not be well to leave her here, amid the turmoil of recruiting and the clashing of weapons, would it?"

"I can't say. My business is in the kitchen; I don't know anything about matters out of it," replied Lisette, still shuffling her cards.

"But I intend to take you out of the kitchen, Lisette," returned the baroness. "I don't intend to let you work any more. You shall live with us over at the manor, in a room of your own, and, if you wish, have a little kitchen all to yourself, and a little maid to wait on you. You will come with us, will you not?"

"I thank your ladyship; but I had rather stay where I am."

"But why?"

"Because I should be a trouble to everybody over yonder. I am a person that suits only herself. I don't know how to win the good will of other people. I don't keep a cat or a dog, because I don't want to love anything. Besides, I have many disagreeable habits. I use snuff, and I can't agree with anybody. I am best left to myself, your ladyship."

"But what will become of you when both your master and mistress are gone from the castle?"

"I shall do what I have always done, your ladyship. The Herr Count promised that I should never want for anything to cook so long as I lived."

"Don't misunderstand me, Lisette. I did not ask how you intended to live. What I meant was, how are you going to get on when you do not see or hear any one—when you are all alone here?"

"I am not afraid to be alone. I have no money, and I don't think anybody would undertake to carry *me* off! I am never lonely. I can't read,—for which I thank God!—so that never bothers me. I don't like to knit; for ever since I saw those terrible women sitting around the guillotine and knitting, knitting, knitting all day long, I can't bear to see the motion of five needles. So I just amuse myself with these cards; and I don't need anything else."

"But surely your heart will grow sore when you do not see your little mistress daily?"

"Daily—daily, your ladyship? This is the second time I have laid eyes on her face in six years! There was a time when I saw her daily, hourly— when she needed me all the time. Is not that so, my little mistress? Don't you remember how I had a little son, and how he called me *chère maman*, and I called him *mon petit garçon?*"

As she spoke, she laid the cards one by one on her snowy apron. She looked intently at them for several moments, then continued:

"No; I don't need to know anything, only that she is safe. *She* will always be carefully guarded from all harm, and my cards will always tell me all I need know about *mon petit garçon*. No, your ladyship; I shall not go with you; I cannot leave the place where my poor Henry died."

"Poor Lisette! what a tender heart is yours!"

"Mine?" suddenly and with unusual energy interrupted Lisette. "Mine a tender heart? Ask this little lady here—who cannot tell a lie—if I am not the woman who has the hardest, the most unfeeling heart in all the world. Ask her that, your ladyship. Tell her, *mon petit garçon*," she added, turning to Marie,—"tell the lady it is as I say."

"Lisette—dear Lisette," remonstrated Marie.

"Have you ever seen me weep?" demanded the woman.

"No, Lisette; but—"

"Did I ever sigh," interrupted Lisette, "or moan, or grieve, that time when we spent many days and nights together in one room?"

"No, no; never, Lisette."

The woman turned in her chair to a chest that stood by her side, opened it, and took out a package carefully wrapped first in paper, then in a linen cloth.

When she had removed the wrappings, she held up in her hands a child's chemise and petticoat.

"What is needed to complete these, your ladyship?" she asked.

"A dear little child, I should say," answered Katharina, indulgently.

"You are right—a dear little child."

"Where is the child, Lisette?"

"That I don't know—do you understand? I—don't—know. And I don't inquire, either. Now, will you still imagine that I have a tender heart? It is years since I looked on these little garments. What did I do with the child that wore them? Whose business is it what I did with her? She was *my* child, and I had a right to do as I pleased with her. I was paid enough for it— an enormous price! You don't understand what I am talking about, your ladyship. Go; take *mon petit garçon* with you; and may God do so to you as you deal with him. Take care of him. My cards will tell me everything, and sometime, when I have turned into a hideous hobgoblin, those whom I shall haunt will remember me! And now, *mon petit garçon*"—turning again to Marie,—"let me kiss your hand for the last time."

Marie came close to the singular woman, bent over her, and pressed a kiss on the fat cheeks, then held her own for a return caress.

This action of the young girl seemed to please the woman. She struggled to her feet, muttering: "She is still the same. May God guard her from all harm!" Then she waddled toward Katharina, took her slender hand in her own broad palm, and added: "Take good care of my treasure, your ladyship. Up to now, I have taken the broomstick every evening, before going to bed, and thrust it under all the furniture, to see if there might not be a thief hidden somewhere. You will have to do that now. A great treasure, great care! And, your ladyship, when you shall have in your house such a little chemise and petticoat, with the little child in them, trotting after you, chattering and laughing, clasping her arms round you and kissing you, and if some one should say to you, as they said to me, 'How great a treasure would induce you to exchange this little somebody in the red petticoat for it?' and if you should say, 'I will give up the child for so much,' then, your ladyship, you too may say, as I say, that your heart is a heart of stone."

Katharina's face had grown very white. She staggered toward Marie, caught her arm, and drew her toward the door, gasping:

"Come—come—let us go. The steam—the heat of—the kitchen makes—me faint."

The fresh air of the court soon revived her.

"Let us play a trick on Ludwig," she suggested. "We will take his canoe, and cross the cove to the manor. We can send it back with a servant."

She ordered her coachman to take the carriage home; then she took Marie's hand and led her down to the lake.

They were soon in the boat. Marie, who had learned to row from Ludwig, sent the little craft gliding over the water, while Katharina held the rudder.

Very soon they were in the park belonging to the manor; and how delighted Marie was to see everything!

A herd of deer crossed their path, summoned to the feeding-place by a blast from the game-keeper's horn. The graceful animals were so tame that a hind stopped in front of the two ladies, and allowed them to rub her head and neck. Oh, how much there was to see and enjoy over here!

Katharina could hardly keep pace with the eager young girl, who would have liked to examine the entire park at once.

What a number of questions she asked! And how astonished she was when Katharina told her the large birds in the farm-yard were hens and turkeys. She had never dreamed that these creatures could be so pretty. She had never seen them before—not even a whole one served on the table, only the slices of white meat which Lisette had always cut off for her. But what delighted her more than anything else was that she might meet people, look fearlessly at them, and be stared at in return, and cordially return their friendly "God give you a good day!"

What a pleasure it was to stop the women and children, with all sorts and shapes of burdens on their heads or in their arms, and ask what they were carrying in the heavy hampers; to call to the peasant girls who were singing merrily, and ask where they had learned the pretty songs.

"Oh, how delightful it is here!" she exclaimed, flinging her arms around the baroness. "I should like to dig and work in the garden all day long with these merry girls. How happy I shall be here!"

"To-morrow we will visit the fields," said Katharina "Can you ride?"

"Ride?" echoed Marie, in smiling surprise. "Yes—on a rocking-horse."

"Then you will very soon learn to sit on a living horse."

"Do you really believe I shall?" breathlessly exclaimed Marie.

"Yes; I have a very gentle horse which you shall have for your own."

"One of those dear, tiny little horses from which one could not fall? I have seen them in picture-books."

"He is not so very small; but you will not be afraid of falling off when you have learned to ride. Then, when you can manage your horse, we will ride after the hounds—"

"No, no," hastily interposed the young girl; "I shall never do that. I could not bear to see an animal hurt or killed."

"You will have to accustom yourself to seeing such sights, my dear little daughter. Riding and hunting are necessary accomplishments; besides, they strengthen the nerves."

"Have not the peasant women got strong nerves, little mama?"

"Yes; but they strengthen them by hard work, such as washing clothes."

"Then let us wash clothes, too."

Katharina smiled indulgently on the innocent maid, and the two now entered the manor, where Marie made the acquaintance of Fräulein Lotti, the baroness's companion.

Marie's attention was attracted by the number of books she saw everywhere; and they were all new to her. Ludwig had never brought anything like them to the castle. There were poems, histories, romances, fables. Ah, how she would enjoy reading every one of them!

"Oh, who is doing this?" she exclaimed, when her eyes fell on an easel on which was a half-finished painting—a study head.

Her admiration for the baroness increased when that lady told her the picture was the work of her own hand.

"How very clever you must be, little mama! I wonder if you could paint my portrait?"

"I will try it to-morrow," smilingly replied the baroness.

"And what is this—this great monster with so many teeth?" she asked, running to the piano.

Katharina told her the name of the "monster," and, seating herself in front of the "teeth," began to play.

Marie was in an ecstasy of delight.

"How happy you ought to be, little mama, to be able to make such beautiful music!" she cried, when Katharina turned again toward her.

"You shall learn to play, too; Fräulein Lotti will teach you."

For this promise Marie ran to Fräulein Lotti and embraced her.

While at dinner Marie suddenly remembered that she had not yet seen the little water-monster, and inquired about him.

The baroness told her that the boy had gone back to his fish companions in the lake; then asked: "But where did you ever see the creature?"

Marie hesitated a moment before replying; a natural modesty forbade her from confessing to Ludwig's betrothed wife that he had taught her how to swim, and had always accompanied her on her swimming excursions in his canoe.

"I saw him once with you in the park, when I was looking through the telescope," she answered, with some confusion.

"Ah! then you also have been spying upon me?" jestingly exclaimed the baroness.

"How else could I have learned that you are so good and beautiful?" frankly returned the young girl.

"Ah, I have an idea," suddenly observed the baroness. "That spy-glass is here now. The surveyor to whom Ludwig gave it sent it to me when he had done with it. Come, we will pay Herr Ludwig back in his own coin! We will spy out what the gentlemen are doing over at the castle."

Marie was charmed with this suggestion, and willingly accompanied her "little mama" to the veranda, where the familiar telescope greeted her sight.

Two of the windows in that side of the Nameless Castle which faced the manor were lighted.

"That is the dining-room; they are at dinner," explained Marie, adjusting the glass—a task of which the baroness was ignorant. When she had arranged the proper focus, she made room for Katharina, who had a better right than she had to watch Ludwig.

"What do you see?" she asked, when Katharina began to smile.

"I see Ludwig and the vice-palatine; they are leaning out of the window, and smoking—"

"Smoking?" interposed Marie. "Ludwig never smokes."

"See for yourself!"

Katharina stepped back, and Marie placed her eye to the glass. Yes; there, plainly enough, she beheld the remarkable sight: Ludwig, with evident enjoyment, drawing great clouds of smoke from a long-stemmed pipe. The two men were talking animatedly; but even while they were speaking, the pipes were not removed from their lips—Ludwig, indeed, at times vanished entirely behind the dense cloud of smoke.

"For six whole years he never once let me see him smoking a pipe!" murmured Marie to herself. "How much he enjoys it! Do you"—turning abruptly toward the baroness, who was smilingly watching her young guest—"do you object to tobacco smoke?"

She seemed relieved when the baroness assured her that tobacco smoke was not in the least objectionable.

Some time later, when reminded that it was time for little girls to be in bed, Marie protested stoutly that she was not sleepy.

"Pray, little mama," she begged, "let us look a little longer through the telescope; it is so interesting."

But even while she was giving voice to her petition the windows in the dining-room over at the castle became darkened. The gentlemen evidently had retired to their rooms for the night.

"Oh, ah-h," yawned Marie, "I am sleepy, after all! Come, little mama, we will go to bed."

Katharina herself conducted the young girl to her room. Marie exclaimed with surprise and delight when, on entering the room adjoining the baroness's own sleeping-chamber, she beheld her own furniture—the canopy-bed, the book-shelves, toys, card-table, everything. Even Hitz, Mitz, Pani, and Miura sat in a row on the sofa, and Phryxus and Helle came waddling toward her, and sat up on their hind legs.

The things had been brought over from the castle while the baroness and Marie were in the park.

"You will feel more at home with your belongings about you," said Katharina, as she returned the grateful girl's good-night kiss.

PART VII
THE HUNGARIAN MILITIA

CHAPTER I

When Count Vavel and the vice-palatine disappeared from the window of the dining-room, they did not retire to their pillows. They went to Ludwig's study, where they refilled their pipes for another smoke.

"But tell me, Herr Vice-palatine," said the count, continuing the conversation which had begun at the dining-table, "why is it that six months have been allowed to pass since the Diet passed the militia law without anything having been accomplished?"

"Well, you must know that there are three essential parts among the works of a clock," returned Herr Bernat, complacently puffing away at his pipe. "There is the spring, the pendulum, and the escapement. The wheels are the subordinates. The spring is the law passed by the Diet. The pendulum is the palatine office, which has to set the law in motion; the escapement is the imperial counselor of war. The wheels are the people. We will keep to the technical terms, if you please. When the spring was wound up, the pendulum began to set the wheels going. They turned, and the loyal nobles of the country began to enroll their names—"

"How many do you suppose enrolled their names?" interrupted the count.

"Thirty thousand cavalry and forty thousand infantry—which are not all the able-bodied men, as only one member from each family is required to join the army. After the names had been entered came the question of uniforms, arms, officering, drilling, provisions. You must admit that a clock cannot strike until the hands have made their regular passage through all the minutes and seconds that make up the hour!"

"For heaven's sake! What a preamble!" ejaculated the count. "But go on. The first minute?"

"Yes; the first minute a stoppage occurred caused by the escapement objecting to furnish canteens; if the militiamen wanted canteens they must provide them themselves."

"I trust the clock was not allowed to stop for want of a few canteens," ironically observed Count Vavel.

"Moreover," continued the vice-palatine, not heeding the interruption, "the escapement gave them to understand that brass drums could not be furnished—only wooden ones—"

"They will do their duty, too, if properly handled," again interpolated Vavel.

"A more disastrous check, however, was the decision of the *Komitate* that the uniform was to consist of red trousers and light-blue dolman—"

"A picturesque uniform, at any rate!"

"There was a good deal of argument about it; but at last it was decided that the companies from the Danube should adopt light-blue dolmans, and those from the Theiss dark-blue."

"Thank heaven something was decided!"

"Don't be too premature with your thanks, Herr Count! The escapement would not consent to the red trousers; red dye-stuff was not to be had, because of the continental embargo. The militia must content itself with trousers made of the coarse white cloth of which peasants' cloaks are made. You can imagine what a tempest that raised in the various counties! To offer Hungarian nobles trousers made of such stuff! At last the matter was arranged: trousers and dolman were to be made of the same material. The Komitate were satisfied with this. But the escapement then said there were not enough tailors to make so many uniforms. The government would supply the cloth, and have it cut, and the militiamen could have it made up at home."

"That certainly would make the uniform of more value to the wearer!"

"*Would have made*, Herr Count; would have made! The escapement suddenly announced that the cloth could not be purchased; for, while the dispute about the colors of the uniform had been going on, the greedy merchants had advanced the price of all cloths to such an exorbitant figure that the government could n't afford to buy it."

"To the cuckoo with your escapement! The men have got to have uniforms!"

"Beg pardon; don't begin yet to waste expletives, else you will not have any left at the end of the hour! The counties then agreed to pay the sum advanced on the original price of the cloth, whereupon the escapement said the money would have to be forthcoming at once, as the cloth could not be bought on credit."

"Well, is there no treasury which could supply enough funds for this worthy object?" asked the count.

"Yes; there is the public treasury for current expenses. But the treasurer will not give any money to the militia until they are mounted and equipped; the escapement will not furnish the cloth for the uniforms without the money; and the treasury will not give any money until the militia has its uniforms!"

"Well, a man can fight without a uniform. If only these men have horses under them and weapons in their hands—"

"Two of these requisites we already have; but the escapement announces that arms of the latest improvements cannot be furnished, because the government has not got them."

"Well, the old ones will answer."

"They *would* if we had enough flints; but they are not to be had, because the insurrectionary Poles have captured the flint depot in Lemberg."

"Each man certainly could get a flint for himself."

"Even then there are only enough guns for about one half of the men. The escapement suggested that to those who had no arms it would furnish— halberds!"

"What? Halberds!" cried Vavel, losing all patience. "Halberds against Bonaparte? Halberds against the legions who have broken a path from one end of Europe to the other with thêir bayonets, and with them carved their triumphs on the pyramids? Halberds against them? Do you take me to be a fool, Herr Vice-palatine?"

He sprang to his feet and began to pace the floor excitedly, his guest meanwhile eying him with a roguish glance.

"There!" at last exclaimed Herr Bernat, "I will not tease you any longer. Fortunately, there is a clock-repairer who, so soon as he perceived how tardily the hands performed their task, with his finger twirled them around the entire dial, whereupon the clock struck the hour. This able repairer is our king, who at once advanced from his own exchequer enough money to equip the militia companies, distributed six thousand first-class cavalry sabers and sixteen cannon, and loaned the entire Hungarian life-guard to drill the newly formed regiments. And now, I will wager that our noble militia host will be ready for the field in less than thirty days, and that they will fight as well as the good Lord permitted them to learn how!"

"Why in the world did you not tell me this at once?" demanded Count Vavel.

"Because it is not customary to put the fire underneath the tobacco in the pipe! The king's example inspired our magnates. Those whom the law compelled to equip ten horsemen sent out whole companies, and placed themselves in command."

"As I shall do!" appended Count Vavel. "I hope, Herr Vice-palatine, that you will not forget the amnesty for Satan Laczi and his men. They will be of special value as spies."

"I have a knot in my handkerchief for that, Herr Count, and shall be sure to remember. The company to be commanded by Count Ludwig Fertöszeg will be complete in a week."

"Why do you call me Fertöszeg?"

"Because a Hungarian name is better for your ensign than your own foreign one. Our people have an antipathy to everything foreign—and we have cause to complain of the Frenchmen who served in our army. Most of them were spies—tools of Napoleon's. Generals Moiselle and Lefebre surrendered fortified Laibach, together with its entire brigade, without discharging a gun. And even our quondam friend, the gallant Colonel Barthelmy, has taken Dutch leave and gone back to the enemy."

"What? Gone back to the enemy!" repeated Ludwig, springing from his chair, and laughing delightedly.

"The news seems to rejoice you," observed Herr Bernat.

"I shout for very joy! The thought that we might have to fight side by side annoyed me. Now, however, we shall be adversaries, and when we meet, the man who did not steal Ange Barthelmy will send her husband to the devil! And now, Herr Vice-palatine, I think it is time to say good night. It will be the first night in six years that I shall sleep quietly."

They shook hands, and separated for the night.

CHAPTER II

From early morning until evening the enrolment of names went on at the Nameless Castle, while from time to time a squad of volunteers, accompanied by Count Vavel himself, would depart amid the blare of trumpets for the drill-ground.

The count made a fine-looking officer, with the crimson shako on his head, his mantle flung over one shoulder, his saber in his hand. When he saluted the ladies on their balconies, his spirited horse would rear and dance proudly. His company, the "Volons," had selected black and crimson as the colors for their uniform. The shako was ornamented in front with a white death's-head, and one would not have believed that a skull could be so ornamental.

The Volons' ensign was not yet finished, but pretty white hands were embroidering gold letters on the silken streamers; lead would very soon add further ornamentation!

When Ludwig Vavel opened the door of his castle to the public, he very soon became acquainted with a very different life from that of the past six years. For six years he had dwelt among a people whom he imagined he had learned to know and understand through his telescope, and from the letters he had received from a clergyman and a young law student.

The reality was quite different.

Every man that was enrolled in his volunteer corps Count Vavel made an object of special study. He found among them many interesting characters, who would have deserved perpetuation, and made of all of them excellent soldiers. The men very soon became devoted to their leader. When the troop was complete—three hundred horsemen in handsome uniforms, on spirited horses—their ensign was ready for them. Marie thought it would have been only proper for Katharina, the betrothed of the leader, to present the flag; but Count Vavel insisted that Marie must perform the duty. The flag was hers; it would wave over the men who were going to fight for her cause.

It was an inspiriting sight—three hundred horsemen, every one of noble Hungarian blood. There were among them fathers of families, and brothers;

and all of them soldiers of their own free will. Of such material was the troop of Volons, commanded by "Count Vavel von Fertöszeg."

Count Vavel had a second volunteer company, composed of Satan Laczi and his comrades. This company, however, had been formed and drilled in secret, as the noble Volons would not have tolerated such vagabonds in their ranks. There were only twenty-four men in Satan Laczi's squad, and they were expected to undertake only the most hazardous missions of the campaign.

Ah, how Marie's hand trembled when she knotted the gay streamers to the flag Ludwig held in his hands! She whispered, in a tone so low that only he could hear what she said:

"Don't go away, Ludwig! Stay here with us. Don't waste your precious blood for me, but let us three fly far away from here."

Those standing apart from the count and his fair ward fancied that the whispered words were a blessing on the ensign. She did not bless it in words, but when she saw that Ludwig would not renounce his undertaking, she pressed her lips to the standard which bore the *patrona Hungaria*. That was her blessing! Then she turned and flung herself into Katharina's arms, sobbing, while hearty cheers rose from the Volons:

"Why don't *you* try to prevent him from going away from us? Why don't you say to him, 'To-morrow we are to be wedded. Why not wait until then?'"

But there was no time now to think of marriage. There was one who was in greater haste than any bridegroom or bride. The great leader of armies was striding onward, whole kingdoms between his paces. From the slaughter at Ebersburg he passed at once to the walls of Vienna, to the square in front of the Cathedral of St. Stephen. From the south, also, came Job's messengers, thick and fast. Archduke John had retreated from Italy back into Hungary, the viceroy Eugene following on his heels.

General Chasteler had become alarmed at Napoleon's proclamation threatening him with death, and had removed his entire army from the Tyrol. His divisions were surrendering, one after another, to the pursuing foe.

Thus the border on the south and west was open to the enemy; and to augment the peril which threatened Hungary, Poland menaced her from the north, from the Carpathians; and Russia at the same time sent out declarations of war.

The countries which had been on friendly terms with one another suddenly became enemies—Poland against Hungary, Russia against Austria. Prussia waited. England hastened to seize an island from Holland. The patriotic calls of Gentz and Schlegel failed to inspire Germany. The heroic attempts of Kalt, Dörnberg, Schill, and Lützow fell resultless on the indifference of the people. Only Turkey remained a faithful ally, and the assurance that the Mussulman would protect Hungary in the rear against an invasion on the part of Moldavia was the only ray of light amid the darkness of those days.

Then came a fresh Job's messenger.

General Jelachich, with his five thousand men, had laid down his arms in the open field before the enemy. Now, indeed, it might be said: "The time is come to be up and doing, Hungary!"

He who had neglected to celebrate his nuptials yesterday would have no time for marriage feasts to-morrow. Hannibal was at the gates! The noble militia host was set in motion. The Veszprime and Pest regiments moved toward the Marczal to join Archduke John's forces. The primatial troops joined the main body of the army on the banks of the March, and what there was of soldiery on the farther side of the Danube hastened to concentrate in the neighborhood of the Raab—only half equipped, muskets without flints, without cartridges, without saddles, with halters in lieu of bridles!

Under such circumstances a fully equipped troop like that commanded by "Count Fertöszeg," with sabers, pistols, carbines, and a leader trained in the battle-field, was of some value.

The days which followed the flag presentation were certainly not calculated to whispers of happy love, while the nights were illumined only by the light of watch-fires, and the glare over against the horizon of cannonading. Count Ludwig had so many demands on his time that he rarely found a few minutes free to visit his dear ones at the manor. Sometimes he came unexpectedly early in the morning, and sometimes late in the evening. And always, when he came, like the insurgent who dashes unceremoniously into your door, there was a confusion and a bustling to conceal what he was not yet to see—Marie's first attempts at drawing, her piano practices, or the miniature portrait Katharina was painting of her. Sometimes, too, he came when they were at a meal; and then, despite his protests that he had already dined or supped in camp, he would be compelled to take his seat between the two ladies at the table. Hardly would he have taken up his fork, however, when a messenger would arrive in great haste to summon him for something or other—some question he alone could decide; then all attempts to detain him would prove futile.

The day he received his orders to march, he was forced to take enough time to speak on some very important matters to his betrothed wife. He delivered into her hands the steel casket, of which so much has been written. When he entered the room where the two ladies were sitting, Marie discreetly rose and left the lovers alone; but she did not go very far: she knew that she would be sent for very soon. Why should she stop to hear the exchange of lovers' confidences, hear the mutual confessions which made *them* so happy? She did not want to see the tears which *he* would kiss away.

"May God protect you," sobbed Katharina, reflecting at the same moment that it would be a great pity were a bullet to strike the spot on the noble brow where she pressed her farewell kiss.

"You will guard my treasure, Katharina? Take good care of my palladium and of yourself. Before I go, let me show you what this casket which you must guard with unceasing care contains."

He drew the steel ring from his thumb, and pushed to one side the crown which formed the seal, whereupon a tiny key was revealed. With it he unlocked the casket.

On top lay a packet of English bank-notes of ten thousand pounds each.

"This sum," explained Ludwig, "will defray the expenses of our undertaking. When I shall have attained my object, I shall be just so much the poorer. I am not a rich man, Katharina; I must tell you this before our marriage."

"I should love you even were you a beggar," was the sincere response.

A kiss was her reward.

Underneath the bank-notes were several articles of child's clothing, such as little girls wear.

"Her mother embroidered the three lilies on these with her own hands," said Ludwig, laying the little garments to one side. Then he took from the casket several time-stained documents, and added: "These are the certificate of baptism, the last lines from the mother to her daughter, and the deposition of the two men who witnessed the exchange of the children. This," taking up a miniature-case, "contains a likeness of Marie, and one of the other little girl who exchanged destinies with her. The Marquis d'Avoncourt, who is now a prisoner in the Castle of Ham,—if he is still alive!—is the only one besides ourselves who knows of the existence of these things. And now, Katharina, let me beg of you to take good care of them; no matter what happens, do not lose sight of this casket."

He locked the casket, and returned the ring to his thumb.

The baroness placed the treasure intrusted to her care in a secret cupboard in the wall of her own room.

And now, one more kiss!

The girl waiting in the adjoining room was doubtless getting weary. Suddenly Ludwig heard the tones of a piano. Some one was playing, in the timid, uncertain manner of a new beginner, Miska's martial song. Ludwig listened, and turned questioningly toward his betrothed. Katharina did not speak; she merely smiled, and walked toward the door of the adjoining room, which she opened.

Marie sprang from the piano toward Ludwig, who caught her in his arms and rewarded her for the surprise. And thus it happened that Marie, after all, was the one to receive Ludwig's last kiss of farewell.

CHAPTER III

The camp on the bank of the Rabcza was shared by the troop from Fertöszeg and by a militia company of infantry from Wieselburg. The parole had been given out for the night. Count Vavel had completed his round of the outposts, and had returned to the officers' tent. Here he found awaiting him two old acquaintances—the vice-palatine and the young attorney from Pest, each of them wearing the light-blue dolman.

The youthful attorney, whose letters to the count had voiced the national discontent, had at once girded on his sword when the call to arms had sounded throughout the land, and was now of one mind with his quondam patron: if he got near enough to a Frenchman to strike him, the result would certainly be disastrous—for the Frenchman. Bernat bácsi also found himself at last in his element, with ample time and opportunity for anecdotes. Seated on a clump of sod the root side up, with both hands clasping the hilt of his sword, the point of which rested on the ground, he repeated what he had heard from the palatine's own lips, while dining with that exalted personage in the camp by the Raab.

At a very interesting point in his recital he was unceremoniously interrupted by the challenging call of the outposts:

"Halt! who comes there?"

Vavel hastened from the tent, flung himself on his horse, and galloped in the direction of the call. The patrol had stopped an armed man who would not give the password, but insisted that he had a right to enter the camp.

Vavel recognized Satan Laczi, and said to the guard:

"Release him; he is a friend of mine." Then to the ex-robber: "Come with me."

He led the way to his own private tent, where he bade his companion rest himself on a pallet of straw.

"I dare say you are tired, my good fellow."

"Not very," was the reply. "I have come only from Kapuvar to-day."

"On foot?"

"Part of the way, and part of the way swimming."

"What news do you bring?"

"We captured a French courier in the marshes near Vitnyed just as he was about to ride into the stream."

"Where is he?"

"Well, you see, one of my fellows happened to grasp him a little too tightly by the collar, because he resisted so obstinately—and, besides, it must have been a very weak cord that fastened his soul to his body."

"You have not done well, Satan Laczi," reproved the count. "Another time you must bring the prisoner to me alive, for I may learn something of importance from him. Did not I tell you that I would pay a reward for a living captive?"

"Yes, your lordship, and we shall lose our reward this time. But we didn't capture the fellow for nothing, after all. We searched his pockets, and found this sealed letter addressed to a general in the enemy's army."

Vavel took the letter, and said: "Rest here until I return. You will find something to eat and drink in the corner there. I may want you to ride farther to-night."

"If I am to go on a horse, that will rest me sufficiently," was the response.

Vavel quitted the tent to read the letter by the nearest watch-fire. It was addressed to "General Guillaume."

That the general commanded a brigade of the viceroy of Italy's troops, Vavel knew.

The letter was a long one—four closely written pages. Before reading it Vavel glanced at the signature: "Marquis de Fervlans." The name seemed familiar, but he could not remember where he had heard it. He was fully informed when he read the contents:

> "M. GENERAL: The intrigue has been successfully carried out. Themire has found the fugitives! They are hidden in a secluded nook on the shore of Lake Neusiedl in Hungary, where their extreme caution has attracted much attention. Themire's first move was to take up her abode in the same neighborhood, which she did in a masterly manner. The estate she bought belonged to a Viennese baron who had ruined himself by extravagance. Themire bought

the property, paying one hundred thousand guilders for it, on condition that she might also assume the baron's name; such transfers are possible, I believe, in Austria. In this wise Themire became the Baroness Katharina Landsknechtsschild, and, as she thoroughly understands the art of transformation, became a perfect German woman before she took possession of her purchase. In order not to arouse suspicion on the part of the fugitives, she carefully avoided meeting either of them, and played to perfection the rôle of a lady that had been jilted by her lover.

"Themire learned that our fugitive owned a powerful telescope with which he kept himself informed of everything that happened in the neighborhood, and this prompted her to adopt a very amusing plan of action. *I* wanted to put an end at once to the matter, and had gone to Vienna for the purpose of so doing. I entered the Austrian army as Count Leon Barthelmy, in order to be near my chosen emissary. But my scheme was without result. I had planned that a notorious robber of that region should steal the girl and the documents from the Nameless Castle,—as the abode of the fugitives is called,—but my robber proved unequal to the task. Consequently I was forced to accept Themire's more tedious but successful plan. The difficulty was for Themire to become acquainted with our fugitive without arousing his suspicions. An opportunity offered. One night, when we knew to a certainty that the hermit in the Nameless Castle would be in his observatory because of an eclipse of the moon, Themire put her plan into operation. The hermit, who is only a man, after all, found a lovely woman more attractive than all the planets in the universe; he was captured in the net laid for him! When the moon entered the shadow, four masked robbers (Jocrisse was their leader!) climbed into the Baroness Landsknechtsschild's windows. The hermit in his observatory beheld this incursion, and, being a knight as well as a recluse, what else could he do but rush to the rescue of his fair neighbor? His telescope had told him she was fair. Jocrisse played his part admirably. At the approach of the deliverer the "robbers" took to their heels, and the brave knight unbound the fettered and charming lady he had delivered from the ruffians. As Themire had prepared herself for the meeting, you may guess the result: the hermit was captured!"

Oh, how every drop of blood in Vavel's veins boiled and seethed! His face was crimsoned with shame and rage. He read further:

"Themire was perfectly certain that the mysterious hermit of the Nameless Castle had fallen in love with her; and *I* am not so sure but Themire has ended by falling in love with the knight! Women's hearts are so impressionable.

"I managed to have my regiment sent to her neighborhood, and took up my quarters in her house. I sought by every means to lure the hermit from his den; but he is a cunning fox, is this protector of fair ladies! I could not get a sight of him. I decided at last to waylay him (when he would be out driving with the veiled lady), to pretend that I was a betrayed husband in search of his errant wife, and ask to see the face of his veiled companion. This, naturally, he would refuse. A duel would be the result; and as he has not for years had a weapon in his hand, and as I am a dead shot, you can guess the result—a hermit against a Spadassin! With a bullet in his brain, the mysterious maid would become my property."

Here an icy chill shook Vavel's frame. He read on:

"That was my intention. But something on which I had not counted prevented me from carrying it out. When I insisted on seeing the face of the veiled lady, after telling him I believed her to be my wife, Ange Barthelmy (I need not tell you that that entire story was an invention of my own; I published it in a provincial newspaper, whence it spread all over Europe), my brave hermit showed a very bold front, and we were on the point of exchanging blows, when the lady suddenly flung back her veil and revealed the face of—Themire! You may believe that I was dumfounded for an instant; then I began to believe that my faith in this woman had been misplaced. Could it be possible that she had been caught in her own trap—that she had found this Vavel's eyes more alluring than the fortune we promised her, and that instead of betraying him to us she would do the very opposite—betray us to him? It may be that she has woven a more delicate web than I can detect with which to entangle her romantic victim the more securely. At all events, when I asked Vavel what relation the lady at his side bore to him, he replied: 'She is my betrothed wife.'

"I confess I am puzzled. But I have the means of compelling Themire to keep her promise. Her daughter is in my power!"

("Her daughter?" gasped Vavel. "Her daughter? Then Katharina is a married woman!")

"But," he continued to read, "it might happen that a woman who is in love would sacrifice her child. So soon as this war broke out, Vavel threw off his hermit's mask, and is now leading a company of troopers—which he equipped at his own expense—against us.

"From Jocrisse's letters I learn that Vavel's treasures are now in Themire's hands. That which our fair emissary was commissioned to find is in her possession. Now, however, the question is, What will she do with it?

"Jocrisse also informs me that Themire is quite bewitched with the amiability of the maid who has been intrusted to her care. If this be true, then matters are in a bad way. If this is not another of Themire's schemes, but actual sympathy, if this girl, whose remarkable loveliness of character (even Jocrisse is compelled to praise her) has won the piquant little Amélie's place in her mother's heart, then it will be more difficult to separate Themire from the girl than to win her from her lover."

This was a solitary ray of sunshine amid the threatening clouds which enveloped Ludwig. He continued to read with rapidly beating heart:

"I must know to a certainty what Themire proposes to do. To-day I sent her a message by a trusty courier, informing her that I should be at a certain place at an appointed time—that I wanted her to meet me and deliver into my hands the treasures she now holds. She will have an excellent excuse for leaving the manor. Our troops are approaching Steiermark, and have already crossed the Hungarian border. Thus it will seem as if she fell by accident into the hands of the enemy."

Vavel's heart almost ceased to beat. The letter shook in his trembling hands.

"I shall not, however," he continued to read, "depend on the fickle mood of a woman, who may be swayed by a tear or a love-letter. If Themire does not appear with the maid and the documents at the designated spot to-morrow evening, then I shall ride with my troop to the manor. My troop, as you know, belongs to the 'Legion of Demons,' and they do not know the definition of the word 'impossible'! If Themire of her own free will delivers the treasures into my hands, I shall thank her becomingly. If, however, she fails to meet me, I shall take the maid and the documents by force."

Vavel did not notice that the firelight by which he was reading the letter had begun to grow dim; he believed the characters on the page before him were swimming in a blood-red mist.

"And now," the letter went on, "I come to my instructions to you, general. You will move with your division toward the southern shore of Lake Neusiedl, and cut off the way of our fugitives toward the Tyrol. There is also another task which you must undertake. The mysterious maid, once she is in our hands, must be treated with the utmost courtesy and respect. A remarkable destiny awaits her. You know the emperor is going to separate from Josephine. A new palace will be built for the new empress. Who is the fortunate lady? As yet, no one can tell. A royal maid who can bring as her dowry the crown of a sovereign. A marriage that would unite the imperial crown with the crown of Hugo Capet would firmly establish Napoleon's throne. The legitimate dynasty would then be satisfied with the sovereign chosen by the people. This fugitive maid is, I hear, lovely, amiable, generous, pure, as only the ideal of a sovereign can be."

Vavel stamped his foot in a paroxysm of fury. Had this miscreant written that Marie was to be imprisoned in a convent, he could have borne it. But to suggest that his idol, his pure, adored image of a saint, might become the consort of the man on whom all the savage hatred of his nature was concentrated—this was more horrible than all the torments of hell. But he must calm himself and read the letter to the end.

"With this probability in view, I request that you send your wife and daughter, with a proper escort, of course, to meet me in one of the border cities, say Friedberg, where the ladies will be prepared to take charge of the maid. You will understand that a lady of her exalted position must travel only in company with distinguished persons. Countess Themire Dealba's rôle is concluded. She must not be allowed, in any character, to accompany our presumptive sovereign to Paris. She will receive her five millions of francs, as promised, and that will conclude our business transactions with her. Pray communicate my desire to your wife and daughter, and bid them prepare for the journey.

"Very truly,

"MARQUIS DE FERVLANS."

Not for one instant did Ludwig Vavel deliberate as to his course of action.

He could not leave his post. For a soldier to quit his post before the enemy is treason. He hurried back to his tent. Satan Laczi was stretched on the bare ground, sleeping soundly.

Ludwig shook him vigorously.

"Awake—awake! You must depart at once."

Satan Laczi sprang to his feet.

"Take my own horse, and ride for your life the shortest way to Fertöszeg."

"And what am I to do there?"

"Do you remember that an officer once asked you to steal the treasure I kept concealed in the Nameless Castle?"

"Yes; but I did n't do it."

"Well, I want you to do it now for me."

"Which do you want, the maid or the casket?"

"Both, if possible; the maid in any case. But you must be sure that she is alone when you approach her. Then say merely the name 'Sophie Botta,' and she will listen quietly to what you have to say. Then show her this ring,—here, put it on your left thumb"—he drew the steel ring from his own thumb and slipped it on to Satan Laczi's,—"and say, 'The person who wears this ring sent me to fetch you away from here. You are to come with me at once.'"

"And where am I to take her?"

"You will have a carriage with four swift horses at the park gate nearest the cemetery, and must drive with the maid to Raab.—Don't stop on any account until you get there. In Raab you will inquire for the house of Dr. Tromfszky, who is our army physician. He will have been advised of your coming, and will take charge of the maid. Then you will return to me here, and report what you have done. Here is a passport; if you are stopped at our lines show it to the guard. And here is a purse; don't spare the contents. And do not speak to a living soul about your mission."

"Your orders shall be obeyed," responded Satan Laczi, as he turned to leave the tent.

Vavel did not go back to the officers' tent. He went out into the night, and stood with folded arms, gazing with unseeing eyes into the darkness.

PART VIII
KATHARINA OR THEMIRE?

CHAPTER I

It was a delightful May evening. Marie was practising diligently her piano lesson, in order to surprise Ludwig with her progress when he should return from the war. That he would return Marie was quite certain.

Katharina had gone into the park for a solitary promenade. She had complained all day of a headache—a headache that began to trouble her after she had read the letter she had received that morning from the Marquis de Fervlans. She held the letter in her hand now, and read it again for the hundredth time.

Yes, she had accomplished her mission successfully; the fugitive maid and the important documents were in her possession; and yet her trembling hand refused to grasp the promised reward. A fortune awaited her for the comedy she had played with such success—a comedy in which she had acted the part of the charitable lady of the manor.

And what if there had been something of reality in the farce? Suppose her heart had learned to thrill with emotions hitherto unknown to it? Suppose it had learned to know the true meaning of gratitude—of love?

But five millions of francs!

If she were alone in the world! But there was Amélie, her dear little daughter, who was now almost fifteen years old—almost a young lady. Should she leave Amélie in her present disagreeable position, a member of "Cythera's Brigade," or should she send for her, and confess to the man whose respect she desired to retain that the child was her daughter, and that she was a widow? Could she tell him what she had once been? Would he continue to respect, to love her?

Five millions of francs!

It was an enormous sum, and would become hers if she should order the carriage, and, taking Marie and the casket with her, drive leisurely along the highway until stopped by a troop of soldiers that would suddenly surround the carriage. A politely smiling face would then appear at the window of the carriage, and a courteous voice would say:

"Don't be alarmed, ladies. You are with friends. We are Frenchmen."

But to renounce the love and respect so hardly won! Ah, how very dearly she loved the man to whom she had betrothed herself in jest! In jest? No, no; it was not a jest!

But five millions of francs!

Would all the millions in the world buy one faithful heart?

Katharina was suffering for her transgressions. She had intended to play with the heart of another, and had lost her own. Besides, she could not bear to think of betraying the innocent girl who loved and trusted her and called her "mother."

But time pressed. Three times already Jocrisse had interrupted her meditations to inquire if her answer to the marquis's letter was ready. And still she struggled with herself. When Jocrisse appeared again, she said to him:

"My letter is of such importance that I cannot think of intrusting it to the hands of a stranger. You yourself, Jocrisse, must take it to the marquis."

"I am ready to depart at once, madame."

Katharina wrote her reply, sealed it carefully, and gave it to Jocrisse, who set out at once on his errand.

In the letter he carried were but three words:

"*Io non posso*" ("I cannot").

Katharina locked herself in the pavilion in the park, and gave orders to the servants not to admit any visitors, whether acquaintances or strangers.

An hour or more had passed when she heard a timid knock at the door, and an apologetic voice said:

"A strange gentleman is here. I told him your ladyship would see no one; then he bade me give your ladyship this, which he said he had brought from Paris."

Katharina opened the door wide enough to receive the object. It was a small ivory locket, yellow with age. Katharina's hand shook violently as she pressed the spring to open it. She cast a hasty glance at the miniature,—the likeness of her daughter Amélie,—then said in a faltering voice: "You may tell the gentleman I will see him."

In a few minutes the visitor entered the pavilion.

"M. Cambray!" exclaimed the baroness.

"Yes, madame; I am Cambray, with my other name, Marquis Richard d'Avoncourt. I am he to whom you once said: 'I shall be grateful to you so long as I live.'"

"How—how came you here?" gasped the baroness.

"I managed to escape from my prison at Ham, went to Paris, where I saw your daughter—"

"You saw my daughter?" interrupted the baroness, excitedly. "Did you speak to her? Oh, tell me—tell me what you know about her."

"You shall hear all directly, madame. I told the countess that I intended to search for her mother, and asked if she had any message to send to her."

"Did she send a letter with you?" again interrupted the baroness.

"She did, madame. But before I give it to you I should like to have a shovel of hot coals and a bit of camphor."

"But why—why?" demanded the baroness.

"I will tell you. Do you know what Napoleon brought home with him from the bloody battle of Eilau?"

"I have not heard."

"The 'influenza.' I dare say you have never even heard the name; but you will very soon hear it often enough! It is a pestilential disease that is rather harmless where it originated, but when it takes hold of a strange region it becomes a deadly pestilence—as in Paris, where a special hospital has been established for patients with the disease. It was in this hospital I found your daughter as a nurse."

"*Jesu Maria!*" shrieked the mother, in a tone of agony. "A nurse in that pest-house?"

"Yes," nodded the marquis. Then he took from his pocket a letter, and added: "She wrote this to you from there."

The baroness eagerly extended her hand to take the letter.

"Would it not be better to fumigate it first?" said the marquis.

"No, no; I am not afraid! Give it to me, I beg of you!"

She caught the letter from his hand, tore it open, and read:

"DEAR LITTLE MAMA: What sort of a life are you leading out yonder in that strange land? Do you never get weary or feel bored? Have you anything to amuse you? *I* have become satiated with my life—lying, cheating, deceiving every day in order to live! While I was a little girl I was proud of the praises heaped upon me for my cleverness. But a day came when everything disgusted me. It is an infamous trade, this of ours, little mama, and I have given it up. I have begun to lead a different life—one with which I am satisfied; and if you will take the advice of one who wishes you well, you, too, will quit the old ways. You can embroider beautifully and play the piano like a master. You could earn a livelihood giving lessons in either. Do not trouble any further about me, for I can take care of myself. If only you knew how much happier I am now, you would rejoice, I know! Let me beg you to become honest and truthful, and think often of your old friend and little daughter,

"AMÉLIE (now SOEUÉR AGNES)."

Katharina's nerveless hands dropped to her lap. This sharp rebuke from her only child was deserved.

Then she sprang suddenly toward her visitor, grasped his arm, and cried:

"Tell me—tell me about my daughter, my little Amélie! How does she look now? Is she much changed? Has she grown? Oh, M. Cambray! in pity tell me—tell me about her!"

"I have brought you a portrait of her as she looked when I saw her last."

He drew from his pocket a small case, and, opening it, disclosed a pallid face with closed eyes. A wreath of myrtle encircled the head, which rested on the pillow of a coffin.

"She is dead!" screamed the horror-stricken mother, staring with wild eyes at the sorrowful picture.

"Yes, madame, she is dead," assented the marquis. "This portrait is sent by your daughter as a remembrance to the mother who exposed her on the streets, one stormy winter night, in order that she might spy upon another little child—a persecuted and homeless little child."

The baroness cowered beneath the merciless words as beneath a stinging lash: but the man knew no pity; he would not spare the heartbroken woman.

"And now, madame," he continued in a sharp tone, "you can go back to your home and take possession of your reward. You have worked hard to earn the blood-money."

Here the baroness sat suddenly upright, tore from her bosom a small gold note-case, in which was the order for the five millions of francs. She opened the case, took out the order, and tore it into tiny bits. Then she flung them from her, crying savagely:

"Curse him who brought me to this! God's curse be upon him who brought this on me!"

"Madame," calmly interposed the marquis, "you have not yet completed the task you were set to do."

"No, no; I have not—I have not," was the excited response, "and I never will. Come—come with me! The maid and what belongs to her are here—safe, unharmed. Take her—fly with her and hers whithersoever you choose to go; I shall not hinder you."

"That I cannot do, madame. I am a stranger in a strange land. I know not who is my friend or who is my foe. *You* must save the maid. If atonement is possible for you, that is the way you may win it. You know best where the maid will be safe from her persecutors. Save her, and atone for your transgression against her. Ludwig Vavel gave you his love and, more than that, his respect. Would you retain both, or will you tear them to tatters, as you have the order for the five million francs? Will you let me advise you?" he asked, suddenly.

"Advise me, and I will follow it to the letter!"

"Then disguise yourself as a peasant, hide the steel casket in a hamper, and take it to Ludwig Vavel, wherever he may be."

"And Marie?"

"You cannot with safety take her with you. The maid and the casket must not remain together. You must conceal Marie somewhere until you return from the camp."

"Will you not stay here and keep watch over her until I return?"

"I thank you, madame, for your hospitality, but I must not accept it. I come direct from the influenza hospital. I feel that the disease has laid hold of me. I have comfortable quarters at the Nameless Castle, where my old friend Lisette will take care of me. Don't let Marie come to see me; and if I should not recover from this illness, which I feel will be a severe one, let me be buried down yonder on the shore of the lake."

When the Marquis d'Avoncourt left the pavilion he was shaking with a violent chill, and as he took his way with tottering steps toward the Nameless Castle, Katharina, broken-hearted and filled with anguish, wept out her heart in bitter tears.

CHAPTER II

Marie had finished practising her lesson, and hastened to join Katharina in the park. She found her in the pavilion, and was filled with alarm when she saw her "little mama" kneeling among the fragments of her fortune. Katharina's tear-stained eyes, swollen face, and drawn lips betrayed how terribly she was suffering.

"My dearest little mama!" exclaimed Marie, hastening toward the kneeling woman, and trying to lift her from the floor, "what is the matter? What has happened?"

"Don't touch me," moaned the baroness. "Don't come near me. I am a murderess. I murdered her who called me mother."

She held the ivory locket toward Marie, and added: "See, this is what she was like when I deserted her—my little daughter Amélie!"

"Your daughter?" repeated Marie, wonderingly. "You have been married? Are you a widow?"

"I am."

Katharina now held toward the young girl the portrait M. Cambray had given her. "And this," she explained in a hollow tone, "is what she is like now—now, when I wanted her to come to me."

"Good heaven!" ejaculated Marie, gazing in terror at the miniature, "she is dead?"

"Yes—murdered—as you, too, will be if you stay with me! You must fly—fly at once!"

"Katharina!" interposed the young girl, "why do you speak so?"

"I say that you must leave me. Go—go at once! Go down to the parsonage, and ask Herr Mercatoris to give you shelter. Tell him to clothe you in rags; and when you hear the tramp of horses, hide yourself, and don't venture from your concealment until they are gone. I, too, am going away from here."

"But why may not I come with you?" asked Marie, in a troubled tone.

"Where I go you cannot accompany me. I am going to steal through the lines of Ludwig's camp."

"You are going to Ludwig?" interrupted the young girl.

"Yes, to deliver into his hands the casket containing your belongings. After that I—I don't know what will become of me."

"Katharina! Don't frighten me so! Do you imagine that Ludwig will cease to love you when he learns you are a widow, and that you had a daughter?"

"Oh, no; he will not hate me because I had a daughter," returned Katharina, shaking her head sadly, "but because my wickedness destroyed her."

"Don't talk so, Katharina," again expostulated Marie.

"Why, don't you see that she is dead? Look at these closed eyes, the white face! Ask these closed lips to open and tell you that I did not murder her!"

"Katharina, this is not true! Your enemies have told you this to grieve you. Look at these two pictures! There is not the least resemblance between them. This pale one is not your daughter. He who told you so lied cruelly."

Katharina sighed mournfully.

"He who told me so does not lie. It was your old friend Cambray."

"Cambray?" echoed Marie, with mingled delight and astonishment. "Cambray is here? My deliverer, my second father! Where is he?"

"He is gone. He accomplished that for which he came,—to crush me to the earth, and to serve you,—and has gone away again."

"Gone away?" repeated Marie, incredulously. "Gone away? Impossible! Cambray would not go away without seeing me! Which way did he go? I will run after him and overtake him."

"No; stay where you are!" commanded Katharina, seizing her arm. "You must not follow him."

"Why not?"

"Listen, and I will tell you. Cambray brought these pictures and this letter from Paris. The letter was written by my daughter in the hospital, where she caught the dreadful disease which caused her death. She had been nursing the sick, like a heroine, and died like a saint. It is well with her now, for she is in heaven. If I weep, it is not for her, but for myself. The deadly disease Amélie died of has seized upon your friend Cambray; and the noble old man is unselfish even in dying. He does not want you to come near him, lest you, too, become affected by the pestilence. He is gone to the Nameless Castle, where Lisette will take care of him—"

"Lisette?" interrupted Marie, excitedly. "Lisette, who was afraid to go near her own husband when he lay dying!"

"Well, what would you? Shall I send some one to nurse him?"

"No—no. *I* am the one to take care of him! He was a father to me. For my sake he was imprisoned, persecuted, buried alive all these years! And I am to let him die over yonder—alone, without a friend near him! No; I am going to him. That which your other daughter had the courage to do, this one also will do!"

"Marie! Think of Ludwig! Do you wish to drive him to despair?"

"God watches over us. He will do what is well for all of us!"

"Marie"—Katharina made a last effort to detain the young girl—"Marie, do you wish to go to Cambray to learn from him that I am the curse-laden creature who was sent after you to capture you and deliver you into the hands of your enemies?"

Marie turned at these desperate words, held out her hand, and said gently:

"And if he were to tell me that, Katharina, I should say to him that, instead of destroying me you liberated me, and instead of hating me you love me as I love you."

She made as if she would kiss Katharina; but the excited woman turned away her face, and held toward Marie the letter Cambray had given her.

"Read this, and learn to know me as I am," she said in a choking voice.

While Marie was reading the letter, Katharina covered her burning face with both hands; but they were gently drawn away and held in the young girl's warm clasp, while she spoke:

"A reply must be sent to this letter, little mother. I shall say to her, through the soul now on the eve of departure to the better land where she dwells: 'Little sister, your mother will wear the pure white garment, as you desired, in mourning for you. Instead of you, she will have me, and will love me, as I shall love her, in your stead. Bless us both, and be happy.' Shall I not send this message to your Amélie with my good friend Cambray?"

"Go, then; go—go," convulsively sobbed Katharina, and fell upon her face on the floor as Marie hastened from the pavilion.

CHAPTER III

When her grief had exhausted itself, Katharina stole back to the manor, where she removed the steel casket from its hiding-place, wrapped it in her shawl, and, passing noiselessly and unseen down a staircase that was rarely used, crossed the park to the farmer's cottage.

Here she told the farmer's wife that she was going to play a trick on her betrothed, that she wanted to borrow a gown and a kerchief. She bade the farmer saddle the mule which his wife rode when she went to the village, and to hang the hampers, as usual, from the pommel. In one of these she placed the steel casket, in the other a pistol, and filled them both with all sorts of provisions. Thus disguised, she mounted the quadruped, and set out alone on her way toward the camp.

Almost at the same moment that Ludwig Vavel had learned of the deceit of the woman he loved, he became convinced that his ambitious designs had come to naught. The rising of the German patriots against Napoleon had ended in their defeat, and not a trace was left of the uprising among the French people themselves.

It was the third day after the battle of Aspern when Master Matyas entered Count Vavel's tent.

The jack of all trades had proved himself a useful member of the army— not, indeed, where there was any fighting, for he much preferred looking on, when a battle was in progress, to taking an active part in the fray. But as a spy he was invaluable.

"I have seen everything," he announced. "I saw the balloon in which a French engineer made an ascent to the clouds, to reconnoiter the Austrian camp. He went up as high as a kite, and they held on to the rope below, down which he sent his messages—observations of the Austrians' movements. I saw the bridge, which is two hundred and forty fathoms long, which can be transported from place to place, and reaches from one bank of the Danube to the other. And I saw that demi-god flying on his white horse. He was pale, and trembled."

"And how came you to see all these sights, Master Matyas?" interrupted Vavel.

"I allowed the Frenchmen to capture me; then I was set to work in the intrenchments with the other prisoners."

"And did you manage to deliver my letter?"

"Oh, yes. The Philadelphians are easily recognized from the silver arrow they wear in their ears. When I whispered the password to one of them, he gave it back to me, whereupon I handed him your letter. I came away as soon as he brought me the answer. Here it is."

This letter by no means lightened Vavel's gloomy mood. Colonel Oudet, the secret chief of the Philadelphians in the French army, heartily thanked Count Vavel for his offer of assistance to overthrow Napoleon; but he also gave the count to understand that, were Bonaparte defeated, the republic would be restored to France. In this case, what would become of Vavel's cherished plans?

It was after midnight. The pole of "Charles's Wain" in the heavens stood upward. Ludwig approached the watch-fire, and told the lieutenant on guard that he might go to his tent, that he, Vavel, would take his place for the remainder of the night. Then he let the reins drop on the neck of his horse, and while the beast grazed on the luxuriant grass, his rider, with his carbine resting in the hollow of his arm, continued the night watch. The night was very still; the air was filled with odorous exhalations, which rose from the earth after the shower in the early part of the evening. From time to time a shooting star sped on its course across the sky.

One after the other, Ludwig Vavel read the two letters he carried in his breast. He did not need to take them from their hiding-place in order to read them. He knew the contents by heart—every word. One of them was a love-letter he had received from his betrothed; the other was the Judas message of his enemy and Marie's.

At one time he would read the love-letter first; then that of the arch-plotter. Again, he would change the order of perusal, and test the different sensations—the bitter after the sweet, the sweet after the bitter.

Suddenly, through the silence of the night, he heard the distant tinkle of a mule-bell. It came nearer and nearer. He heard the outpost's "Halt! Who comes there?" and heard the pleasant-voiced response: "Good evening, friend. God bless you."

"Ah!" muttered Ludwig, with a scornful smile, "my beautiful bride is sending another supply of dainties. How much she thinks of me!"

The mule-bell came nearer and nearer.

By the light of the watch-fire Vavel could see the familiar red kerchief the farmer's wife from the manor was wont to wear over her head. The mule came directly toward the watch-fire, and stopped when close to Vavel's horse. The woman riding the beast slipped quickly to the ground, emptied the provisions from the hampers, then, lifting the object which had been concealed in the bottom of one of them, came around to Vavel's side, saying:

"It is I. I have come to seek you."

"Who is it?" he demanded sternly, recognizing the voice; "Katharina or Themire?"

"Katharina—Katharina; it is Katharina," stammered the trembling woman, looking pleadingly up into his forbidding face.

"And why have you come here?"

"I came to bring you this," she replied, holding toward him the steel casket.

"Where is Marie?"

"She is safe—with the Marquis d'Avoncourt."

"What?" exclaimed Vavel, in amazement, flinging his carbine on the ground. "Cambray—d'Avoncourt—*here?*"

"Yes; he is at the Nameless Castle, and Marie is with him."

"After all, there is a God in heaven!" with deep-toned thankfulness ejaculated Ludwig. Then he added: "Oh, Katharina, how I have suffered because of—Themire!"

"Themire is dead!" solemnly returned the baroness. "Let us not speak of her. Here, take these treasures into your own keeping; they are no longer safe with me. Open the casket and convince yourself that everything is there."

"I cannot open it; I have not got the key."

"Have you lost your ring?"

"No. I have trusted the most notorious thief in the country with it. I have sent him with the ring to Marie. I bade him show it to her, and tell her that she was to follow him wherever he might lead her. Satan Laczi has the ring."

Katharina covered her eyes with her hand, and stood with drooping head before her lover.

"I have deserved this," she murmured brokenly.

Vavel passed his hand over his face, and sighed. "It was all a dream! It was madness to expect impossibilities," he murmured. "I am familiar enough with the stars to have known that there are constellations which never descend to the horizon. The 'Crown' is one of them! Of what use are these rags now?" he exclaimed, with sudden vehemence, pointing to the casket, which Katharina still held on her arm. "Whom can they serve? They have brought only sorrow to him who has guarded them, and to her to whom they belong. I cannot open the casket; but I need not do that to destroy the contents. Pray throw it into the fire yonder."

Katharina obeyed without an instant's hesitation. After a while the metal casket began to glow in the midst of the flames. It became red, then a pale rose-color, while a thin cord of vapor trailed through the keyhole.

"The little garments are burning," whispered Vavel, "and the documents, and the portraits, and the heap of worthless money. From to-day," he added, in a louder tone, "I begin to learn what it is to be a poor man."

"I have already learned what poverty means," said Katharina. "Look at these clothes! I have no others, and even these are borrowed."

"I love you in them," involuntarily exclaimed Vavel, extending his hand toward her.

"What? You offer me your hand? Do you believe that I am Katharina — only Katharina?"

"That I may wholly and entirely believe that you are Katharina, and not Themire, answer one question. A creature who calls himself the Marquis de Fervlans and Leon Barthelmy is lying in ambush somewhere in this neighborhood, waiting for you to settle an old account with him. If you are the same to me that you once were, and if I am the same to you that I was once, tell me where I shall find De Fervlans, for it will be *my* duty then to settle with him."

Katharina's face suddenly blazed with eager excitement. She flung back her head with a proud gesture.

"I will lead you to the place. Together we will seek him!" she cried, with animation in every feature.

"Then give me your hand. You *are* Katharina—*my* Katharina!"

He bent toward her, and the two hands met in a close clasp.

Count Fertöszeg ordered the drums to beat a reveille; then he selected from his troop one hundred trusty men, and galloped with them in the direction of Neusiedl Lake. Katharina on her mule, without the tinkling bell, trotted soberly by his side.

PART IX
SATAN AND DEMON

CHAPTER I

There was a notorious troop with Napoleon's army, the sixth Italian regiment, which was called the "Legion of Demons."

The troop was made up of worthless members of society—idlers, highwaymen, outcasts, and desperate characters, who had lost all sense of respectability and morality. The majority of them had sought the asylum of the battle-field to escape imprisonment or worse.

When their commander led his "demons" to an attack, he was wont to urge them thus:

"*Avanti, avanti, Signori briganti! Cavalieri ladroni, avanti!*" ("Forward, forward, Messieurs Highwaymen! My chivalrous footpads, forward!")

A division of this legion of demons had made its way with the vice-king of Italy thus far through the belt-line, and had been intrusted with the mission mentioned in De Fervlans's letter to General Guillaume. The marquis commanded this body of the demons, he having, as Colonel Barthelmy in the Austrian army, become thoroughly familiar with that part of Hungary.

Lisette and Satan Laczi's little son were living alone at the Nameless Castle.

When Marie, who was come in quest of her friend Cambray, rang the bell, the door was opened by the lad.

"Is there a strange gentleman here?" she asked.

"I don't know. He went to see Lisette, and I did not see him come away," was the reply.

"Then let me come in," said the young girl. "I want to speak to Lisette, too."

"She will beat me if I let you come in," returned the boy, opening the door after a moment's hesitation.

The fumes of camphor were perceptible even in the vestibule; and when Marie's little conductor knocked at the door of the kitchen, a heaping shovelful of hot and smoking coals was thrust toward him, and a scolding voice demanded irritably:

"What do you want again? Why do you keep annoying me, you little torment!"

"Excuse me, Lisette," humbly apologized the lad, "but our young mistress from the manor is here."

At this announcement Lisette hastily shut the door again, and opened a small loophole in an upper panel, through which she spoke in a sharp tone:

"Why do you come here? Has the Lord forsaken you over yonder, that you come back to this pest-house? Get out of it as quickly as you can. Go down and hide yourself in the Schmidt's cottage—perhaps they will not betray you. Anyway, you can't stop here with us."

"That is just what I mean to do, Lisette,—stop here with you," smilingly responded Marie. "Where is my friend Cambray?"

"How should I know where he is? A pretty question to ask me! He is n't anywhere. He has gone to bed, and you can't see him."

"I shall hunt till I find him, Lisette."

"Well, you will do as you like, of course; but you will not find M. Cambray, for he does n't want to see you."

"Very well," returned Marie. Then to the lad by her side, "Come with me, Laczko; we will hunt for the gentleman."

Lisette was beside herself with terror at the danger which threatened Marie; but before she could utter another word, the young girl and her little escort had disappeared down the corridor.

There was a great change everywhere in the castle. The floors were covered with muddy foot-tracks; huge nails had been driven into the varnished walls, and great heaps of dust, straw, and hay lay about on the inlaid floors of the halls and salon. Marie hardly recognized her former immaculate asylum.

She called, with her clear, soft-toned voice, into every room, "Cambray! father! art thou here?" but received no reply.

Then she mounted the staircase to her own apartment. The door was open like all the rest, but a first glance told Marie that the room had not been used until now. Lisette, beyond a doubt, had lodged her respected guest in this only habitable chamber.

Marie entered and looked about her. The metal screen was down!

She hastened toward it. There was a light burning in the alcove, and she could see through the links by placing her eyes close to them. The noble old knight was lying on the bare floor, with his hands forming a pillow for his head. His glassy eyes were fixed and staring, and burning with a startling brightness. His parched lips were half-open, as if he were speaking.

"Cambray! father!" called Marie; in a tone of distress.

"Who calls? Marie?" gasped the fever-stricken man, making a vain attempt to rise. He fell back with a deep groan, but flung out his hand as if to ward off her approach.

"Let me come in, Cambray. It is I, your little Marie. Please let me come in. There, close to your right hand, is a button in the floor. Press it, and this screen will rise."

The sick man began to laugh; only his face showed that he was laughing, no sound came from his parched throat. He was laughing because he had prevented his favorite from coming to his pestilential resting-place.

Marie deliberated a moment, then decided to resort to stratagem:

"If you will not let me come in to you, papa Cambray," she called, simulating a petulant tone, "I shall go away, and not come back again. If you should want anything there will be a little boy here, outside; you can summon him by pressing that button. Good night, dear papa Cambray!"

The sick man turned his face toward the screen and listened in dreamy ecstasy to the sweet voice. He raised his hand, waved it weakly toward the speaker, then clasped it with the other on his breast, while his lips moved as if in prayer.

"Go fetch candles, and the tinder-box," whispered Marie to the little Laczko. "Place them here by the sofa, then light the lamp in the corridor."

"May I fetch my gun, too?" asked the boy.

"Your gun? What for?"

"I should n't be afraid if I had it with me."

"Then fetch it; but don't come into the room with it, for I am dreadfully afraid of guns. Leave it just outside the door."

It was quite dark when Laczko returned with the candles and a heavy double-barreled fowling-piece. He carefully placed the latter in the corner, then asked:

"Shall I light the candles now?"

"Certainly not. I don't want the gentleman to know that I am here. Maybe he may want something, and open the screen. I am going to lie down on this sofa, and you are to stand close by the alcove and watch the gentleman. If he should lift the screen, and I have fallen asleep, you must waken me at once."

Marie wrapped herself in her shawl, and lay down on the leather couch. Laczko took up his station as directed, close by the metal screen, through which he peered from time to time.

But there was no danger of Marie falling asleep. She could not even keep her eyes closed. Every few moments she would sit up and ask in a cautious whisper:

"What is he doing now?"

"He is tossing from side to side."

This reply was repeated several times.

At last the answer came that the invalid was perfectly quiet, whereupon Marie decided not to inquire again for an hour.

Suddenly she heard the lad say, in a trembling voice:

"I am dreadfully frightened."

"What of?" whispered Marie.

"The gentleman lies so still. He has n't stirred for a long time."

"He is asleep, I dare say."

"If he were sleeping his breast would rise and fall; but he is perfectly still."

Marie rose, and hastened to the screen. The smoking wick in the night-lamp near Cambray's head illumined his ghastly face. Marie had already seen one such pallid countenance—that of the old servant Henry when he lay dead on his bier.

She shuddered, and retreated with trembling limbs, drawing the lad with her.

"You may light the candle now," she whispered; "then we will go back to Lisette."

Laczko lighted the candle, then shouldered his gun, and preceded his young mistress down the staircase to the lower story.

They had almost reached the door of Lisette's room when Marie, who had been peering sharply ahead, stopped abruptly, and exclaimed in a startled tone:

"There is a man!"

Even as she spoke a dark form stepped from a doorway into the corridor in front of them. Marie retreated several steps; but her little escort proved that he was made of sterner stuff. He placed himself valiantly in front of his young mistress, laid his gun against his cheek, and aiming directly for the stranger's breast, said, in a brave tone:

"Halt, or I will shoot you."

"That's my brave lad," commented the stranger. "But don't shoot. It is I, your father."

"Don't come any nearer, I tell you!" responded the lad, threateningly.

"Why, I am not moving a muscle, lad; don't be foolish."

"What do you want here?" demanded Laczko. "I will not let you do any harm to my mistress."

Here Marie, who had recovered from her alarm, came forward, and laid her hand over her small defender's eyes.

"Take down your gun, Laczko," she commanded. Then turning to the stranger asked: "What do you want, my good man?"

For answer the man merely pronounced a name:

"Sophie Botta."

Without an instant's hesitation, and although she shuddered involuntarily when her eyes fell on the stranger's repulsive countenance, the young girl went close to his side, and said calmly:

"What do you wish me to do?"

Satan Laczi held the thumb-ring toward her, and said:

"The person who wears this sent me to fetch you away from here. Are you ready to come with me at once?"

"I am," replied Marie, who seemed unable to remove her eyes from the hideously ugly face before her.

"My master," continued the ex-robber, "also bade me fetch a little steel casket. Do you know where it is hidden?"

"The person who had it in her care has already taken it to your master," was Marie's response.

"Ah, she has taken it to him?" repeated Satan Laczi. "Then it is all right. I know now what I have to do. My master bade me convey you to a place of concealment; but my face is not exactly the sort to win anybody's confidence. Besides, I know some one who can perform this errand as well as I. The way to Raab is clear. Instead of taking you there myself, my wife will go with you. I think you would rather have her for a companion?"

"Yes, I think I would rather go with a woman," diplomatically assented Marie.

"As an additional protection, take this little lad with you." Here the ex-robber laid his hand on his son's shoulder, and looked proudly down on him. "His heart is already in the right place. And then he is not a wicked rascal like his father."

He was silent a moment, then added: "But I intend to reform. When my master has spoken with the woman to whom he intrusted his treasures, and if she has not betrayed him, then I know where he will be to-morrow. And Satan Laczi will be there, too! Then I and my comrades will show them what we can do. But come, we must make haste, and get on as far as possible while the moon is shining."

"But I am not properly clad for a journey," interposed Marie.

"My wife brought a nice warm *bunda* to wrap you in; it is in the carriage out yonder," returned the ex-robber.

"One word first: you are acquainted with the man who made the metal screen in my apartments. Could you see him?"

"He is in Count Vavel's service, and I can see him when I return to the camp."

"Then tell him to come to the Nameless Castle at once. He understands the secret spring of the screen, behind which he will find a dead man. This man was a very good friend, and I want him properly buried."

"I will give Master Matyas your order."

Marie now took leave of the Nameless Castle, feeling that she would never again come back to it. But she had not the courage to enter her apartments again.

The four-horse coach waited at the park gate. Marie entered it, wrapped the warm sheep-skin around her, and tied a cotton kerchief over her head in peasant fashion. Satan Laczi's wife took a seat by her side; the little Laczko climbed to the coachman's box, where he sat with his gun between his knees. Then the coachman cracked his whip, and the vehicle rattled down the road amid a cloud of dust. Satan Laczi looked after the coach until it disappeared around a turn in the road. Then he blew a shrill blast on his whistle, whereupon a number of wild-looking men, each armed to the teeth, emerged from the shrubbery and came toward him. Whispered orders were given, then the men in a body moved toward the willow-copse on the shore of the lake. Here were two flatboats drawn up on the beach. These were pushed into the water; the men entered them, each took an oar, and the unwieldy vessels were propelled along the shore toward the marshes.

The Marquis de Fervlans had camped with his company of demons on the shore of Neusiedl Lake. The marquis himself had taken quarters at the inn in the nearest village, where, assisted by two companions of questionable respectability but of undoubted valor, he was testing the quality of the fiery wine of the region, when a peasant cart, drawn by three horses, drew up before the inn, and Jocrisse, Baroness Katharina's messenger, alighted.

"Ah, here comes a sensible fellow," exclaimed the marquis. "I wonder what news he brings."

He was very soon enlightened.

"Hum! '*Io non posso!*'" he repeated, after reading the brief message Jocrisse delivered to him. "Very well, madame, I think I shall know what to do if you 'cannot'! Jocrisse, how is the country around Odenburg garrisoned?"

"A division of militia cavalry occupies every town,"

"That is exasperating! Not that I fear these militiamen might give my demons too much work; but I am afraid I may alarm them; then they will scamper in all directions, and frighten the entire Neusiedl region, so that when I arrive at Fertöszeg I shall find the birds flown and the nest empty. We must take them by surprise. Have you ever before been in this part of the country, Jocrisse?"

"I accompanied the county surveyor once as far as Frauenkirchen."

"Is the road practicable for wheels?"

"To Frauenkirchen it is good for wagons; but beyond the city it is in a wretched condition."

"Very well. You will engage a post-chaise here, and follow us to Frauenkirchen, where you will wait for further orders. What time did you leave Fertöszeg?"

"About noon."

"Listen. I suspect that your mistress will try to escape with the maid. If that is the case, we must bestir ourselves. But women are afraid to travel by night; and even if they have already left the manor, they cannot have gone very far. The water in the Danube was unusually high on the day of the battle at Aspern; that would cause the Raab to rise, and overflow the bridges crossing it. I shall doubtless overtake the fugitives at Vitnyed."

"It will be rather risky crossing the Hansag at night," observed Jocrisse, "and no amount of money would induce one of these natives about here to act as guide. They are a peculiar folk."

"Yes; but I shall not need a guide. I have an excellent map of the neighborhood, which I used when I was in garrison here. I used to hunt all over this region after wild boars and turkeys, and never had any difficulty finding my way, even at night."

De Fervlans now sent orders to his troop to break camp at once, with as little stir as possible; and before twilight shadows fell upon the land, the demons were riding toward the Hansag.

If we assume that Marie left the Nameless Castle in company with the wife of Satan Laczi at midnight, we can easily see that she would have but a few hours' advantage of the demons, who broke camp at sunset. If the latter met with no hindrance on their way, they would overtake the coach of the fugitives at the crossing of the Raab. As it was after midnight when Ludwig Vavel learned of the danger which threatened Marie, he could not, even if he had set out at once, have reached the Hansag before noon of the following day, by which time De Fervlans and his demons would have accomplished their errand. Therefore nothing short of a miracle could save the maid.

CHAPTER II

The miracle happened—a true miracle, like the one of the biblical legend, when the Red Sea obstructed the way of the persecutor Pharaoh.

Those who may doubt this assertion are referred to the "Monograph on Lake Neusiedl," in which may be read a description of the phenomenon. In the last years Lake Neusiedl had been drained, and where it had joined the lakes of the Hansag, a stout dam had been built. When the waters of the Hansag chain rose, the muddy undercurrent threw up great mounds of earth, like enormous excrescences on a diseased body. One of these huge mounds burst open at the top and emitted a black, slimy mud that inundated the surrounding morass for a considerable distance.

Already in the neighborhood of St. Andras this slimy ooze was noticeable when the troop of demons galloped over the plantain-covered flats which here and there bent under the weight of the horsemen. As they proceeded, the enormous numbers of frogs became surprising, as if this host of amphibia had leagued against the invading demons. Then flocks of water-fowl, with clamorous cries and rustling wings, rose here and there, startled from their quiet nests by the approaching inundation, which by this time had completely hidden what was called in that region the public road. De Fervlans, at a loss what to make of this singular freak of nature, sent a horseman to the right, and one to the left, to examine the ground, and learn whence came the sea of slime, and how it might be avoided. Each of his messengers returned with the information that the slime was flowing in the direction he had ridden. The source, then, must be near where they had halted.

"This is bad," said De Fervlans, impatiently. "This eruption of mud will hinder our progress. We can't run a race with it. We must look up another route, and this will delay us perhaps for hours. But we can make that up when on a hard road again."

De Fervlans, who was familiar with the neighborhood, now led his troop in the direction of the path which ran through the morass toward the village of Banfalva, hoping thus to gain the excellent highway of Eszterhaza. Here and there from the swamp rose slight elevations of dry earth which were overgrown with alders and willows. On one of these "hills" De Fervlans concluded to halt for a rest, as both men and horses were weary with the toilsome journey over the wretched roads.

Very soon enough dry wood was collected for a fire. There was no need to fear that the light might attract attention; the camp was far enough from human habitation, and neither man nor beast ever spent the night in the morass of the Hansag. Besides, they could have seen, from the top of a tree, if any one were approaching. They could see in the bright moonlight the long poplar avenue which led to Eszterhaza; and even a gilded steeple might be seen gleaming in the Hungarian Versailles, which was perhaps a two hours' ride distant.

Suddenly the sharp call, "*Qui vive?*" was heard. It was answered by a sort of grunt, half-brute, half-human. Again the challenging call broke the silence, and was followed in a few seconds by a gunshot. Then a wild laugh was heard at some distance from the hill. De Fervlans hurried toward the guard.

"What was it?" he asked.

"I don't know whether it was a wild beast or a devil in human form," was the reply. "It was a strange-looking monster with a large head and pointed ears."

"I 'll wager it is my runaway fish-boy!" exclaimed the marquis.

"When I challenged the creature he stood up on his feet, and barked, or grunted, or whatever you might call it; and when I called out the second time he seemed to strike fire with something; at any rate, he did not act in the proper manner, so I fired at him. But I did n't hit him."

"I should be sorry if you had," responded the marquis. "I am convinced that it was my little monster. I taught him to strike fire; and he was evidently attracted by the light of our camp-fire."

Perhaps it would have been better had the guard shot the amphibious dwarf. Hardly had De Fervlans returned to his seat when the adjutant called his attention to a suspicious flashing in the morass a short distance from the hill on which they were resting. Suddenly, while they were watching the flashes of light, a column of flame rose toward the sky, then another, and another—the morass was on fire in a dozen places.

"Hell, and all devils!" shouted De Fervlans, springing toward his horse. "The little monster has set the marsh-grass on fire, and it was I who taught the devil's spawn how to use touchwood! Give chase to the creature!"

But the order for a chase came too late. In ten minutes the reeds growing about the hill were burning, and the demons were compelled to use their spurs in order to speed their horses from the dangerous conflagration.

They did not stop until they had reached the Valla plain—driven to their mad gallop by the caricature of the "militiaman"!

"This is a pretty state of affairs!" grumbled De Fervlans. "Mire first, then flames, bar our way. *Quis quid peccat, in eo punitur*—he who sins will be punished by his sin! I sinned in teaching that monster to strike fire. It has made us lose four more hours."

The four hours were of some consequence to the fugitive maid and Ludwig Vavel.

Dawn broke before the demons found the road between the groups of hills, and when they reached it, they still had before them that half of the Hansag which is formed by a series of small lakes.

De Fervlans now became anxious to shorten their route. A lakelet of fifty or sixty paces in width is not an impassable hindrance for a horseman. Therefore it was not necessary to ride perhaps a thousand paces in making a detour of the lakelets—the demons must ride through them. How often had he, when following a deer, swam with his horse through just such a body of water. Only then it was autumn, and now it was spring.

The flora of this marsh country has many species which hide underneath the water, and in the springtime send their long stems and tendrils toward the surface. De Fervlans was yet to learn that even plants may become foes. Those of his demons who were the first to plunge into the water suddenly began to call for help. Neither man nor beast can swim through a network of growing plants; at every movement they become entangled among the clinging tendrils and swaying stems, and sink to the bottom unless promptly rescued. The men on shore were obliged to grasp the tails of the struggling horses and draw them back to land. De Fervlans, who could not be convinced that it was impossible to swim across the narrow stretch of water, came very near losing his life among the aquatic growths. There was now no likelihood of their reaching the highway before sunrise.

There was still another hindrance. The fire in the morass had alarmed the entire neighborhood, and the inhabitants were out, to a man, fighting the flames which threatened their meadows. Therefore De Fervlans, who wished to avoid attracting attention to his troop, was obliged to make his way through thickets and over rough byways, which was very tedious work.

It was noon when they arrived at the bridge which crossed the Raab half a mile from Pomogy. At the farther end of this bridge was the custom-house, which was also a public inn.

"We must rest there," said De Fervlans, "or our worn-out beasts will drop under us."

Just as the troop rode on to the bridge, two men ran swiftly from the custom-house toward the swampy lowland. Before they entered the marsh they stopped, and bound long wooden stilts to their feet; and, thus equipped, stepped without difficulty from one earth-clod to another. No horseman could have followed them across the treacherous ground. De Fervlans's adjutant became uneasy when he saw these two men, whose actions seemed suspicious to him; but the marquis assured him that they were only shepherds whose herds pastured in the marshes.

The troop dismounted at the inn, and demanded of the host whatever he had of victuals and drinks. He could offer them nothing better than sour cider, mead, and wild ducks' eggs. But when a demon is hungry and thirsty, even these will satisfy him. De Fervlans, who had not for one instant doubted that his expedition would be successful, spread out his map and planned their further march. General Guillaume would have received one of his letters at least,—he had sent two, with two different couriers in different directions,—and would now be waiting at Friedberg for the arrival of the demons and their distinguished captive. Therefore the most direct route to that point must be selected. It was not likely that any militia troops would be idling about that cart of the country; and if there were, the demons could very easily manage them.

CHAPTER III

One of the two men who crossed the morass on stilts was Master Matyas, whose distance marches during this campaign were something phenomenal. Matyas found Count Vavel with his troop already at Eszterhaza, and apprized him at once of De Fervlans's arrival at the bridge-inn. The Volons had not yet rested, but they had traveled over passable roads, and were not so exhausted. Their leader at once gave orders to mount.

When Ludwig saw that Katharina also prepared to accompany the troop, he hurried to her side.

"Don't come any farther, Katharina," he begged. "Remain here, where you will be perfectly safe. Something might happen to you when we meet the enemy."

Katharina's smiling reply was:

"No, my dear friend. I have paid a very high entrance-fee to see this tragedy, for that you will kill Barthelmy Fervlans I am as certain as that there is a just God in heaven!"

"But *your* presence will make me fear at a moment when I must not feel afraid—afraid for your safety."

"Oh, don't trouble about yourself. I know you better. When you come in sight of the enemy you will forget all about *me*. As for me, I am going with you."

The troop now set out on the march through the poplar avenue. When they drew near to Pomogy, Vavel sent a squad in advance to act as skirmishers, while he, with the rest of his men, took possession of a solitary elevation near the road, which was the work of human hands. It was composed of the refuse from a soda-factory, and encircled on three sides a low building. Vavel concealed his horsemen behind this artificial hillock, then, accompanied by Katharina, he ascended to the top to take a view of the surrounding country.

He could see through his field-glass the bridge across the Raab and the inn at the farther end. The entire region was nothing but morass. A trench ran from the highway toward Lake Neusiedl; it could be traced by the dense growth of broom along its edges.

"You are my adjutant," jestingly remarked Vavel to Katharina. "I am going down now; for if I should be seen here it will be known what is behind me. You are a farmer's wife, and will not arouse suspicion; stop here, therefore, and take observations with my glass, and keep me informed of what happens."

The Marquis de Fervlans was enjoying a tankard of foaming mead when his adjutant came hastily into the room with the announcement that some troopers were approaching the bridge on the farther side of the river. De Fervlans hurried from the inn and gave orders to mount. As yet only the crimson hats of the troopers could be seen above the tall reeds on the farther shore.

"Those are Vavel's Volons," said De Fervlans, taking a look through his glass. "I recognize the uniform from Jocrisse's description. Madame Themire has turned traitor, and sent the count to deal with me instead of coming herself. Very good! We will show the gentleman that war and star-gazing are different occupations. He was a soldier once; but I don't think he paid much attention to military tactics, else he would not have neglected to occupy yon hill, on which I see a peasant woman with a red kerchief over her head. That is an old soda-factory—I know the place well. I should n't wonder if Vavel had concealed some men there after all! That small body coming this way is evidently bent on a skirmishing errand. Well, our tactics will be to lure him from his concealment."

He held a consultation with his subordinates; after which he turned toward the waiting demons, and called:

"Signor Trentatrante!"

The man came forward—a true type of the gladiator of the Vatican.

"Dismount," ordered the marquis. "Take thirty men, and proceed on foot to the farther side of yon thicket, where you will lie in ambush until I have begun an assault on the soda-factory over yonder. The men in hiding there will show up when we approach; I shall then pretend to retreat, and lure them toward the thicket. You will know what to do then—fall upon them in the rear. When you have arrived at the thicket let me know. Set fire to that tallest clump of reeds near the willow-shrubs."

"All right!" returned the signor. Then he selected thirty of his companions, who also dismounted, and they started at once to obey the orders of their leader.

The "peasant woman with a red kerchief over her head," who was standing on the soda-factory hill, called in a low, clear tone to Ludwig:

"De Fervlans is coming with his troop."

"Then we must prepare a greeting for him," responded Vavel. He ordered his men into their saddles, then sallied forth with them to meet the enemy.

The two bodies of soldiers moving toward each other were very nearly alike in numbers. Neither seemed to be in a particular hurry to begin an assault. Suddenly a column of smoke rose from the thicket near the bridge—it was the signal De Fervlans was waiting for. He gave orders to halt. The next instant there was a rattling salute from the demons' carbines. The "peasant woman" on the hill covered her face with both hands and shivered. The messengers of death flew about the head of her lover, but left him unharmed.

Vavel now moved nearer to the attacking foe, and himself made straight for the leader. One of De Fervlans's lieutenants, however, a thick-set, sun-browned Sicilian, met the count's assault. There was a little sword-play, then Vavel struck his adversary's blade from his hand with a force that sent it whizzing through the air, and with his left hand thrust the Sicilian, who was reaching for his pistols, from the saddle.

Nor had Vavel's companions been idle the while. The first assault was a success for the count's troop. De Fervlans now ordered a retreat. The death-heads looked upon this as a victory, and eagerly pursued the retreating foe. But the woman on the hill had already perceived that the retreat was but a feint. She saw the demons crouching among the reeds in the thicket, and guessed their intention.

"Vavel!" she shouted at the top of her voice, "Vavel, take care! Look to your rear!"

She imagined that her lover would hear her amid the tumult of the fight.

But Vavel had ears and eyes only for what was in front of him. Nearer and nearer he approached to the trap De Fervlans had laid for him. He was in it! The trench was behind him now, and the demons in ambush were preparing to spring upon their prey.

Katharina could look no longer. She ran down the hill, sprang on her mule, and galloped after her lover.

De Fervlans's retreat was conducted in proper order, step by step, from earth-clod to earth-clod.

Suddenly Katharina discovered that a mule was an obstinate beast. The one she was riding stopped abruptly, and would not advance another step. In vain she urged and coaxed. At last she sprang from the saddle, and on foot made her way toward the scene of the fray.

At this moment the demons creeping steathily along the trench sprang from their concealment, their bayonets ready for action. They were on the point of firing a volley into the black backs of the Volons, when a rattling fire in their own rear brought down half of them dead and wounded. The uninjured on turning found themselves confronted by Satan Laczi and his comrades, who, black and slimy from their passage through the morass, sprang like tigers upon the foe.

"Strike for their heads!" commanded Satan Laczi, as, with sabers drawn, the ex-robbers rushed upon the bewildered demons, who had at last met their match.

When De Fervlans heard the firing in the neighborhood of the trench, he believed it to come from the muskets of his own men, and quickly sounded an attack. The demons, who had been feigning to retreat, now turned and met their pursuers, and a hand-to-hand conflict began.

Vavel also had heard the firing behind him, and believed himself surrounded by the enemy. He beckoned to his trumpeter, to whom he wished to give orders to sound a retreat, but the man's horse unfortunately stumbled, and threw his rider to the earth. Three demons, at once sprang to capture the fallen trumpeter; but Vavel, who knew how necessary the man was to him, hastened to his assistance.

De Fervlans in amazement watched this unequal encounter. A masterly conflict arouses admiration even in an enemy; and Vavel certainly proved himself a master in the art of fighting.

He fought in cold blood; he was not in the least excited. He made no unnecessary thrusts, but wounded his three adversaries in the hand, the elbow, the forearm, whereby he rendered them incapable of further combat. De Fervlans saw how his skilled demons gave way before Vavel's masterly thrusts, while the Volons drew their unfortunate trumpeter from beneath his horse, and assisted him to mount again, after they had also helped the horse to his feet.

But the trumpet was now useless; it was filled with mud. Consequently a signal for retreat could not be sounded.

A dense mass of wild-hop vines inclosed the eastern side of the scene of action. De Fervlans glanced impatiently toward this green wall. The armed men who should penetrate it would decide the victory.

Even as the thought flashed through his brain, the tangle of vines began to shake violently; but the first man to appear therefrom was not Signor Trentatrante, as De Fervlans had expected, but Satan Laczi, with his ferocious followers.

The attack from this point was so unexpected that De Fervlans for a moment seemed stupefied; then quickly recovering himself, he dashed into the thick of the fight, Vavel following his example. By this time the trumpet had been cleansed, but no orders were received for a retreat signal; instead, the sound it shrilled above the fearful turmoil was: "Forward! forward!"

With the blood pouring from a gaping wound in his head, Satan Laczi, swinging a saber he had captured from a foe, now rushed to meet De Fervlans, who at once recognized the former robber.

"Ah!" he exclaimed, preparing to meet the furious onslaught, "you have not yet found your way to the gallows!"

"No; here in Hungary only traitors are hanged," retorted Satan Laczi, in a loud voice, as, with a mighty leap that would have done credit to a horse, he sprang toward the marquis, caught the reins from his hands, and with true robber-wit called: "Surrender, brother-rascal!"

De Fervlans raised himself in his stirrups and brought his saber savagely down on the robber's head. This was the second serious cut Satan Laczi had received that day, and was evidently enough to calm his enthusiasm. He staggered to one side, made several vain attempts to straighten himself, then fell suddenly to the earth. His own blade, however, remained in the breast of De Fervlans's horse, where he had thrust it to the hilt.

The marquis hardly had time to leap from the saddle before the poor beast fell under him.

All seemed lost now. His men were confused and thrown into disorder. In desperation he tore his pistols from the saddle of his fallen horse. Only a single shrub separated him from his enemy,—twenty paces,—and De Fervlans was a celebrated shot.

Count Vavel saw what was coming, and he too drew his pistol.

"Good night, Chevalier Vavel!" in a mocking tone called De Fervlans, as his finger pressed the trigger. There was a sharp report, the ball whistled through the air—but Vavel did not fall.

"Accept *my* greeting, marquis!" responded Vavel, He raised his pistol, and fired without taking aim. De Fervlans fell backward to the ground.

CHAPTER IV

When De Fervlans's men saw that their leader had fallen they retreated toward the bridge, where a portion of the troop alighted and held at bay their pursuers, while the rest tore up and flung into the stream the planks of the bridge. Then the men who had prevented the Volons from following crossed on foot the narrow lengthwise beam to the opposite shore—a feat impossible for a man on horseback.

The spot where the fiercest fighting had occurred was already cleared when Katharina arrived upon it. She shuddered with horror, and staggered like one who walks in his sleep as she moved about the desert place.

Suddenly she came upon a large wild-rose bush covered with bloom. Close by it lay a horse with the hilt of a sword protruding from his breast. Near the dead animal lay a metal helmet ornamented with the gilded imperial eagle, and a little farther on lay a mud-stained form in a uniform of coarse gray cloth, with a gaping wound in his head; his left hand clutched the rushes among which he had fallen. As Katharina, in her peasant gown, moved timidly across the open space, she heard a voice say faintly in Hungarian:

"For God's sake, good woman, give me a drink of water."

Without stopping to question whether he was friend or foe, Katharina caught up the metal helmet to fetch the water.

There was water everywhere about her, but it was the filthy water of the morass.

Katharina remembered having heard that the shepherds of the Hansag, when they were thirsty, cut a reed and thrust it deep into the swampy earth, when clear, drinkable water would rise from the lower soil. She therefore thrust a long cane into the moist earth, then put her lips to it, and sucked up the water. On removing her lips a clear stream shot upward from the cane. She held the helmet under this improvised fountain until it was full, then returned with it to the rose-bush.

The wounded man was lying on his back, his bloodstained face upturned toward the sky. Katharina knelt by his side, and held the helmet to his lips.

"Themire!" gasped the wounded man.

At sound of the name a sudden fury seemed to seize the woman.

"De Fervlans!" she cried, in a hoarse voice. "*You!* you, the accursed destroyer of my daughter! May God refuse to forgive you for making of me the wretched creature I am!"

As she spoke she raised the helmet, of water above her head, as if she would dash it upon the dying man's face; but he turned his head away from her furious gaze, and did not stir again.

Slowly Katharina lowered the helmet, and struggled with her excited feelings. She looked about her, and saw another motionless form lying across a clump of turf. Perhaps he was still alive. Perhaps she might help him.

She stepped quickly to his side with the helmet of water and washed the blood and mud-stains from his face. Ah, what a hideous face it was! All the same, she carefully washed it, then bathed the gaping wounds in his head. They were horribly deep, and she was almost overcome by the fearful sight. But she looked upward for a moment, and it seemed to her as if she recognized amid the fleecy clouds a snow-white form, and heard an encouraging voice say:

"That is right, mother. I, too, performed such work."

Then she took her handkerchief and bound it around the wounded man's head. While so doing her eyes fell on the steel ring on his thumb.

"Satan Laczi!" she exclaimed.

She put her arms around him, and lifted him to a more comfortable position, wondering the while how he came to be there. Had he failed to find Marie, whom he was to accompany to Raab? Had Cambray, perhaps, prevented her from leaving the castle?

She bent over the wounded man and said:

"Satan Laczi, awake! Look up—come back to life!"

And Satan Laczi was such an obedient fellow, he opened his eyes and saw the lady kneeling by his side.

Then he opened his lips, and said in a very weak voice:

"I should like a drink of water."

Katharina made haste to fill the helmet again at her fountain.

"Thank you, sister."

"Look at me, Laczi bácsi;" commanded Katharina, in a cheerful tone. "Don't you know me? I am the woman who gave shelter to your wife and child. I am little Laczko's foster-mother."

The wounded man smiled faintly, and murmured: "Yes, yes—Laczko—Laczko is a fine lad! He came near—shooting me because—because of the maid."

"Tell me what you know about the maid," eagerly questioned Katharina. "Where is she?"

The wounded man opened his eyes, and seemed to be trying to recall something. After a pause, he said slowly, and with evident difficulty:

"You need n't—trouble about the—pretty maid. Laczko is a brave lad—and my wife—my wife is—an honest woman."

"Yes, yes, I know," returned Katharina. "A good lad, and an honest woman. But tell me, in heaven's name, where is the maid?"

"The maid—Sophie Botta went with—my wife to Raab—they are there now—and Laczko too."

How gently the lady bathed the wounded man's face and hands! How carefully she renewed the bandages on the horrible wounds!

Ludwig Vavel, who hart approached noiselessly, stood and watched her perform the labor of love. He saw, heard, and admired. Then he came close to the kneeling woman, and clasped his arms around her.

"My Katharina! Oh, what a woman art thou!"

PART X
CONCLUSION

CHAPTER I

When Count Vavel returned from his skirmish with De Fervlans's demons, he sent his betrothed at once to Raab, with instructions not to separate herself again from Marie.

He had not been able to accompany Katharina on her journey, as he had received marching orders immediately on his return to camp. On parting with his betrothed, however, he had promised to pay a visit to her and Marie at an early day, and to write to both of them daily.

The first part of his promise he had not been able to fulfil; his time was too fully occupied with the duties of the field. But he sent frequent messages to his loved ones; while every day, no matter where he might be, he would be sure to receive his letter from Raab—one sheet covered to the edges with Katharina's writing, and the other with Marie's.

Their letters were always cheerful, and filled with hope and confidence for the future. Ludwig fancied he could see the scene as Katharina described it, when Marie had opened the steel casket.

He knew just how delighted the young girl had been when she beheld nothing but ashes instead of the little garments, the documents, the portraits, the bank-notes; and he could hear her joyous laugh on finding herself relieved of the burden of her greatness. But what he could not hear was Katharina reciting his brave exploits during the fierce struggle on the Hansag, a recital Marie insisted on hearing every day.

Then the two, Marie and Katharina, would go every morning to church, to pray for Ludwig, to ask God to protect him, and bring him safely back to them. This was their daily pleasure and consolation.

Then came the bloody days of Karako, Papa, Raab, and Acs. The militia troops took active part in all these battles, and proved themselves valiant warriors.

Vavel with his Volons had been assigned to Mesko's brigade, and had shared its adventurous march from Abda, around Lake Balaton to Veszprim. Here he found his spy and scout, Master Matyas, awaiting him.

For weeks he had not had a word from his loved ones. When he had sent them to Raab he believed he had selected a secure haven for them, but the course which events had taken proved that he had made a mistake in his calculations. Katharina and Marie were now surrounded on all sides by the enemy.

It was while he was oppressed with these gloomy thoughts that his spy and scout suddenly appeared before him. Noah in his ark had not looked more longingly for the dove than had he for his brave Matyas.

"Well, Master Matyas, what news?"

"All sorts, Herr Count."

"Good or bad?"

"Well, mixed. Both good and bad. I will leave the good till the last. To begin: Poor Satan Laczi was buried yesterday—may God have mercy on his sinful soul! They fired three salvos over his grave, and the primate himself said the prayers for his soul. If Satan Laczi himself could have seen it all, he could hardly have believed that so much honor would be shown to his dead body. Poor Laczi! His last words were a greeting to his kind patron."

"His life closed well!" observed the count. "He got what he longed for—a soldier's death. But tell me what you know about Raab."

"I know all about it. I come from there."

"Ah, did you see them? Has not the enemy besieged the city?"

"Yes; the city as well as the fortress is in the hands of the enemy, and the baroness and the princess are both in it."

"Who told you to call her a princess?" demanded Count Vavel, his face darkening.

"I will come to that all in good time," composedly replied Matyas, who was not to be hurried. "Colonel Pechy," he went on, "bravely defended the fortress for ten days against the Frenchmen; but he had to yield at last—"

"Where are Katharina and Marie?" impatiently interrupted Vavel. "What became of them when the city capitulated?"

"All in good time, Herr Count, all in good time! I can tell you all about them, for I am just come from them."

"Were they in any danger?"

"Danger? No, indeed! When the city surrendered they were concealed in a house where they passed as the nieces of the Herr Vice-palatine Görömbölyi."

"Is the vice-palatine with them now?"

"Certainly. He has surrendered, too."

"Excellent man! Who commands the Frenchmen at Raab?"

"General Guillaume—"

"General Guillaume?" excitedly interrupted Vavel.

"Yes, certainly; Guillaume—that is his name. And he is a very polite gentleman. He does not ill-treat the citizens; on the contrary, the very next day after he entered the city he gave a ball in the large hotel, and invited all the distinguished citizens with their wives and daughters. The Herr Count's dear ones also received an invitation."

"As the nieces of the vice-palatine, of course?"

"Not exactly! I saw the invitation-card, and it was to 'Madame la Comtesse de Alba, avec la Princesse Marie.'"

"Princess Marie?" echoed Vavel.

"As I tell you; and that is how I come to know she is a princess."

Vavel's brain seemed paralyzed. He could not even think.

"The vice-palatine," nonchalantly continued Matyas, "protested that a mistake had been made; but the French general replied that he knew very well who the ladies were, and that he had received instructions how to treat them. From that day, two French grenadiers began to guard the baroness's door, day and night, just exactly as if they were standing guard over a potentate."

Vavel paced the floor, mute with rage and fear.

"Why did I desert them!" he exclaimed at last, in desperation. "Why did I not do as Marie wished—flee with her and Katharina into the wide world—we three alone!"

"Well, you see you did n't, and this is the way matters stand now," responded Master Matyas. "The general's adjutant visits the house twice every day to inquire after the ladies; then he reports to his superior."

"If only Cambray had not died!" ejaculated the count.

"Yes, but I helped to bury him, too," added Matyas, shaking his head.

"Yes, so I was told. How did you manage to get the body from behind the metal screen?"

"Oh, that was easy enough. You know the spring is connected with the bell in your study; when the screen unrolled, the bell rang. It was only necessary to reverse the operation: by pulling the bell-wire in the Herr Count's study the screen was rolled up."

"A very simple arrangement, indeed," observed Count Vavel, smiling in spite of his gloom. "Ah, Master Matyas, if only you were clever enough to open for me the locks which now imprison my dear ones! That would be a masterpiece, indeed!"

"I can do that easily enough," was the confident rejoinder.

"You can? How?"

"Did n't I say I would leave the good news until the last?"

"Yes, yes. Tell me what you have in view."

"I must whisper the secret in your ear; I have often overheard important secrets listening at the keyhole or while hiding under a bed, and what I have done another may be doing."

Vavel bent his head so that Master Matyas might whisper the important information in his ear.

The words were few, but they served to restore Vavel to a cheerful mood.

He laughed heartily, slapped Master Matyas on the shoulder, and exclaimed:

"You are truly a wonderful fellow!" Then he took a roll of bank-notes from his pocket, and pressed it into Matyas's hand. "Here—take these, and buy what is necessary. We will make the attempt at once."

Master Matyas thrust the money into his own pocket, and darted from the room as if he had stolen it. Ludwig hastened to his general, to beg for leave of absence.

CHAPTER II

"Everything is ready," said Master Matyas to Vavel, pointing toward three covered luggage-wagons, which the Volons had captured from the Frenchmen at Klein-Zell.

The "Death-head troop," as Vavel's Volons were designated, marched in the rear of the brigade; consequently they could drop out from it any time without attracting special notice.

To-day the brigade marched toward Palota, and the Volons turned into the road which led to Zircz. They seemed, however, to have been swallowed up by the Bakonye forest, for nothing was seen again of them after they entered it. The inhabitants of Ratota still repeat tales of the handsome troopers—every man of them a true Magyar!—who rode through their village to the sound of the trumpet, nodding to the pretty girls, and paying gold coin for their refreshment at the inn. But the dwellers in Zircz complained that, instead of Magyar troopers, a squad of hostile cavalry passed through their village—Frenchmen in blue mantles, with cocks' feathers in their helmets, with a commandant who had given all sorts of orders that no one could understand. Luckily, the prior of the Premonstrants could speak French, and he acted as interpreter for the French commandant. And everybody felt relieved when he marched farther with his troop.

These were the transformed Volons. They had exchanged their crimson shakos in the dense forest for the French helmets, and wrapped themselves in the blue mantles taken from the luggage-wagons. No one would have doubted that they were French *chasseurs*—even the trumpeter sounded the calls according to the regulations in the armies of France.

Master Matyas hurried on in advance of the troop to learn if the way was clear. It would have been equally unpleasant to have met either Hungarian or French soldiery. They encountered neither, however; and at daybreak on the second day arrived at the village of Börcs, on the Rabcza, where is an interesting monument of times long past—a redoubt of considerable extent, in the center of which stands the village church.

Vavel's troop camped within this redoubt, where they could escape attracting attention. The country about them, for a long distance, was occupied by French troops.

The highway which led to Raab might be seen from the steeple of the church, and here Vavel took up his station with a field-glass.

He had not been long in his tower of observation when he saw a heavy cloud of dust moving along the highway, and very soon was able to distinguish a body of horsemen. It was a company of cuirassiers, whose polished breastplates glittered in the sunlight like stars. The company was divided into two squads: one rode in front of a four-horse traveling-coach, the other in the rear of it.

There were two ladies in the coach. The elder of the two shielded her face from the dust with a heavy veil; the younger lady wore no veil over her pale face, but held in front of it a fan, from behind which she took an occasional look at the variegated plain, where the ripening grain, blended with the green of the meadows, formed a rich, carpet on either side of the road.

The young officer riding beside the coach sought to entertain the elder lady with observations on the country through which they were passing, and from time to time exchanged tender glances with the younger. These ladies were the wife and daughter of General Guillaume. They were on their way to Raab, where they expected an addition to their party in the person of *la Princesse Marie*, whom they were going to accompany to Paris. The troop of cuirassiers was their escort.

"There come some *chasseurs* on a foraging expedition," observed the young officer, pointing toward a body of horsemen that was approaching across the green plain.

And, judging from the appearance of the riders, he was right; for the Volons, in order to deceive the Frenchmen, were bringing with them a couple of loaded hay-wagons, which they were dragging through the middle of the highway.

While yet a considerable distance away from the approaching *chasseurs*, the postilions began to blow their horns for a clear way.

The hay-wagons were turned, in obedience to the signal, but, in turning, the second one ran into the one in advance with such force that the pole was broken clean off.

In front of the barricade thus formed Vavel halted his men, and commanded them to throw off their French cloaks and helmets. In a second the order was obeyed; the crimson shakos with their grim death-heads were donned, and the troop dashed forward upon the escort accompanying the coach.

The astonished cuirassiers, who were wholly unprepared for the assault, were soon overpowered by the Volons, who also outnumbered them.

The youthful leader had at once placed himself in front of the coach, ready for combat with the leader of the attacking foe, and Vavel was obliged to exercise all his skill to disarm without injuring him.

At the moment when the young French champion's sword flew from his hand, the younger lady, forgetting all ceremony, cried in terror:

"*Oh mon Dieu, ne tuez pas Arthur!*"

Ludwig Vavel turned toward her, bowed courteously, and said in Talma's most exquisite French:

"Do not be alarmed, ladies. You are perfectly safe. We are Hungarian gentlemen!"

"But what do you want of us?" demanded the elder lady, haughtily surveying the count. "What business have we with you? We do not belong to the combatants."

"I will tell this brave young chevalier what I want," replied Vavel, turning toward the youthful leader. "First, let me restore your sword, monsieur. You handle it admirably, only you need to grasp it more firmly. Then, let me beg of you to mount your horse—a beautiful animal! And third, I beg you to ride as quickly as possible to Raab, and give General Guillaume this message: 'I, Count Vavel de Versay, have this day taken captive the wife and daughter of General Guillaume. The general holds as prisoners my betrothed wife, Countess Themire Dealba, and my adopted daughter, Sophie Botta, or, if he prefers, *la Princess Marie*. I demand my loved ones in exchange for Madame and Mademoiselle Guillaume.' I have no further demands, monsieur, and the sooner you return the better. I shall await you in yonder redoubt, where you see the church-steeple. Adieu."

The younger lady, with hands clasped pleadingly, mutely besought the youthful officer to assent. As if he would not do everything in his power to urge the general to consent to the exchange! The young Frenchman galloped down the road toward Raab. Count Vavel took his place beside the coach, and ordered the postilions to drive to Börcs. At first, the general's wife heaped reproaches on her captor.

"This is a violation of national courtesies," she exclaimed irately. "It is brigandage, to waylay and take as prisoners two distinguished women."

"Madame's husband has also detained as prisoners two distinguished women," in a respectful tone responded Vavel.

"But my daughter is so nervous."

"There is not a more timid creature in the world than my poor little Marie."

"At all events, monsieur, you are a Frenchman, and know what is due to ladies of our station."

"In that respect, madame, I shall follow General Guillaume's example."

They were now among the gardens of Börcs, where the cherry-trees, heavily laden with fruit, rose above the tall hedges; and very soon they turned into a beautiful street shaded by walnut-trees, which led to the redoubt. The parsonage was the only house of importance in the village. The pastor was standing at his door when Vavel ordered the coach to stop. He assisted the ladies to alight, and begged the pastor to grant them the hospitality of his roof. The request was not refused, and the ladies were made as comfortable as possible.

"Do you care to see the sights of the village, madame?" asked Vavel of the mother, after they had partaken of the lunch prepared by the pastor's housekeeper. The young lady, who was exhausted by the journey, had gone to her room. "There is a very old church here which is interesting."

"Are there any fine pictures in it?" inquired madame.

"There is one,—a very touching scene,—'The Samaritan.'"

"Ancient or modern?" queried the lady.

"The subject is old—it dates back to the first years of Christianity, madame. The execution is modern."

"Is it the work of a celebrated artist?"

"No; it is the work of our clerical host."

The lady shook her head; she was uncertain whether Count Vavel was making sport of her or of the pastor.

But she understood him when she entered the church. The house consecrated to the service of God had become a hospital, and was crowded with wounded French soldiers. The women of the village, as volunteer nurses, were taking care of them, and performed the task as faithfully as if the invalids were their own sons and brothers. The pastor himself supplied the necessary medicines from his own cupboard; for no army surgeon came here at a time when twenty thousand wounded Frenchmen lay at Aspern, and twenty-two thousand at Wagram.

"Is it not an affecting tableau, madame?" said Count Vavel. "It would be a suitable altar-piece for Notre Dame—and the name of its creator deserves perpetuation!"

CHAPTER III

Monsieur le Capitaine Descourcelles rode an excellent horse, was a capital rider, and was plainly very much in love. These three circumstances combined brought back the gallant soldier from Raab by five o'clock in the afternoon.

The captain of the cuirassiers was not a little surprised to find the general's wife playing cards with the hostile leader.

"General Guillaume agrees to everything," he announced immediately, on entering the room. "He will release the ladies he has been holding as prisoners."

Vavel hastened to shake hands with the bearer of these glad tidings, who was, however, more eager to kiss the hand of Vavel's partner, and to inquire:

"I hope I find the ladies perfectly comfortable?"

"Very comfortable indeed," replied madame. "*Messieurs les Cannibales* are very polite, and *leur Catzique* plays an excellent hand at piquet."

"And where is mademoiselle? I trust she is not suffering from the fatigue of the journey?"

"Oh, no; she is very well. She is making her toilet, and will soon join us. I hope we shall leave here very soon."

Madame now rose, and left the two soldiers alone in the room.

"Here," observed the French captain, handing Vavel a paper, "is the *sauf conduit*."

The pass contained the information that "Vavel de Versay, expatriated French nobleman and magnate of Hungary, together with the Countess Themire Dealba (alias Baroness Katharina Landsknechtsschild) and Sophie Botta (pretended Princess Marie Charlotte Capet), with attendants, were to be allowed to travel unmolested by any French troops they might chance to meet."

Ludwig Vavel looked at this document a long time.

"Do you doubt the assurance of a French officer, monsieur?" asked the captain.

"No; I was just unable to understand why a word had been used here. I dare say it is a mistake. But no matter. I am greatly obliged to you."

"Pray don't speak of it," responded the Frenchman, cordially shaking the hand Vavel extended toward him. "I must not forget to tell you that a four weeks' armistice was agreed upon to-day."

The ladies now entered the room, prepared to continue their journey. The face of the younger one wore a more cheerful expression than on her arrival at the parsonage. Madame thanked Vavel for his courtesy, then, with her daughter, entered the carriage and drove away.

Madame Guillaume was forgetful: she neglected to take leave of her host the pastor, and of her wounded countrymen in the church.

Vavel communicated the news of the armistice to his adjutant, and commanded him to return at once with the Volons to Fertöszeg, there to quarter themselves in the Nameless Castle, and await further orders. Then he mounted his horse, and, accompanied by Master Matyas, galloped out of the village.

Twilight had deepened into night when the two men arrived at Raab. The clocks were striking eight, and the French trumpets were sounding the retreat at every gate. Vavel, therefore, would not be allowed to enter the city until the next morning; but Master Matyas, who did not stop to inquire which was the proper way when he wanted to go anywhere, knew of a little garden that belonged to a certain tanner, and very soon found an entrance along a rather circuitous route among the tan-vats.

Vavel had already seen battered walls, and dwellings ruined by bombs and flames, yet the thought that he should find his loved ones amid these smoke-blackened ruins oppressed his heart.

The two men attracted no attention. In the last days there had been many strangers in the city, deputations from the militia camps, to assist in establishing the line of demarcation. Master Matyas, without difficulty, led the way among the ruins to the neat little abode where the worthy vice-palatine had established his protégés. When they came within sight of the house Matyas observed:

"The two Frenchmen with their bearskin caps are not on guard to-day. The vice-palatine's servant seems to be doing sentry-duty."

Vavel applied his spurs and cantered briskly toward the house, but moderated his speed when he came nearer. He remembered how easily Marie was frightened by the clatter of horse-hoofs.

At the corner of the street he alighted, and cautioning Matyas to exercise slowly the fatigued horses, proceeded on foot to the house.

The servant on guard at the door saluted in military fashion with drawn sword. Ludwig hurried into the house. In the hall he encountered the little Laczko, who, at sight of the visitor, dropped the boot and brush he held in his hands, and disappeared through a door at the end of the hall. Vavel followed him, and found himself in the kitchen, where the widow of Satan Laczi also dropped to the floor the cooking-utensil she had in her hand.

The count did not stop to question her, but went on into the adjoining room, whence proceeded the sound of voices, and here he found three acquaintances—the vice-palatine, Dr. Tromfszky, and the surveyor, Herr Doboka. The three started in alarm when they beheld Vavel. The doctor even made as if he would rush from the room—as when in the Nameless Castle the furious invalid had seized his groom by the throat.

The expressions on the three startled countenances brought a sudden fear to Ludwig's heart.

"Is any one ill here?" he asked.

The vice-palatine and the doctor looked at each other, but did not speak; the surveyor began to stammer:

"I say—I say that—"

"Is Marie ill?" interrupted Vavel, excitedly.

Herr Bernat silently nodded assent, and pointed toward the door leading into the next room.

Vavel did not stop to inquire further, but strode into the adjoining chamber.

What a familiar little room it was, another fairy-like retreat like that of the Nameless Castle! Here were Marie's toys, her furniture; the four cats were purring in the window-seat, and the two pugs lay dozing on the sofa.

A canopy-bed stood in the alcove, and among the pillows lay Marie. Katharina was sitting by the bedside.

"Oh, God!" cried Vavel, in a tone so full of anguish that every one who heard it, man, woman, and child, burst into tears. The invalid among the pillows alone laughed—laughed aloud for joy.

And had she not cause to rejoice? Ludwig—*her* Ludwig—did not hasten first to embrace and kiss his betrothed wife. No, *she*, his little Marie, was the first!

He flung himself on his knees by the bed and covered the pale face with kisses and tears.

"Oh, my dearest! My adored saint! My idol!" he sobbed, while Marie's face glowed with the purest earthly happiness.

She pressed Ludwig's head to her breast and whispered soothingly:

"Don't grieve, Ludwig; I am not going to die. I have not got that horrid influenza poor papa Cambray brought with him from Paris. I took a little cold the night we ran away from the bombs; but I shall soon be well again, now that you are come. I want to live, Ludwig, and you, who rescued me from death once before, will know how to do it again."

Katharina laid her hand tenderly on the maid's head, and said gently:

"Don't talk any more now, dearest; you know you must not excite yourself."

Marie grasped the white hand and drew it down to Ludwig's lips.

"Kiss it, Liadwig; kiss this dear, good hand. Oh, she has been a good little mother to me! She has wept so much because of me. If only you knew what she had planned to do when they were going to tear me away from her! But that danger is past, and now that you are come everything will be well. We have been reading about you, Ludwig. What a hero you are—our knight, St. George! I have n't been really ill, you know, Ludwig; it was only anxiety about you. I shall soon be well again. Please tell the doctor I don't need any more medicine. I want to get up—I feel strong already. I want to put on my gown; then I will take your arm and Katharina's, and we three will promenade to the window. I want to see the evening star. Please send Frau Satan to me; she can lift me more easily than Katharina, for I am very heavy. Ludwig, take Katharina into the next room while I am dressing. I know you have much to say to each other."

Frau Satan now entered in answer to the summons. The doctor had ordered that the invalid's wishes must be obeyed.

Ludwig and Katharina went into the next room. They looked long into each other's eyes, and in the gaze lay many of the thoughts which, if they cannot be told to the one person on earth, are never heard by any one else. Suddenly Katharina, without word of warning, dropped on her knees at her lover's feet, seized his hand, and laid her face against it.

"You are my guardian angel," she whispered (the invalid in the next room must not be disturbed by the sound of voices); "you have rescued that saint from her enemies and saved me from perdition. Oh, Ludwig, if only you knew what I have suffered! Marie's every sigh, the feverish words uttered in her delirium, have been so many accusations oppressing my heart. These have been terrible days! To be compelled hourly to dread either of two horrible blows, and to have to pray to God that, if both could not be averted, to let the milder one fall! Death would have been welcome, indeed, compared to the other one. To listen tremblingly, hour after hour, for the knock at the door which would announce the messenger sent to bear Marie to Paris, or death with his scythe to bear her to the grave! And then to have to look on her sufferings, and hear her pray for her betrayer! Oh, it was terrible, terrible! Ludwig, you are just—as God is just. I have suffered as any woman in the Bible suffered. You have taken my load of sorrow from me, have released my heart from the tortures of perdition. All the evil I have done, you have made good. Therefore, do you pronounce judgment on me. Condemn me or forgive me. I deserve both; I will accept either at your hands."

Without a word Ludwig Vavel raised the woman to her feet, clasped her in his arms, and pressed his lips to hers in a long, long kiss. In it were forgiveness, love, union.

From the adjoining room came the sounds of a piano. Some one was playing the hymn of the Hungarian militia.

Ludwig and Katharina hurried into the room. Marie was seated at the piano, arrayed in her favorite blue gown. Her transparent hands hovered over the ivory keys, and lured from them the melancholy air, to which she sang, in a voice that seemed to come from the distant clouds:

"Was kleinliche Bosheit ausgedacht,
Hat unserer Liebe ein Ende gemacht."

At the last word her arms sank to her sides; the exertion had completely exhausted her. But she struggled bravely to overcome her weakness. She smiled brightly at Ludwig and Katharina, and said:

"This melancholy song was not intended for you two. It was only to show Ludwig how I have improved. You two will love each other very dearly, won't you? And you will go far, far away from here, and leave 'Marie' buried in her tomb. I don't mean myself; I mean the troublesome girl who has made so much ill feeling in the world, because of whom so many people have suffered; the girl whose ashes rest there in the steel casket, and whose life was so sad that she had no desire to live longer. But 'Sophie' is going with you out into the world. She will see how happy you two can be. And now, help me to the window; I want to look at the evening star,"

They rolled her arm-chair to the window, and Vavel opened the sash to admit the fresh air from the garden.

Marie clasped Ludwig's and Katharina's hands in both her own, and whispered in a faint voice:

"You will forget the past, will you not? or think of it only as a dream—a disagreeable dream. And don't go back to the Nameless Castle. The veiled woman, the locked doors, the silent man, the telescope, the lonely promenades in the garden—all, all were dreams. Don't think of them! Forget them all! The clanking swords, the thunder of cannons—all these were not. We only dreamed it. We never lived under the shadow of a throne. Who was Marie? A sovereign of cats, and crown princess in the realm of little dogs and birds—a nursery tale to tell naughty little children who will not go to sleep! But Sophie Botta will be here to-morrow, and the next day, and always; she will be with you, the silly, stupid little maid, who can do nothing but obey those whom she loves with all her heart."

Vavel with difficulty refrained from giving voice to his overwhelming grief.

"Just see," Marie continued in a gay tone, "how much better I am! Heretofore, when the hour came for the evening star to appear, the fever would come too, and to-day it has failed to come with the star. Joy has cured me. Don't take your hands away from me, Ludwig—Katharina. They will— hold me—hold me—fast."

But they did not "hold her fast."

And why should such a being remain on this earth—a being that could do naught else but love and renounce, adoring her nation even when it persecuted her?

A dark thunder-cloud rose above the horizon out over the Hansag. The sky looked like a vaulted ceiling hung with mourning draperies. From time to time a distant flash of lightning illumined the cloud-curtain, then would be heard the rumbling of thunder, like the deep tones of a distant organ.

Under the threatening sky lay the glittering lake. Its surface of quicksilver was streaked here and there with black shadows—the track of the wind-gusts racing across it. The trees were rustling in the wind, making a sound like a distant choral.

On the shore of Lake Neusiedl stood the Volons in rank and file. They were waiting for something that was coming from the farther shore of the little cove.

Presently the glistening surface of the water was ruffled by a black object that pushed out from the shore. It was a boat. Six men were rowing, a seventh held the rudder. There was a coffin in the boat, covered with a simple pall. No ostentatious trappings ornamented the coffin; only a myrtle wreath lay on it. A woman, sat at the head of it, another at the foot—the former a lady, the latter a peasant wife.

The six men, with even and powerful strokes, sent the craft through the ripples which occasionally leaped into the boat, as if they would salute her who had so often toyed with them.

At the moment the boat touched the shore the storm burst. Vivid lightning illumined the heavy downpour of rain, and it seemed as if the black-robed forms bore the coffin to its grave amid a flood of harpstrings that reached from heaven to earth.

The two weeping women followed the coffin; at a little distance they seemed two shadows. The helmsmen of the funeral boat now stepped to the head of the grave and opened his lips to speak, but a heavy peal of thunder drowned his voice. When it had ceased he said:

"My brave comrades, you are here to pay a last honor to your patroness. There is nothing left for us to fight for. Peace has been proclaimed. The conqueror takes from you a plot of ground twenty-four hundred square miles in extent. The one lying here takes from you only six feet of earth. To you remain your tattered flag and your wounds. Return to your homes. My sword has finished its work, and will accompany the saint for whom it was drawn!"

As he spoke he broke the keen blade in twain and cast the pieces into the grave, adding impressively, "May God give us forgetfulness, and may we be forgotten!"

The Volons fired three salvos over the grave, the reverberating thunder and the flashing lightning mingling with the noise of the muskets.

When the storm had passed the moon rose in a cloudless sky. Only the waves, which had been stirred by the tempest, continued to murmur to their favorite who was sleeping peacefully in her grave on the shore.

Marie had asked to be buried on the grassy slope by the side of her old friend the Marquis d'Avoncourt, and that no other monument should mark her resting-place save the imperishable tree which turns to stone after it dies.

And what could have been graven on her tomb? A name that was not hers? A history that was not true?

Or would it have been well to carve on the marble her true life-history, that those who would not believe it might wage a lawsuit against an epitaph?

No; it was better so. No one would ever learn what had become of her.

Vavel had prayed for forgetfulness—that he might be forgotten.

His prayer was granted.

For a few years afterward tales were repeated about Sophie Botta, and some of her kinsfolk came from a distance to claim the sum of money Vavel had placed in the hands of the authorities for the young girl's heirs. But none of the claimants could produce satisfactory proofs of kinship, and after a while Sophie Botta was forgotten by all the world, as were Count Vavel and Katharina.

The Nameless Castle as well vanished from the face of the earth, as have entire villages which once stood on the treacherous shores of Lake Neusiedl.

Gradually, imperceptibly, the castle disappeared; gradually, imperceptibly, bastion after bastion vanished, until not even the stone hand which held aloft the sword in the noble escutcheon, or the towering weathervane, could be seen above the placid waters of the lake.